Pamela Bennetts

The Barons of Runnymede

ROBERT HALE & COMPANY
63 Old Brompton Road, London, S.W.7

© Pamela Bennetts 1974

First published in Great Britain 1974

ISBN 0 7091 3991 8

Printed in Great Britain by
Clarke, Doble & Brendon Ltd.
Plymouth

P7

The Barons of Runnymede

When John, with the reputation of a feckless, untrustworthy libertine, comes to the throne, the mighty Angevin empire is already crumbling. Bellicose magnates are calling for a revision of the feudal contract which will clip the sovereign's wings and give them the rights they demand.

After the loss of Normandy to Philip Augustus of France, John's main ambition is to secure his continental possessions. But the English barons will not support him and he is forced to rely on foreign allies and mercenaries. By a stroke of genius he prevents the invasion of England by the French king and wins the undying support of Pope Innocent III. But he cannot keep his beautiful, voluptuous wife, Isabella of Angouleme, who flaunts her lovers before her jealous husband's eyes.

Even though he is clever, imaginative and indefatigable, John's personal failings widen the gulf between himself and the great men of the realm who continue to press for a charter to establish their rights. Although their motives are purely selfish, they are aided by Archbishop Stephen Langton, who can see that by broadening the clauses of the charter it can bring justice and relief to all free men. When the rebels seize London, John is forced to meet them at Runnymede and affix the Great Seal to the Articles of the Barons. But as he rides away from the water meadow by the Thames he is already planning to repudiate the document, later known as the Magna Carta, whilst England shuffles uneasily to the brink of civil war.

ACKNOWLEDGEMENTS

King John. A bad king; a worse human being? A clever, capable, imaginative ruler who inherited insoluble problems from his father and brother and who never learned how to use his natural talents or gain the trust of those who served him? Historians differ in their opinions, but I am grateful to the following scholars for helping me to form my own opinion, and for making this book possible:

King John	W. L. Warren
John Lackland	Kate Norgate
John King of England	John T. Appleby
King John and Magna Carta	J. A. P. Jones
The Reign of King John	Sidney Painter
King John	Maurice Ashley
Domesday Book to Magna Carta	A. L. Poole
William Marshal	Sidney Painter
Magna Carta	J. C. Holt
History of the English-Speaking Peoples	Winston S. Churchill
Angevin Kingship	J. E. A. Jolliffe
Stephen Langton	Maurice Powicke
The Plantagenets	John Harvey
The Rise of the Feudal Monarchies	Sidney Painter
From Alfred to Henry III	Christopher Brooke
The Medieval Papacy	Geoffrey Barraclough
Medieval France	Gustave Masson
Lives of the Queens of England	Agnes Strickland
The Capetian Kings of France	Robert Fawtier
Makers of the Realm	Arthur Bryant

P.B.

CHAPTER ONE

THE snow began to fall at the hour of four. Since early dawn the day had been full of intangible threats as it hung sombre clouds over the soaring keep of Winchester Castle and sent long icy fingers probing spitefully through the narrow slits of windows in the solid stone walls.

A serving girl, Joie de Pec, hurried along the corridor which led to the private apartments, a jug of wine in one hand and a fur-lined wrap in the other, pausing for a moment by one of the larger windows latticed with stout iron to gaze out into the gloom. Down below in the hall and in the bustling kitchens there was noise and laughter and shouted orders whilst, in the cobbled courtyard beyond, horses clattered to the stable buildings led by squires whose round young cheeks glowed like red apples as the anvils of the smiths rang out like a dozen carillons in the frosty air.

Joie was glad to be alone for a moment, for solitude was a rare luxury which did not often come her way. At night she had to share a thin palliasse with three other maids, and her every waking hour was spent rubbing shoulders with the throng of servants, soldiers and hangers-on who followed the king's court wherever it went. But now she stood by herself and watched the whirling flakes mingling with the oncoming darkness, trembling slightly, for her simple gown and cloak of homespun wool were no real protection against the determination of the elements.

She screwed up her eyes as she tried in vain to distinguish the familiar outlines of the cathedral in the valley below, but the torrent of white specks and the misty dusk blinded her as much as the trace of tears which moistened her lashes.

If King John had scoffed and made light of the interdict laid upon England in the previous year, Joie had not. To her, the awful sentence imposed by Pope Innocent III had brought terror and distress, for not a mass could be said, not a bell rung, not a confession heard nor absolution given. Marriages were held at the church door and such sermons as were preached were delivered in the churchyard. The newly-born were bereft of sacraments as harshly as the newly-departed, for finally the pontiff had grown impatient with the king's intransigence and condemned his realm to the ultimate punishment.

Joie shivered again. There was something almost ghostly about the great church lying down there so still and silent. All its quick and thriving life was gone, as if its very soul had departed, and there were no longer any mellow lights to flicker through its windows nor sound of chanting voices to rise from its choir, nor yet the shuffle of feet as men and women crowded in to offer their prayers to God. All it could boast now were thick wooden beams hammered over the west door to keep out the faithful, as encroaching weeds and brush began to tangle its pathways and creep insidiously up its buttresses and walls.

Joie forced herself to stop her dreaming and began to scurry towards the queen's chamber. Her moment of peace and privacy was over and it would not do to keep her grace waiting, for although her second son had been born not more than five hours ago, the queen had already recovered from her ordeal and was making her normal and exacting demands upon her women and maids.

When Joie opened the door of the chamber all the gloom and silence of the dark corridor vanished as if by magic, and she was in another world warmed by a roaring log fire and lit by a score of fat wax candles in silver holders. Joie thought the room was the most beautiful she had ever seen, for its walls were lined with glowing tapestries and even the fresh straw beneath her feet was scented with herbs to sweeten it. On one side there were tall perches on which the queen's robes were hung and on the other two chests carved by a master-hand which held more of the royal finery. At the foot of the bed there was a long bench piled with coloured cushions and at one side of it a table bearing a brass ewer and basin which had been burnished until it shone like the sun. But it was the bed itself which dominated the room with its sturdy wooden posts and fine white linen sheets under rugs of marten and sable and an elaborately embroidered quilt of vert silk.

She often wondered what it would be like to sleep on a mattress filled with soft down, and what warmth one would feel from such luxurious coverings. As her feet rustled gently through the straw her eyes widened as they always did at the magnificence of the coverlet. It was so dazzling that the jug shook in her hand and for a moment she hardly saw the occupants of the room until a sharp reprimand brought her back to reality and to the presence of the women grouped about the bed.

Beatrix de Gresby, the oldest of the queen's women, with black eyes which snapped with impatience and a round face swathed in wimple and veil to hide the sagging chin; Petronilla Asterby, tall, thin, neither beautiful in face nor body, but possessed of a sharp intelligence which frightened the king's nobles a good deal more than her lack of charm; Alina de la Celle, only recently come to court, and very young. Her fresh appeal had already caused much ribald comment and speculation amongst the barons and some sour remarks from their women-folk. She wore a worried look as if she was not quite sure what was required of her as she sat on the edge of a stool by the side of the bed, her hands folded meekly in her lap, her eyes downcast.

Out of the corner of her eye Joie could see the solid oak cradle by the fire rocked by Eva, nurse to the infant prince. Eva's garb was plain, as befitted one of her rank, but under it her body was splendidly ripe and mature and her face had the calm, unworried serenity of a madonna.

"Come along, girl, where have you been? Am I to wait all night for a sip of wine?"

Joie turned scarlet and bobbed a curtsy to the queen, retreating hurriedly to one corner of the room lest the sharpness of her grace's tongue should lash out at her again.

Isabella of Angoulême lay back against the plumped up pillows, her silky hair falling like a dark cloud about her white shoulders. At twenty-one her loveliness was almost breath-taking, for her skin was pure alabaster, her eyes almost black, her mouth full, red and warmly inviting, whilst her body was shaped with such perfection that it was hard to believe she was a mere mortal of flesh and blood. That she was a beauty was beyond doubt; what was not so certain was the quality of her virtue and Joie had heard many rumours of the queen's lovers and the almost maniacal jealousy of the king when such tales reached his ears.

Joie watched with bated breath as Isabella sipped the wine and then stretched voluptuously, the wide sleeves of her camise falling back to reveal her smooth, rounded forearms.

"Well! My lord the king cannot complain. I have given him two sons in fifteen months which is more than Berengaria could do for his brother Richard." Isabella's chuckle was malicious. "But then perhaps it was not entirely Berengaria's fault, for it is said Richard's taste did not favour women and that he preferred his pages' company to his wife's." She took another mouthful of wine and handed the goblet back to Petronilla. "How I wish I had known him, the handsome Coeur de Lion. Perhaps I could have made him change his habits, eh, Beatrix?"

Lady de Gresby's thin lips moved fractionally as she smoothed the coverlet with her plump hand.

"Perhaps you might have done, madam, for I have yet to meet the man who could resist you, but since his grace cannot bear you even to look at another, maybe it is as well that King Richard was not exposed to your witchcraft."

"Faith, Beatrix, do you call me a witch?"

Isabella gave a mock frown but she was not annoyed, for nothing pleased her more than an acknowledgment of her power over men, and her glance was affectionate as she looked at Beatrix.

"And do you say you are not, your grace?"

The queen and Lady de Gresby shared an intimate moment of mirth: then Isabella's eyes slid to Alina de Celle whose flush betrayed her acute embarrassment. Alina had not wanted to come to court at all but her father had made short work of her nonsense. It was an honour to serve the queen, he had told her brusquely as he packed her off without listening to her nervous whispers. But she had been right to be afraid, for the king's glance had been uncomfortably inquisitive when she had made her bow to him, and Isabella was clearly a wanton who delighted in dangerous, clandestine meetings with reckless, infatuated men.

"We have shocked the Lady Alina." Isabella's lips curved in renewed amusement. "Perhaps we have even made her fearful with our talk of witches."

Alina's colour deepened and she had difficulty in making her protest.

"No, no, madam. I am not . . . that is to say . . . I do not. . . ."

"There you see! We have all but brought the poor girl to tears. Shame on you, Beatrix, for frightening an innocent so."

Lady de Gresby cast the unfortunate Alina a contemptuous look. In her opinion it was high time the girl grew up. Perhaps she was only fifteen, but that was quite old enough to understand the way of things, and her perpetual air of shy bewilderment was something of an irritation.

"She had best dry her tears." Beatrix was short. "The court is no place for them and the sooner she learns it the better."

"Oh come, you are too harsh." Isabella laughed again and stretched out her slender fingers to cover Alina's hand. "At her age she wants to hear tales of romance and why not? Never mind, child, dry your eyes and you shall have a true story of love at first sight which will drive all thoughts of witches from your mind. I will tell you how I came to meet the king and of his wooing. Will you like that?"

The mortified Alina managed to choke back her sobs and raised her head.

"Y . . . yes, your grace."

"Good, then you shall hear how it came about." Isabella gave Beatrix a sly, conspiratorial wink and motioned her to take a seat by the bed. "Come, Beatrix, sit by me so that you can remind me if I forget any of the details and you, Petronilla; you can listen too. Doubtless you have heard the story before but it will not hurt you to hear it again."

Petronilla Asterby curled up on the bench at the end of the bed and watched the queen through her pale sardonic eyes. She thought Isabella and Beatrix were cruel to make fun of the little Alina and regretted that their spite would soon make the child as hard as they were, but then if it were not the queen and Beatrix who spoiled her sweet, untouched air it would be one of the hot-blooded gallants now feasting in the great hall below. One way or the other, Alina would soon grow up.

By now Isabella was satisfied that her audience was sufficiently attentive and she was smiling reminiscently as she said softly:

"It was in the summertime when I first saw him. I was twelve years old and already betrothed to the son of Hugh de Lusignan, the Count de la Marche. My future husband was also called Hugh. I thought him rather handsome and I was pleased when it was arranged that I should be sent to the count's home to be brought up with my betrothed until it was time for us to be bedded." The dark eyes were mocking as they dwelt for a moment on Alina's still face. "I had no doubt that I was already old enough, but it was as well that Hugh's father did not agree, for who would want to marry a mere count when one could have a king for the asking?

"My betrothal to young Hugh was important to my family and to his. For many years our families had quarrelled bitterly and this pleased King Richard, for while we were divided and at war we were no threat to him, but when John became king my father's feud with the Lusignans was done and the marriage would have healed old wounds and made a powerful alliance.

"Then one day John came to Aquitaine to receive the homage of his vassals. As I was my father's sole heiress it was John's wish that I too should attend upon him, and word was sent to the Count de la Marche's castle. He was away with his wife and young Hugh at the time but I was in the care of the Count of Eu, Lusignan's brother. Later they were angry with him and

12

said he should not have let me go, but after all who could blame him? My father's request was a reasonable one and John, as Duke of Aquitaine, had said I should make my own fealty to him."

Her voice grew quieter as her eyes dreamed.

"That summer the Angoumois was at its most beautiful. The air was soft and scented with flowers, the sky without a single cloud, the grass like green silk under the horses' hooves as we rode along the banks of the Charante. Such a lovely place, Alina. There the wheat grows tall and golden when it is ripe and the fruit is rich and plentiful. I remember how the sun shone and how pleased I was that I had so magnificent a dowry to carry to Hugh's son, for one day my father's province would be his. Ah well!"

She sat up and her voice grew brisker.

"When I made my obeisance to the king he could not take his eyes off me. I heard people whispering at the way he stared at me and how he kept me by his side, paying no attention to the others about him. He said afterwards that he had fallen in love with me at the first moment of our meeting. He had already had his marriage to Isabel of Gloucester put aside because they were cousins and she bored him. It was said he sought the hand of a Portuguese princess for political reasons, yet once he had seen me he soon forgot her."

Petronilla gave an unseen sigh of impatience. She had heard all this many times before and it moved her no more now than it had done at its first telling. She had often wondered whether it was mere lust which had moved John to marry the precocious little daughter of Count Aymer of Angoulême or whether it was the acute political sense which the king had inherited from his father. The balance of power in Aquitaine would have been seriously disturbed by the union of the houses of Lusignan and Angoulême and John would not have been blind to the dangers.

Yet he had had to pay a high price for Isabella just the same, for he had made undying enemies of the Lusignans and by removing Isabella from the care of one of his own vassals had committed a serious breach of feudal law, and that was all that the wily Philip Augustus of France had needed.

13

Philip had returned from the Holy Land determined to destroy the Angevin empire. He had not succeeded during Richard's lifetime but when a stray arrow brought about Coeur de Lion's death, Philip's ambitions quickened. He had not hurried. Indeed, he moved very cautiously at first, pretending to plead with John to heed the Lusignans' complaints and to make proper restitution but John had ignored him, and since Philip could not allow himself to be flouted in that manner, he had finally summoned John to his own court in Paris. When John refused to go, the French court pronounced him contumacious and declared him forfeit of Aquitaine, Poitou and Anjou, whilst Philip, seizing the opportunity for which he had waited so long, broke the feudal ties between himself and his rebellious vassal and began to fight for Normandy, the duchy for which he had hungered for many years.

John, already at odds with his English barons, had had difficulty in finding enough money to support his campaign and appeared to many to be more interested in his child-bride than the project on hand, but in fact the real problem lay within the duchy itself. The truth of it was that the Normans had grown weary of Angevin rule. Old King Henry had kept too tight a rein on them; Richard had bled them white for his crusades and filled the duchy with savage mercenaries who treated his subjects like hated enemies. More and more the Norman baronage was beginning to look towards the cool, subtle states-man in Paris whose reputation for astute judgments, painstaking diligence, and steely, disciplined determination measured favourably against the name which John had made for himself as a frivolous, weak and idle playboy.

The fight was a long one but the outcome was never really in doubt, for time and natural circumstances were on Philip's side and all he had needed was patience, of which he had ample reserves, and resolution, which he possessed in unlimited quantities. By June 1204 the whole of the duchy of Normandy, with the exception of the Channel Islands, was lost to the English crown and Philip Augustus was triumphantly master of Rouen.

Petronilla came out of her reverie as Isabella finished speaking and grimaced. Perhaps if John had not married Isabella he would have held Normandy. Or, if he had come to terms with the Lusignans once the deed was done, perhaps Philip would not have found an excuse to run his royal sword through the duchy with such ease. But then again, perhaps it would have made no difference. Even Henry Plantagenet and his warrior-son might have done no better against a disaffected people, and it was clear that the vast Angevin empire was already crumbling by the time John had been crowned at Westminster.

"Is that not romantic?" asked Isabella artlessly. "My poor Hugh. How his heart must have broken when I wed John. I often wonder if he still thinks of me, for he once said that if he could not marry me he would take no other woman."

She leaned forward and pointed to the cradle.

"Beatrix, give me my son; I want to hold him again."

She waited impatiently until the infant was laid in her arms, laughing ruefully as the tiny red face puckered and contorted.

"He is not very handsome is he? Did you know that the king has decided to call him Richard?" Her tone was mildly derisive. "Poor John. He hated his father and his brother, yet our first child he named Henry and this one he calls Richard. It is as though even in death they will not let him go nor permit him to forget the ties between them which he tried so hard to sever."

Beatrix nodded. "Yes, I had heard of his grace's decision. Has the Bishop of Winchester agreed to baptize the child?"

"Of course. Peter des Roches is our good friend and was he not the only bishop to remain in England after the interdict?" Isabella was scornful. "All the others scuttled off to France or Rome to save their immortal souls, but Peter is loyal to John and believes him right in the stand he has taken against the pope. Yes, he will christen my sweet Richard in the chapel here, although, alas, there will be few to witness it."

Joie had crept out of her corner in the hope of catching a glimpse of the king's son. She was glad to hear that he would not be deprived of the protection of the Church, and was too

15

simple to ask herself whether the powerful Bishop of Winchester, who was the king's right hand, did wrong to defy the Holy Father. It had been a sad Christmas and now, on the Eve of the Epiphany 1209, the blanket of sorrow had not been lifted, for all that Isabella's child could hope for was a quick and hurried service in the cold seclusion of the castle chapel.

When the baby had been returned to his warm nest, Isabella gave a yawn.

"Oh, how tired I am. My eyelids feel so heavy I can scarce keep them open."

"I am not surprised." Beatrix was a trifle tart. "You have talked too much when you should have been resting."

"Do not scold so." Isabella sighed as she slid down in the bed. "Put out some of the candles so that I can sleep, and when I wake we will have supper together, for I doubt that the king will be minded to leave his celebrations to sit with me."

Beatrix was quick to soothe, her sharpness gone as she saw the chagrin in her mistress.

"He has more sense, your grace; he knows you must rest. Now close your eyes and sleep. I shall not be far away."

She snuffed out the candles so that the bed retreated into shadows, gesturing to Alina and Petronilla to follow her to the fire.

For a moment Isabella watched the dark outlines of their heads against the blaze. It was a comfort to feel them near and she was growing deliciously drowsy under the warmth of the covers. She was glad she had given John another boy. It would keep him sweet-tempered for many weeks to come and nowadays John was not always good-humoured. Sometimes his frantic rages terrified her, although she was always careful not to show her fear, but he would not be angry now, and when he came to see her on the morrow he would probably bring her some valuable trinket to show his pleasure and gratitude.

Outside, black night had chased the last of the feeble daylight away as howling winds whipped the snow into a white frenzy about the castle perched on its rocky hill, but inside the quiet chamber Isabella smiled in her sleep as she dreamed

16

of Angoulême in summer, where birds had sung from morn till dusk and where she had been carefree and happy until that fateful day when John, Duke of Aquitaine, Count of Poitou, and King of England, had summoned her to her father's capital city to pay homage and suddenly and unexpectedly had made her his bride.

While Isabella slept, John was preparing for the evening meal. His chamber was a hive of activity as Petit, his body-servant, laid out a new dalmatica of crimson silk powdered with small knots of gold and a mantle of deep blue lined with vair, and Florence, the royal washer-woman, bustled about collecting the discarded linen and hose which John had worn that day.

Petit smoothed the rich garments with a complacent hand. Yes, the king would look well in these, and he was glad that Ralph, the tailor, had put the finishing touches to them the night before. It would never have done for John to celebrate the birth of a son in robes which had been worn before.

Petit was a short gnome-like man with not a hair to bless his shining bald pate and small alert eyes which never missed anything which went on around him. His thin body was neatly garbed in decent black and his hands were scrubbed spotlessly clean, for John, personally fastidious to the point of mania, was equally concerned to see that those who served him were without stain or blemish.

Petit did not mind John's eccentricities: indeed, he rather approved of them, proud that where some of the court nobles scarcely knew the feel of water on their bodies, the king took frequent baths and even employed a bathman, William, paying him the generous sum of five pence a day for his services. Beyond the iron-bound door William was at that very moment pouring more cans of steaming water into the tub housed in the king's garderobe, and presently John would emerge clean and pink in the long gown he wore in his chamber, whistling cheerfully or singing snatches of some racy song.

Of course John was not always so sunny of disposition, and

no one knew it better than Petit who had served him for many years but, on the other hand, when things were going well, no man was more affable or silver-tongued than the king and in such moods he could be very generous.

Petit hummed to himself as he selected hose of woven silk and precious slippers stitched with patterns of small diamonds and rubies, rubbing the toes lightly with a clean cloth until the jewels winked and gleamed like fire. He was just reaching for the casket which contained the king's choicest gems when he heard the door open and turned quickly to bow to the man who strode into the room with a firm, decisive step.

John grinned amiably at Petit as he crossed to the bed, nodding in approval at his servant's handiwork.

"Excellent, Petit, excellent. I shall make heads turn tonight shall I not? I must remember to thank Ralph for his industry."

Petit murmured a brief reply and put his head on one side to regard his master for a moment.

John was not tall, no more than five foot five, but his body was solid and strong under the flowing gown and he moved as if every inch of him was charged with fierce, pulsating energy. His hair which had once been thick and curly was now growing thin, his face sallow in hue, the eyes of dark blue slanting oddly under arched brows. His nose was true Plantagenet, with its curiously blunted tip, but the mouth, wide and sensual, was peculiarly his own.

John was undoubtedly a libertine and Petit was the first to admit it, but he took a vicarious pride in the number of women the king had managed to lure to his bed, marvelling at the zest and stamina which John brought so cheerfully to his task. He sometimes thought his master was a trifle unwise to seduce the wives and daughters of his own barons, for he had made an unnecessary number of enemies that way, but it was, of course, no business of his and he was never seriously critical of John.

"A great occasion, sire," said Petit conversationally as he got the king into his thin, pleated shirt and well-fitting breeches. "It is not every day a man has a son."

"Nor every day a king has another heir." John sat on the side

18

of the bed as Petit began to pull on the hose. "If anything should happen to young Henry, I shall have a second string to my bow and there will be no question as to the succession when I am gone."

"Indeed, lord king, and he's a fine child I hear."

"The women think so and, praise be to God, he's healthy."

"Well, the queen is young and strong and. . . ." Petit broke off as the light behind the king's eyes changed. "And you, sire, are. . . ."

He fell silent as John's lips tightened, knowing full well what was passing through the king's mind. Although his own attention strayed only too often, John was still passionately jealous where Isabella was concerned and was constantly on the watch for any sign that she was betraying him with another man. No one could fail to see that, for all her regal beauty and grace, the queen was a strumpet and it was no wonder that the king glowered with fury when she turned her smile on some handsome stripling or squire, for if she had her way a smile would not be all which they would exchange. Once or twice John had driven men from the court because he thought Isabella favoured them too well, and often Petit had heard his master screaming his rage at his wife behind their chamber door. He cursed himself for mentioning her name and driving the contentment from the king's eyes, but the moment of danger had already passed and John was shrugging calmly enough.

"Yes, he comes of sound stock. Now the robe, Petit."

Swiftly the body-servant pulled the folds into place, leaving visible just a hint of the embroidered tunic below, and then set the mantle carefully about the king's shoulders, fastening it with a huge jewelled morse. When they were both fully satisfied with the effect John began to turn over the rings in the casket holding them up one by one and admiring them by the light of the candles.

"They are beautiful, Petit, beautiful," he said softly. "As lovely as any woman and a good deal less trouble."

"But not always so satisfying, your grace?" suggested Petit slyly. "An armful of warm flesh in bed on a cold winter's night is more comfort than a fistful of diamonds."

19

The king laughed. "What do you know about women, eh?" He shot Petit an amused glance. "One would think to hear you talk that you had much experience of them."

Petit was not in the least offended.

"No personal knowledge, sire, but then I have learned a lot from you."

John threw back his head and roared with approval.

"Well said, Petit; I asked for that. And talking of women. . . ." The tilted eyes had an almost wolfish look about them now as one hand stroked the short, neatly trimmed beard with reflective fingers. "That woman who nurses my son: she's a comely baggage right enough."

"Eva, my lord?"

"Yes, Eva, that's the one."

Petit raised his shoulders negligently. He thought Eva decidedly fat, and she looked too slumberous for his taste, but it was clear that she had taken the king's fancy and after all it was his job to be helpful.

"Aye, she's shapely enough and her skin is fresh and clean."

John leered. "And how much of it have you seen, my friend?"

Petit tittered. The king liked to have his little joke.

"Not much, I confess, but there are others who might be more fortunate."

"Like me, for example?"

"Why not? She'd be honoured."

"Would she?" John's lips curved into a faintly unpleasant smile. "Could she be dragged away from the whelp and that pack of chattering females?"

"Easily enough. After all, they cannot expect her to work day and night. There is another to take her place at midnight."

John looked sharply at his servant.

"You are well-informed."

Petit cackled again.

"Of course, my lord, that is why you employ me, is it not? Anyone could lay out a garment or two, but it takes more than that to know what really pleases you. I saw you look at her this

20

morning when you went to see the child. If you recall, you bade me accompany you, and I noticed."

"You're a sly old fox and sometimes I think you see too much for your own good, but I confess she interests me and after all it would be a tame end to a night of celebrations to go to a cold bed and sleep. You're right, Petit, a handful of diamonds would not be enough. Send the girl to my chamber when she is free, and tell her she has nothing to fear. I'm generous enough when I'm satisfied as you can testify."

"Indeed, and I will see to it."

John slipped three rings on to his strong, stubby fingers and considered them for a moment. Then, with a brief word of thanks, he turned on his heel and left Petit to tidy the chamber.

As he folded the discarded robe, Petit was thoughtful. Men said that the king had a sense of humour which was both bawdy and spiteful, and it was well in character that on the very day when his wife had given him a much-wanted son, John should elect to bed the woman hired to nurse the infant. On the other hand, however, it was equally likely that as the queen lay resting in her downy nest she too was planning some light intrigue ready for the time when she had recovered from the birth, for there were a number of very comely knights at court at present and Isabella would not have failed to notice them. Yes, they were a well-matched pair right enough; each deserving the other's blatant and uncaring infidelity.

Petit sighed once more, glancing round the room now meticulously neat and ready for the king's secret assignation with his son's wet-nurse. Yes, it would do, and now he could make his way down to the kitchens where Berthe, who had a soft spot for him, would have put aside a special delicacy or two for him to sample and would have made ready a jug of cool wine to slake his thirst.

With another nod of satisfaction Petit picked up a smoking candle and made his way downstairs, pausing for a second by the great hall to listen to the roar of approval as barons, knights and their exquisite, perfumed ladies rose to their feet to lift their goblets to the king in a quick, congratulatory toast.

When Petit had finished his leisurely meal he made his way into the hall, wincing slightly as the noise struck his ear like a blow. When the hall was empty it seemed a vast, hollow place, cold and unwelcoming, but that night it was scarcely large enough for the crowds which filled every corner to capacity.

At one end the king's table had been raised on a dais to a commanding position and those most favoured by the monarch sat with him in front of a snowy cloth scarcely visible beneath the many dishes and platters which an army of servants had borne in, fragrant and piping-hot, from the kitchens behind the screens. The remainder of the company sat on either side of long trestles running through the length of the hall, but in addition to John's guests, his household servants and the guards who made merry between the tables and at the end of the chamber, vast numbers of beggars and poor folk had been allowed into the castle to share in the joyous celebrations.

In front of the royal board jesters in bright motley decorated with tiny jangling bells romped with dwarfs no higher than a man's knee, as tumblers and acrobats twisted their lithe bodies into incredible shapes to entertain the clapping audience. High above in the minstrels' gallery the court musicians were playing on harp and guitar, blowing their pipes and beating their drums with untiring vigour in an effort to make themselves heard above the deafening roar of laughter and voices. To add to the confusion the barons' much-prized hunting dogs were roaming happily under the tables, condescending every now and then to accept the favour of a choice portion of meat from an indulgent master, barking enthusiastically to show their pleasure and appreciation, adding new depths to the ear-splitting din.

Petit leapt out of the way as a sturdy cellarer pushed his way through the mob with a fresh load of wine jugs, making his way to the far corner where the squires were carving the great sides of beef and haunches of venison. For a while he stood and watched them, admiring the swift dexterity of their slim young hands as their sharp knives sliced the blood-red meat into neat portions to be laid carefully on hot silver dishes by their side.

They were the sons of some of the noblest houses in England, sent to court to endure the exacting rigours of the training for knighthood, and amongst the manifold things which they had to master was the correct way to culpone a salmon, portion out a crane or heron, or carve a boar's head with exact precision. It was no menial task and they were proud of their skill, for it was yet another step along the road they trod with such enthusiasm.

Finally Petit moved on and found himself in the company of Fulk de Peche and Robert de Houbridge, two of the mercenaries serving under one of John's Flemish captains, and Gerold Fitz-Hubert, a peppery and aged doctor whose job it was to care for the sick and wounded in the royal household.

FitzHubert heartily disapproved of John and criticized him with such frequency and lack of discretion that it was a wonder to all that the king had not done away with him long since. Now he took a long draught of ale and said sourly:

"And what have you been doing, Master Petit? Acting as procurer for your master again, I suppose."

Petit ignored the gibe. Sometimes he grew angered at FitzHubert's outspokenness, but it had to be admitted the old man was very shrewd, and tonight he was in no mood for quarrels.

"Never you mind. What I do for his grace is between him and me and I talk to no man of our business."

"Just as well for the pair of you." The thin shoulders hunched up in disdain. "You've neither of you anything to boast about."

"Hush, old man, are you bereft of your wits?" De Houbridge was half-laughing but he cast a quick look about him for he had a strong instinct of self-preservation. "What if someone hears you?"

"Amidst this?" Gerold threw up his hands in scorn. "They can hear nothing but the clacking of their own tongues as they flatter and fawn upon the king. And he's no fit sovereign either. If Richard had lived he would not have let Normandy go."

"That's in the past." Fulk de Peche leaned back against the

23

wall turning his beaker slowly between his hands. "What's done is done, and Richard is dead."

"More's the pity. Now there is only Softsword left to lead us."

"That's no way to speak of your liege-lord." Petit was sharp in spite of his determination not to be goaded by the truculent physician. "Robert is right; you'll come to a bad end with that tongue of yours."

"Softsword is what men called him when he made peace with Philip Augustus, and the name fits him well. He should not have agreed to terms; he should have fought as his brother would have done. And much good it did him, he and his treaties. In the end the Frenchman won."

"John had too much sense to try to fight in the beginning. He could see that peace was his only hope. His father's empire was too big to hold with his resources and he knew it. He had neither the money nor the troops to make war on Philip."

Gerold made a rude noise.

"He had sufficient. Lackland he was at birth and Lackland he will end, mark my words."

"It was not his fault he had no inheritance," returned Petit hotly. "Was he to blame because there were no territories remaining? His eldest brother, Henry the young king, had been promised Anjou, Maine, Touraine, Normandy and England; Richard, his mother's duchy of Aquitaine, and Geoffrey was married off to Constance of Brittany to provide him with valuable lands. When John was born there was nothing left for for him but his father's love, and the old king did love him, better than any other of his sons."

"And how did _Jean sans Terre_ repay that love?" demanded Gerold shortly. "By betraying his father when Richard and Philip Augustus made war on him. It broke the old king's heart and he had no will to live thereafter."

"Men do not die of broken hearts." De Peche roused himself from his contemplation of a serving wench with full soft breasts and hips which made his loins ache. "You should know better than that, since you profess to cure our ills. The old king was mortally ill."

24

"Then what of Richard?"

"What of him?" De Peche watched regretfully as the girl moved away and out of his sight.

"John betrayed him too. Once Philip Augustus had returned from the Holy Land, leaving Richard to fight Saladin alone, John was quick to ally himself with his brother's enemy."

Petit gritted his teeth. A dozen protests trembled on his lips and he longed to hurl a fierce rebuttal at the tiresome old creature who was smiling triumphantly at the strength of his argument, but it was difficult to put a defence of John into words.

It was easy enough to dismiss John as a traitor to his father and brother, for that was how the whole of Europe had seen him, but few took the trouble to wonder why he had acted as he did.

John, born on Christmas Eve 1167, the eighth and youngest child of Henry II and Eleanor of Aquitaine, had had a poor beginning. His parents were soon separated and quarrelling violently with one another, whilst he was thrust into the Abbey of Fontevrault in the hope that he might become an oblate. It was, of course, a completely forlorn hope and John soon went back to his father's court where he grew up spoiled and pampered, more interested in fine clothes, jewels, and backgammon than in jousting and the manly arts of war. Always conscious that he had nothing to look forward to, it was not surprising that the boy had become bitter and that that bitterness had grown and festered as time went on, for everything which came within his grasp seemed to shatter like fragile glass in his hand. First, the chance of a rich marriage with the daughter of the Count of Maurienne, but the count had demanded certain castles and territories as the price of the match and young Henry, to whom these had belonged, had refused to part with them. Then there had been the glorious opportunity of the crown of Jerusalem. The Patriarch had come to England, because King Baldwin IV was dying of leprosy, to plead with Henry that one of his sons should be allowed to become the next ruler. Petit had heard how John had knelt at

25

his father's feet, begging with tears in his eyes to be given the chance but Henry, either because he would not let the darling of his heart leave him or because he knew his stripling too well, refused to agree and John was given the unimportant lordship of Ireland instead.

That had been a disaster too. With no leaning towards matters military, and even less towards statesmanship, John, egged on by his gay young companions, had spent his time pulling the long beards of the Irish chieftains and mocking them for their crude and unsophisticated ways. The old king had had to recall his cub in haste, but not before John had done much to disturb the hard-won peace of that troublesome island.

It was true that when Richard became king he had been generous to John in the matter of titles and fiefs and had permitted him to wed Isabel of Gloucester, a wealthy heiress, but he had not trusted his brother and would have kept him out of England whilst he was in the Holy Land but for the intercession of Queen Eleanor.

After his abortive plotting with the French king, John had taken refuge in Normandy and there Richard had found him and forgiven him as if he were a fractious, misguided child. As John was then a man of seven and twenty years, it had done nothing to sweeten his temper nor to soften the gnawing, passionate grievances he nursed broodingly to his heart.

Yes, John had been disloyal, but life had made him so. His father had had nothing but love to offer him; his brilliant brother could produce no more than a tolerant regard mingled with scorn. John had learned early that if he wished to succeed he would have to use his own wits and fight with whatever weapons he could find and by any method which was open to him.

And even when Coeur de Lion was dead the way was still not clear, for whilst England and Normandy declared for John, Anjou, Maine and Touraine had acclaimed Arthur of Brittany as the rightful heir, for Arthur's father, Geoffrey, was John's elder brother. John had managed to win the crown of England

and the ducal coronet of Normandy, but his troubles had by no means come to an end.

"And not only is he a betrayer." FitzHubert smirked at Petit's nonplussed face. "He's a murderer too, for did he not put to death with his own hand that innocent child Arthur?"

"Christ! Have a care, you'll get us all hanged." Fulk de Peche swore under his breath and nudged the doctor with a sharp elbow. "If you are tired of life, I am not. No one knows who killed Arthur of Brittany."

"William de Briouze knows and that's why he's out of favour with the king. Oh, John would have it that it's because de Briouze failed to pay his debts to the crown, and because his son was one of the bishops charged by the pope to pronounce the interdict, but there are stronger reasons than these which have stirred up such a hatred."

He motioned his companions to draw nearer, his eye brightening as he lowered his voice.

"I once spoke to a squire in the service of de Briouze. It was clear to me that something troubled his mind for he was pale and watchful and his hands shook like a man well advanced in years. As I am not one to let a man suffer when I can give him aid, I asked him what ailed him."

He ignored the sceptical glances of his audience as he paused to bask in complacent self-righteousness.

"Well?" asked de Houbridge finally. "What did ail him? Could he not get sufficient women to cool his blood?"

"You have a coarse mind, Master Robert." The smugness was gone and FitzHubert looked irritated. "It had nothing to do with women. The boy was frightened."

"Of what? His own shadow?" De Peche looked bored. "If you've nothing more important to tell us than that. . . ."

"Be quiet!" FitzHubert quivered with indignation at the interruption. "How can I tell you anything when you keep chattering? Listen! The squire was frightened because he could not forget what had happened in Normandy. He had learned how the king sent men to Falaise, where Arthur was first imprisoned, with orders to blind and castrate him so that he could no longer be a threat, but when the castellan of the castle, Hubert de Burgh, refused to let the men do their evil work, Arthur was moved to the stouter fortress of Rouen. There, on that night in April, the squire saw John at supper. The king had drunk so much that his speech was slurred and when he rose he staggered wildly and almost fell."

Petit stirred defensively. "All men drink deeply at times. Who has not got sorrows to drown?"

FitzHubert's thin lips curved derisively.

"It was not his sorrows your master wanted to drown, my friend, as you know full well. As I was saying, the squire watched John as he left the hall and followed him as he lurched down the stairs and along the passages to where his nephew was housed. He was careful not to let the king see him, for he had some premonition of what was to come. He could not see anything, of course, for the door was all but closed but he heard the terrible screams and groans of the boy, the scuffling, and the curses of his grace. Then he fled, for he could stand no more, but after that no word of Arthur came until his body was dragged out of the Seine some time later by fishermen. An innocent child! How can you defend a man who would do that?"

"It is only rumour that says he did," snapped Petit furiously. "Your squire was probably drunker than the king. How can you claim that Arthur was an innocent child; he was a dangerous rebel vassal. And do not forget how he was taken prisoner in the first place, this pure-hearted youth over whom you would have us weep. He was besieging his own grandmother at Mirebeau but, fortunately, Queen Eleanor was made of sterner stuff than he and she held Arthur and his knights at bay whilst she sent word to the king at Le Mans.

Petit's anger was fading and now it was his turn to look mildly triumphant.

"John raced his army over those eighty miles in less than two days, fell upon the besiegers, and took them all prisoner."

"Mere good fortune," grunted FitzHubert testily. "The weather favoured him and he had fast horses."

"No such thing! He proved then, to any with eyes to see, that he knew how to fight if he had to. It was his father all over again, springing out from nowhere when men least expected him; as spectacular an appearance as any Coeur de Lion had contrived. No, no, you cannot call that good fortune. That was the mark of a fine general and you know it."

"I know no such thing. It was luck, nothing more."

"And was his plan to save Château Gaillard luck? That was a masterly design if you like."

"Which failed." Gerold's blackened teeth bared. "That is nothing to boast about, Master Petit."

"It failed, but through no fault of the king's. Each step was planned with meticulous care and it was a brilliant piece of strategy. Could the king be blamed because the tide was not full at the right time, so that his water-borne troops and land forces did not arrive together? If it had not been for Nature's whim, the garrison would have been relieved and Richard's 'Saucy Castle' at Les Andelys would have held." Petit looked sad. "If the king could have held the castle he could have held Normandy, for Château Gaillard guarded the way to Rouen and was the lock which secured the duchy."

"But he did not relieve it and eventually it fell." FitzHubert was tetchy. "John was not even there to watch it fall; he had scuttled back to England. Richard would not have done that. Richard would have stayed and defended that which was his with his own sword."

"There were reasons why John could not stay."

"You always make excuses for him. Next you will tell us that he is faithful to his wife." The old doctor chortled with mirth at his own devastating wit and Petit's discomfiture. "Will you tell us that?"

"He's as faithful to her as she is to him, and you have said enough for one night. If you despise the king so, why do you stay and take his money?"

"Why shouldn't I? I do my work well. I earn what he gives me, and where else would I find good food, a comfortable bed, and warmth to cosset my old bones in winter?"

"Nowhere, so be done with your spite." Petit scowled. "He's a good master to serve; you prove it yourself with your own words. He does not stint his servants and he does them no ill."

"Not those who can do him no harm, I agree." FitzHubert was entirely unmoved by Petit's censure, clutching his cup in his skinny hands, reluctant to sip the last of the wine it held. "But those who are powerful lords have no such security, for if John rewards them with one hand he's quick to bring them down with the other, for he distrusts them heartily and is fearful that they mean him harm."

"Perhaps with reason." De Houbridge stretched his arms above his head and yawned. He had not found the doctor's tale of suspected murder of much interest, and cared not a whit whether John had made an end of Arthur or not. Had he been in the king's shoes he thought he probably would have done the same. Arthur had been a tiresome, petulant boy, well-pleased with his own importance, and a ward of John's enemy, Philip Augustus. "There are precious few of the barons with whom the king finds favour."

"Can you wonder, since he puts all his trust in mercenaries?" The doctor waxed indignant. "It is the great lords to whom the king should look for aid and advice, but does he? No, by my faith, he does not! He hires brigands and cut-throats from the Low Countries and Poitou to give him counsel and support."

"Watch what you say," said de Houbridge curtly. "We come from Flanders and so does our captain. If John is prepared to ignore your insolence, we shall not."

FitzHubert paused long enough to contemplate the sinewy strength of the two men now eyeing him in a far from friendly manner, and became instantly conciliatory.

"Come, come, good sirs, I meant no reflection on you, for it is clear enough that you are fighting men of top quality. I simply meant that when the old king was alive, he kept the confidence of the great men of the realm. They respected him and, if he bade them do such and such a thing, they would do it. With John it is different. Even before they agreed to support his claim to the crown they began to make demands of him.

30

They wanted their ancient rights they said, although what those were none could really say."

"The privileges which the old king had taken away from them bit by bit." Petit was acid. "I would say no ill of Henry, for he was a fine king, but he was quick to exercise his authority, and his laws and administration left the barons vastly poorer. When he died, they saw a chance to get something back from Richard. When that plan failed, they hoped for more success with John."

"But he has not given them what they want." Finally Fitz-Hubert drained his cup and smacked his lips appreciatively. "Not one iota more than he has had to, and they are strangely restive. They come to court, but only because custom demands it and they are afraid to ignore the summons. They are not easy with the king, nor he with them. He prefers your foreign masters."

"He knows them to be loyal to him." De Peche smiled thinly. "Maybe we are cut-throats, Master Gerold, but we keep our bargains. If we take the gold of the English king, our swords are his and we look to no other. The Norman barons paid John homage but, when Philip began to fight, they deserted their master. You scorn him because he did not stay to defend the duchy, but how could he when he was surrounded by traitors?"

"And he'll not have forgotten it," broke in de Houbridge, "and nor would I. Were I in John's place, I'd look hard at these English earls who paid lip service to my face and sent their messengers to Paris behind my back. I'd not put my faith in any one of them."

"There are some to be trusted." Petit gave de Houbridge a brief look. "The king's half-brother, Longspée, is true; so is William Marshal of Pembroke, and a few others besides."

"Precious few." De Houbridge was caustic. "You'd be hard put to it to name them. No, if John is suspicious and full of doubts I reckon he's got good cause." He yawned again. "Well, I've had enough of talk for one night." He got to his feet and brushed his tunic free of the strands of clinging straw. "After all, this is a celebration and I've a mind to take another draught

31

of wine and find me a wench who's prepared to be accommodating. What say you, Fulk?"

De Peche scrambled up with alacrity, murmuring his approval, and Petit watched them thrust their way boldly through the crowd. Then he too rose to his feet and his eyes slid to the malcontent still crouching over his empty cup.

"A good night to you, sir," he said with quiet malevolence. "Sleep well on that soft couch which the king has provided for you, and dream in comfort of the goodly meals he'll furnish for you tomorrow. And if by chance you should hear footsteps in the night, or strange rustlings by your side, do not fear too much. Not all the enemies of the king disappear as Arthur did, and not all die by violence. Perhaps you will survive to grow older still and meet your Maker in a peaceful end. Who knows?"

And with that he walked off in search of Eva, glad to have robbed the malignant old doctor's face of colour, not bothering to turn back to watch him shudder under his black robe which he hugged about him as the full significance of Petit's words broke upon him with uncomfortable and sinister clarity.

CHAPTER TWO

"GOD's teeth, William! That's another hundred marks you have lost and another hundred which I have won." The king chuckled with delight as he gathered up the dice from the table in front of him and rattled them triumphantly in his hand. "Well, this is no time to stop, so let us play another game."

William Longspée, Earl of Salisbury, pulled a face.

"I fear luck is against me tonight, sire, and I've nothing left to wager save my horse. And should you win that from me, how shall I ride off from here to do your bidding?"

John laughed again and gave the earl a look of affection. He was strangely content that night. The Christmas court of 1209 had been a most splendid one and every nobleman worth the name had travelled to Windsor to pay his homage and to eat and drink the gargantuan meals provided at the monarch's expense. John had not stinted them for, if he had a streak of meanness in him, he never showed it on such occasions and the tables had brought forth cries of astonishment and approval which had warmed John's heart. He had made them expensive gifts of new cloaks and jewels, smiling at them blandly as he calculated with his cool blue eyes the likely taxes he could take from them in the following year, wondering which of them bowing before him now was planning some fresh treachery in his heart.

But he had no such reservations about William. William, the natural son of Henry II and his mistress, the Fair Rosamund, had always been completely loyal to his half-brother, demanding nothing of him and offering him steadfast friendship and unswerving support. With William, John could relax, for there were no suspicions to cloud the words between them and the king was never happier than when the earl was at court, for then he could drink a measure of wine with him, exchange a bawdy jest or two, and rob him of his silver in a game of dice.

"Never mind, the night is young and your luck will change. Meanwhile, here is something to mend your fortunes."

John threw a heavy bag of coins across the table to his brother and grinned at Master Alexander who sat watching the game with benevolent interest, signalling to Petit hovering solicitously in the background to call for more wine.

The earl's eyebrows rose at the weight of the pouch, but John dismissed his hesitancy with a wave of his hand.

"What is mine is yours, you know that. Do you begrudge me the pleasure of a game? And how can we play if you have no money?"

Longspée shrugged. He was a tall, heavy man with a thatch of red-gold hair and bright blue eyes. Splendid on the field of battle and tireless in the chase, he was notorious for the regularity with which he lost at the gambling table, yet he had never learned his lesson and as Master Alexander watched, he emptied out the silver pennies and began to arrange them in neat piles.

Alexander's mouth twisted slightly. He would like to have laid hands on such wealth with so little effort, and had he been fortunate enough to do so, he would not have wasted it as William was doing. It was quite clear that John would win again; he always did. He would claim back every last coin on the scarred oak table, and leave Longspée still heavily in debt.

Master Alexander professed to be a theologian, although most men regarded him as a trickster and charlatan. The interdict had been a God-send to him, for he had seized the chance to denounce the pope for his action, and to lay the blame for the disaster on the wickedness of the people of England. Naturally, John had been intrigued by such utterances and had soon sent for the man who held the view that the king was innocent, and before very long Alexander had wormed his way into John's confidence and become his most valued and highly-respected counsellor.

With sufficient education and wit to hold his own in conversation with men more learned than himself, Alexander had feathered a comfortable nest for himself at court, clothing his plump person with the expensive garments which John provided and making the most of the excellent fare which was put before him with almost monotonous regularity.

As he watched the king and his brother roll the dice again he pursed his lips reflectively. John had had a good year, and it was no wonder that he was in an expansive mood. The interdict had not worried the king at all, for in an age when faith was a man's most precious possession, John had neither time for sermons nor for the men who preached them. He was a cynic who had grown tired of prayers long before he had left childhood, and seldom bothered to hear mass or observe the Church's laws of fasting and self-denial.

He had managed not to quarrel openly with the Church until 1205 when Archbishop Hubert Walter had died. Since it was recognized that there was much advantage to a monarch in having clergy for his administrative officers, it was natural enough that John had sought to press his own candidate, John de Gray, his former secretary, as the new primate.

John had hurried off to Canterbury to inform the monks of his desires, ignoring the insistence of the bishops of the province that they had a right to share in the election. As the monks refused to admit the bishops' claim either, they had not been outwardly opposed to the king's suggestion until they had learned that his agents were already on their way to Rome to put de Gray's name before the pope. This was not to be tolerated, for the minster men had had a very difficult time under the last two archbishops and were determined that the new primate should be a man of their own choice. Secretly, and under the cover of darkness, the younger and more militant monks had elected their sub-prior, Reginald, and had sent him to Rome, swearing him to secrecy as they bade him farewell. But Reginald could not keep a still tongue in his head and was soon boasting of his election, rumour of which had quickly reached John through his royal agents. In a fury John had stormed down to Canterbury again, demanding an explanation, and the monks confronted by a display of true Angevin temper quivered in fear and denied hastily that an election had ever taken place. By then John's mind was made up and brusquely he told the monks to be done with their appeals to Rome and forced them to elect John de Gray as the new archbishop.

Pope Innocent III, faced with the many claims and counter-claims of the various parties clamouring for his approval, had not allowed the chaos to confuse him too much or to under-mine his own judgment, and with crisp words he dismissed both Reginald and John de Gray, stating firmly that their elections had been patently irregular, and ordering the cathedral delegates to make a fresh election. When the monks divided equally between the cause of the sub-prior and de Gray, Innocent, unperturbed and by no means displeased with the outcome, had put forward his own suggestion.

Stephen Langton, he had said smoothly, was the ideal solution to the problem. An Englishman of mature years who was a cardinal-priest of St. Chrysogonus and lately a tutor of great distinction at the University of Paris, Stephen was clearly the most suitable person to fill so important a role. The pope had not thought it necessary to add that Langton would also carry out the programme of reforms so near to Innocent's heart, but he expressed great pleasure when the monks had accepted his nominee unanimously, and wrote enthusiastically to John to tell him of the proceedings, seeking his confirmation of the appointment.

John had exploded in fury, and since he had no particular respect for the powerful and much-revered pontiff, he had written him a sharply-worded missive refusing flatly to accept Stephen Langton as archbishop or to permit him to land on English soil. Innocent's reply was equally curt as he chided John for his insolence and short-sightedness in rejecting so suitable a candidate.

After twelve months had elapsed, during which time John had turned the Canterbury monks out of their home, Innocent consecrated Langton at Viterbo in June 1207 without waiting for John's agreement, and ordered the bishops of London, Ely and Worcester to try once more to make the king see sense or, if this task proved impossible, to warn him of the dire consequences which would follow.

Needless to say, the unfortunate bishops had failed entirely to move the implacable king, and were forced to proclaim the interdict but if Innocent had thought to terrorize John's soul by such a sentence, he was sadly disappointed. Once John's initial rage had died down, he set to work calmly and collectedly to make capital out of the situation.

His first move was to confiscate all clerical property and estates on the grounds that such worldly possessions had been given to the clergy to enable them to perform certain tasks. Since they had now ceased to fulfil their undertakings, he argued, they could no longer lay claim to their temporalities, and sent his men under the chief justiciar, Geoffrey FitzPeter, Earl of Essex, to relieve them of their goods.

There had been a good deal of violence, for John's men had not bothered to show either courtesy or restraint, and not a single baron had stirred himself to rise to the defence of the clergy. Many of them felt John in order in defying the pope, for it was beyond doubt the monarch's right to confirm the appointment of the Archbishop of Canterbury, a right which Innocent had not given the king a chance to exercise. Besides, the wealth which flowed into John's coffers from the confiscation of the clergy's goods was so vast that it seemed unlikely the king would trouble his barons with heavy taxation whilst such bounty was available, and they had shrugged their shoulders and turned a blind eye to John's activities.

John had threatened to turn every priest out of England but such a task was beyond even him, and after a week or two the king and clergy had reached an agreement whereby the clergy would farm their benefices and other holdings on behalf of the crown, and would receive in return a small allowance on which to live. This suited John well, for it saved the labours of his own men, whilst the clergy had accepted it philosophically as the only way to prevent the total destruction of their property.

Innocent did not take John's intransigence lying down. His retort was swift and to the point. If the interdict was not enough, worse could follow; John himself could be excommunicated and cut off from the body of the Church and from every living Christian. This time John did not respond with further threats. By now he had things well in hand, and there could have been no clearer testimonial to his father's administrative genius than the ease with which John had been able to use the state machinery to take charge of clerical lands and property until, as an act of grace, he had permitted the unfortunate owners to return as his tenants. If there had been any doubt about his strength as king at the time of his coronation, those doubts were now dispelled, for neither clergy nor barons had opposed him, and from this enviable position John had kept open negotiations with Innocent until November 1209 when the pope finally lost patience and excommunicated him.

And not only had John weathered the storm of interdict and excommunication, of which few took any heed, but he had also succeeded in obtaining the submission of William the Lion, King of Scotland, in April of that year, and had forced the hostile princes of north and south Wales to pay homage to him at Woodstock in October.

Yes, John had had a good year, and suddenly Alexander gave a rich chuckle which made the king look up in enquiry.

"Share your joke with us, Master Alexander. I grow weary of winning silver so easily. I swear you are right, William. Dame Fortune does not sit with you tonight."

"Nor any other time, sire, when I toss the dice." Longspée was resigned. "Should I foreswear such pastimes do you think?"

"And deprive us both of pleasure? Never! Now, Master Alexander, why do you laugh? Is it at the sight of your monarch?"

Alexander's rubicund face crinkled up.

"Nay, lord king, and you know it is not so. No, I was pondering on things which had happened since the interdict was proclaimed. A sudden thought came to me of the priests

38

and their hearth-mates, and I swear I could not control my laughter. Do you recall how you ordered your men to seize the priests' women and keep them safely locked up until sufficient bail was found?"

John gave an appreciative shout of mirth.

"Clearly, Master Alexander. Most clearly do I recall how the clergy tumbled over one another in their anxiety to pay for the privilege of buying back their lady-loves. And these same priests presume to judge me and call me a lecher, though I am not in orders and have made no promises to pope or God to remain celibate. Do you wonder that I have small regard for their cant? It is said that their homes are full of cradles and screeching infants, smelling of warm milk and worse. What kind of priests are they who preach one kind of morality and practise another?"

"Beneath contempt." Alexander nodded vigorously. "You do well to ignore their censure, sire, for it is as worthless as their virtue. Do you not agree, my lord?"

Salisbury gave Alexander a brief look. He disliked the squat, corpulent man whom the king favoured so, for he shared men's view that he was both dishonest and greedy. He did not often consider his brother a fool, but in this he felt John had shown a considerable lack of wisdom and wondered why the king could not see through the transparent falsehood of his newly-found adviser.

"They do no harm," he replied gruffly. "In truth, they haven't much to give them comfort. Small stipends, poor houses, hardly sufficient food to fill their stomachs. Who am I to judge them when they take a woman to their beds?"

John snorted.

"I would not judge them either, William, were they not so quick to judge me, but that was not why I took their mistresses from them. It was a jest, no more, for as you say they are harmless." His smile faded. "But there are others who are more dangerous."

Petit shifted uncomfortably from one foot to another. He had heard the grating note in the king's voice which always heralded trouble, and was wondering whether he could slip away before John's temper rose to the surface.

"Others?" Longspée tilted one eyebrow. "Whom, sire?"

"Do you need to ask? William de Briouze and that trollop Matilda, his wife, of course."

Petit took a nervous step backwards. It was as he had feared. John was touching on a subject which was like an aching tooth and it would only be a matter of time now before the sallow skin flushed with rage and the blue eyes burned red with fire.

Salisbury began to rearrange his remaining pennies in a new pattern, keeping his voice quiet and casual.

"William swears he means you no harm."

"Then he lies." John sat upright. "I knew well enough when the interdict came that I should be made excommunicate and that many of my barons who swear so faithfully to serve me would turn over in their minds the possibility of breaking their vows to me. Thus, I demanded of each of them a hostage to ensure their continued loyalty."

"And you got them."

"Save from de Briouze."

"It was not he who defied your men."

"No, it was his sharp-tongued vixen of a wife." The flush was deepening. "She dared to refuse my men and, what is more, said she would never let any of her sons fall into the hands of one who had murdered his own nephew. God's blood, she deserves to die for that."

Petit could see the sweat standing out on John's forehead as the memory of the bold Matilda came back to him, but cautiously he braced himself to move forward and refill the king's goblet in the hope of averting the oncoming storm.

"She was hysterical and filled with fear for the safety of her children." Salisbury did not look up from his counting. "She did not mean what she said, and later William gave her a severe rebuke for her insolence. Did he not plead with you to tell him how he had offended you, in order that he could offer full satisfaction?"

"Yes he did, but he already knew how he had offended me,

for it was not only that witch's words which had caused hurt. He owed me money. I gave him the honour of Limerick for five hundred marks a year but, in six years, he has repaid less than seven hundred marks. And is he not the father of Giles of Hereford, one of those craven bishops who pronounced the interdict?"

"He had no choice. The pope. . . ."

"To the devil with the pope!" John got up and thrust his chair away with a rough hand. "I do not care a fig for him or his proclamations, and neither should William or his son have done so. They should have stayed loyal to me, for I am right in this argument and Innocent is wrong. And where is William now? Is he here, seeking to gain my pardon. No! He has fled with his family to Ireland and is sheltering under the wing of the Lacys."

Longspée gave a faint sigh.

"Gently, lord king, I pray you, gently. William was afraid. He did not have the money with which to pay his debts, and the acts of his son were beyond his control. Doubtless he beat Matilda for her insult but by then it was too late and it would be a brave man who would venture hence to face your wrath."

For a moment John was silent, clenching and unclenching his fists as he stared angrily at his brother. Then, to the vast relief of Petit and Master Alexander, who was as terrified of John's spleen as the next man, the king gave another snort and sat down again.

"They are not really of importance." Salisbury was quick to take advantage of the moment." What is of concern, sire, is the progress you are making with the emperor and the Rhineland princes. How do these matters go?"

In a second John's anger had melted and he was all smiles again as he pulled up his chair to the table and took a mouthful of wine.

"Well, William, very well. Now that my nephew, Otto, has been crowned Holy Roman Emperor we can really begin to make progress again!" He rubbed his hands together with satisfaction. "It is the only way to withstand Philip Augustus,

41

of that I am sure; a coalition of England, Germany and the Lowlands against France. Richard saw this and at his death he was making splendid plans with the princes but then, just when I needed their aid, they sailed off to the East on some foolish crusade." His frown was fleeting and soon his voice was calm once more. "Now their follies are done, and Otto has promised me full support. It will not be long before I can challenge Philip and lay claim to that which he has stolen from me."

Longspée nodded but he thought the king was a trifle optimistic. John might have been making good progress with the Rhineland princes but his relationship with his own barons was growing steadily worse, and without their co-operation the chance of wresting back his lost continental possession was negligible.

Salisbury pulled his long upper lip thoughtfully. It was a pity that John had failed so signally to reach any rapport with the English nobility. One could not blame him for all the ills which made the baronage grumble so restively, for a good many of these were the work of Henry and Richard. John had been unfortunate in inheriting not only dissatisfactions which were fast reaching boiling point, but were also made much worse by the sharp rise in prices. The old king had been able to hire a good, stalwart mercenary for eightpence; John now had to pay two shillings for such a man. Henry and Richard had had much demesne land; John had far less, for his father and brother had given a good deal away in royal grants.

Scutage was an accepted practice, for few of the great barons wanted to go to war themselves, and although they muttered when John, in the first year of his reign, had raised the knight fee from twenty shillings to two marks, they had made no violent objection for such increases were easily passed on to their own knights. What did infuriate them was John's insistence that they themselves should pay a fine for personal exemption, and they cursed him heartily, conveniently overlooking the fact that it was Richard who had introduced the practice and John who had merely increased the rate.

42

It was not all a matter of money: had it been so perhaps some solution might have been found. Salisbury's eyes moved back to John. No, it was John himself who was the root cause of the trouble. William was fond of his half-brother but he was not blind to his shortcomings. Henry and Richard had had faults too, of course, and not even their most devoted admirers would have denied it but somehow the defects of John's character were more obvious, more rasping, more petty and exacerbating, and less palatable to swallow since he could not dazzle like Richard had done nor evoke the admiration and respect accorded to Henry.

By and large Henry and Richard had got on well with the great men of the realm who were their natural advisers. They had not always agreed with them and they had bullied them harshly enough when they had had to, but they had not cut themselves off from them, and they had trusted them.

John did not trust any of them. He had learned a searing lesson in Normandy which he found it impossible to forget and with few exceptions visited the sins of the Norman baronage on their English brethren. When the great barons found John so markedly suspicious of them it was inevitable that in turn they grew suspicious of him. The mutual distrust was fed by the fact that John had refused to abide by his promise to reinstate the privileges which Henry and Richard had taken from them, nor would he allow them to reclaim many of their castles, those vastly important symbols of baronial power.

No, the boy had not been wise. He could not fight them forever, and he could never gain their support without their trust, and unless he were prepared to trust them in turn, the gap between the throne and the lords would merely grow wider and more dangerous.

William almost smiled to himself. Odd how he still thought of John as a boy. He wasn't a boy any longer, of course, and in many ways, despite his military failures, he had proved remarkably efficient. Old Henry had laid down the foundations of an administration which was the envy of Europe, based on the Chancery and the Exchequer. So strong were the sinews of the machinery of state that although Richard had spent only six months of his reign in England, the day to day business of running the kingdom had not faltered once during his absence.

But John was not content to sit idle in his palace at Westminster and let his officials do the work. John, who had failed to measure up to his father's greatness or his brother's glory, had at least inherited Henry's talent for administration and was equally adept at dealing with the smallest detail of a minor law case as he was at handling vital matters of high policy.

Nor was he satisfied simply to take over what his father had established and make no further progress. His lively, intelligent and imaginative mind was quick to adapt and improve and to find new uses for the various departments of state. Horrified at the chaos he had found in the handling of the Chancery documents, he had quickly instituted a method whereby every writ and deed was carefully entered into the records and neatly filed away in the archives.

He did not consider it enough merely to receive reports from the itinerant judges; he wanted to see for himself and to watch the law in action with his own eyes. It was hard work but John, despite his enemies' insistence to the contrary, was not a lazy man. Indefatigably he trundled his wagons and carts carrying the royal bed, the bath-tub, the portable chapel, the kitchen equipment and the official records from one side of the realm to the other. Up to the north, into the Fens; to the west, the south-west and across to the east coast again. Nothing was too much trouble and no problem too small for his personal attention. He worked hard and he made his high officials work equally hard. If they did their jobs well they earned his praise. If they failed they felt the lash of John's tongue, for he had no time for slackness.

It was a privilege to have one's case heard before the king, and men would travel many miles in order to present their problems to him. It was not simply because he was the sovereign; they respected John's judgment and applauded the conclusions of his shrewd, penetrating mind. Yet it was not only monied merchants or knightly litigants who caught John's ear. In this context at least he was not interested in money and was always prepared to hear a simple plea from a humble farmer for no more than a mark or two, for the king's justice was available to all men and, to John, one legal conundrum was as fascinating as another no matter who brought it to court.

Longspée nodded slightly to himself. There was no doubt about it, John had done well in many ways. A true Angevin, with all his forebears' passion for orderly, effective government and steady, impartial justice. True some claimed that like his father he sold justice to the highest bidder but this was merely pique that John contrived to lure cases out of the magnates' courts and into his own and though on occasions he may have used the law to gain his own ends, he had never tampered with the basic source of justice.

And he had been quick to see other needs as well. Swift to recognize that when Normandy was lost and, for the first time in one hundred and thirty-eight years, there was an enemy coastline on the other side of the Channel a navy was needed to protect and guard his own ports and coastal towns. Henry himself could not have made a better job of building up a fleet with strong galleys, broad-beamed cogs, and heavy, capacious busses to support them.

"Well, Master Alexander, shall I succeed?"

John's voice broke through Salisbury's thoughts as he reached out for his goblet, freshly filled by the attentive Petit.

"Of course, sire." Alexander beamed on the king, his fat face wreathed in an unctuous smile. "It is only a matter of time. I can forecast without hesitation that before many months have passed by, you will be fighting the French king again."

"Let us hope the months will not be too many, eh William?"

"Indeed, your grace." Salisbury stretched comfortably, holding one hand out towards the burning logs. "Do you play again tonight?"

"Yes, but not with dice."

Salisbury looked up quickly. The shadows played odd tricks at times and in the flickering light of the candles John's eyes had an almost satanic slant, whilst the red fury of the fire reflected strangely on his cheek as if it were stained with blood.

"Sire?"

John's chuckle was low. "There are other games to play besides the rolling of dice, and she'll not wait all night for me."

Longspée bit his lip. He wondered whether John's attention had strayed again to one of the women of the court, or whether he would content himself that night with a comely servant, but John did not trouble to set his brother's mind at rest as he waved a hand in farewell and made off to his own chamber.

The girl curled up on the bed, her dark head resting against the pillows, was a lovely creature. Her skin was the colour of a peach and her wide brown eyes watched the king with interest as he crossed the room to give her a friendly slap on the rump.

She giggled delightedly and made a feeble effort to struggle out of his grasp.

"Sire! You should not . . . it is not proper. . . ."

"Of course it is not proper." John made short work of her pretence. "Did you imagine I had you brought here to observe proprieties? If you would rather go back to the kitchens. . . ."

Her face fell and John gave a quick laugh.

"No? Then have done with your nonsense and get your gown off. It may do well enough to scrub floors in but it's no fit garment for my bed. Besides I would see what you conceal beneath it."

She gurgled again and wriggled her body invitingly.

"It is the only one I have."

"One body shaped like yours is enough for any wench."

"I meant the kirtle."

"But I did not. Will you be rid of it or must I tear it from you?"

"What should I wear tomorrow if you did?"

"A piece of sacking."

"Oh!"

He grinned and caught her to him, feeling the softness of her bosom pressed against him. Despite the coldness of the night she was as warm as the fire he had just left, and desire began

46

to quicken his breath as he watched her pink tongue moisten her lips.

"Never fear." His voice was low now, and one hand was on the ties which held her shabby garment together. "I'll find you another gown. Perhaps one of the queen's, eh? What would you think of that?"

"What would she say, my lord?"

She could afford to be pert, for now she was mistress of the situation. She could see the hunger in his eyes and feel the urgent demand of his hands. He wanted her and he would not worry about her insolence until he had got what he wanted.

"We must take care to see she does not find out."

John pulled the kirtle down to the girl's waist and his mouth moved in sudden satisfaction.

"Almighty God, I was right! You are a well-formed hussy for one so young."

His hand was on the girl's breast, fondling it gently until she gave a sudden shiver.

"Aye, now you're as hot for it as I am, but you'll be more eager still ere I am done with you."

He ripped the gown completely away, staring for a moment at the gentle swell of her stomach and the generous curve of her hips. Then he smiled grimly.

"They would have me content myself with creatures like you, d'you know that?"

"My lord?"

She looked puzzled, baffled by his words, wishing that he would get undressed. She had almost forgotten that he was the king and that she was greatly honoured to have been called to his bed. All that she was conscious of was her own nakedness and longing, and the fact that John was a man who had known how to rouse her with an unerring and experienced hand.

"Never mind. You would not understand."

He began to take off his clothes, folding them quickly and neatly, for John was never careless or untidy no matter the circumstances.

"What is your name, girl?"

"Alis."

"A pretty name for a pretty wench."

"You think me pretty?"

"Pretty enough."

She frowned. "That is poor praise. Do I not please you?"

He chuckled.

"Why do you women need so much reassurance? You're all alike, forever demanding confirmation of your own charms." He leaned over and slowly ran a hand along her satin-smooth thigh. "Well, if you must deal in words; yes, you please me, and I've no doubt you'll give me fair satisfaction."

"But my face." She half sat up, tossing her thick curls over her shoulder, her lips pouting. "What of that?"

"Well, what of it? I didn't bring you here to look at your face, and in the dark such things don't matter."

He laid the last garment on the bench and turned to blow out the candles.

"But, my lord. . . ."

"Hold your tongue, Alis," he advised softly as the faint candlelight was doused to leave them in total darkness. "This is no time for talking."

She prepared to argue, for king or no king, he had pricked her vanity, but then she felt the strenght of his arms and his loins pressed against hers as his mouth sought hers greedily, and before many moments had passed she had lost all interest in the issue.

John was a passionate and enthusiastic seducer, well-versed in the art of making love, and as generous in giving sexual pleasure as he was at taking it, and she completely forgot her momentary irritation as happily she gave herself up to the king's fierce but wholly enjoyable demands.

In June 1210 John turned his attention to Ireland where, in his youth, he had failed entirely to impress upon the native chieftains the supremacy of the English crown. Since the death of Rory O'Connor, the last high king of Ireland, the native princes had not been able to stand their ground against the thrusting Norman nobility who had fought one another as ceaselessly as they had battled with the Irish.

A year after Rory's death in 1199, John had sent to Ireland his cousin Meiler FitzHenry, a bastard son of Henry I, as his justiciar, but Meiler's stay had not been of long duration and by 1208 the Lacy brothers, Walter and Hugh, the lords of Meath and Ulster respectively, had driven the unfortunate justiciar back to England with his tail between his legs. Meiler's place was taken by John de Gray, Bishop of Norwich, whom John had tried to get appointed as primate, but de Gray's skills were not of a warlike nature, and the Lacy brothers took no more notice of him than they had done of Meiler.

There were a number of reasons which made John sail to Ireland with the feudal levy of England and several companies of Flemish mercenaries. First, he was determined to make an end of the Lacys' power, not least because Walter was William de Briouze's son-in-law and had been sheltering that fugitive since his flight from England. Secondly, he wished to come face to face with the insolent Matilda and make her choke on her own words, for John could never forget an insult of this kind and was totally bereft of the ability to forgive with generosity. Thirdly, he wanted to see for himself how many of the Anglo-Norman nobles who disported themselves like petty kings in Ireland were truly loyal to the English crown, and lastly he was determined to exercise his own mastery and force the various warring parties to acknowledge him as their sole suzerain.

The mere sight of John's host was enough to bring twenty Irish chieftains running to Dublin to do him homage and when he had received their fealty and reduced the number of castles from which they could conduct their warfare, he marched into Meath in search of William and Matilda de Briouze.

William had already fled into Wales upon learning that John was on his way, leaving Matilda and his eldest son in Meath Castle. Walter and Hugh Lacy did not stop to protect Matilda, for they had no illusions as to their fate should John succeed in catching them, and by the time John started to besiege the

49

castle, they were already in Scotland and preparing to sail for France.

Matilda managed to escape John's net by the skin of her teeth and fled with her son to Scotland, only to fall into the hands of Duncan of Carrick, who promptly turned them over to the king. Matilda offered the sum of forty thousand marks to ransom herself, but John brushed aside her plea and sent the erring noblewoman and her son to Windsor Castle in heavy chains.

When John had settled his business in Ireland and had effected such changes as he felt necessary, he left matters in the capable hands of the Bishop of Norwich and returned to London to find that William de Briouze was pleading for an audience.

John received de Briouze with no small amount of pleasure, and took malicious delight in the fact that the unfortunate William had grown thin and gaunt with worry and despair since he had last seen him.

"Well, my lord?" John was very cool. "So you have come at last."

De Briouze rose from his knee and met John's eye. He knew his mission was a hopeless one, but with Matilda and his son imprisoned in Windsor Castle he had no alternative but to make one last effort to soften the unforgiving anger of the king. He straightened his shoulders, bent with fatigue and care, and said hesitantly:

"I would have come before, your grace, but I feared to do so."

"As well you might, seeing how you have offended us."

"No offence was meant. I am willing to pay all that is owed, as I have said more than once."

"Saying is not enough. We want marks, not words."

"You shall have them, if you will but give me time."

"Time we have already given you."

"I need more. Now I have to raise further sums to ransom my wife."

John's chin was resting in his hand, his elbow propped on

the arm of his chair. He had taken particular trouble with his attire that day for the sole purpose of emphasizing the shabbiness which he knew he would find in de Briouze and he had not been disappointed. William's tunic was badly stained, his cloak torn, his shoes scuffed and discoloured by mud. A gratified smile curled the corners of John's mouth for a second. Then he said gratingly:

"We have not yet said that we would accept ransom."

The eyes of the two men met again and William's heart sank. He had not really expected John to let Matilda go, for he knew John only too well. If only Matilda had held her tongue, John might have forgiven the matter of the debt, but a direct accusation that John had killed his nephew was a very different thing.

"I . . . I . . . had hoped, lord king."

"Had you indeed? You seek generosity in us which you do not look for in your own heart."

William bit his lip, but he knew he would have to crawl.

"That is so, yet I do not think I shall look in vain for you do not have my weakness and are great enough to offer pardon."

John showed his teeth. He was well aware of the tactics which William was adopting and did not suppose for one moment that William thought him either great or forgiving, but the words must have been like gall in de Briouze's throat and that was pleasing.

"Flattery?"

"I swear it is not."

"Your assurance rings hollow, but no matter." John sat upright. "Very well, we will give you a few days but no more for we have waited long enough. You are free to go and find the forty thousand marks at which the Lady Matilda values herself. For our part, we should have considered some smaller sum appropriate."

William reddened.

"She bitterly regrets her words. They were spoken in the heat of the moment and she did not know what she was saying."

51

"Ah, but you did, William, did you not? Matilda was not at Rouen when Arthur disappeared, was she?"

De Briouze's colour fled as suddenly as it had come.

"Your grace? I . . . I . . . do not understand."

"You understand us very well. If Matilda was not at Rouen, how is it that she is so well-versed in this matter?"

William swallowed with difficulty. John's eyes were like hard, bright stones and his mouth was a straight, ugly line. Whichever path de Briouze chose to tread now there was nothing but quicksand waiting for his foot.

"They . . . they were only rumours. No one could seriously believe that you had killed your own nephew, sire. It is unthinkable."

"Philip Augustus did not consider it impossible and he was not alone in his belief."

"He would say anything to blacken your grace's fair name."

"Our fair name!" John gave a short laugh. "Christ! Do you mock us?"

"On my oath I do not, and as for Rouen. . . ."

"Yes?" John's voice was as smooth as silk. "What of Rouen?"

"I was there, but I do not know . . . that is . . . I. . . ."

"You do not know whether we killed Arthur?" The king's tone grew softer still. "No, you do not, do you? Nor will you or any other man ever be sure. But knowledge was not necessary for you, was it? You accused us without proof and taught that screeching harlot of a wife of yours how to condemn as well."

William was perspiring freely now, the sweat standing cold on his wrinkled brow and dampening the thin grey hair at his temples.

"It is not true. I. . . ."

"Enough!" John made a curt gesture with his hand. "You have said enough. Be off with you and find the money if you would see your wife again."

And shaking like an old man de Briouze withdrew with a low bow, but despite his fears for Matilda and his son, his terror for his own skin was greater still. He did not linger in England to wait for John's nemesis to overtake him but took ship to France within a week.

Eleven days after the dungeon door had been closed upon the Lady Matilda and her son William, gaolers went for the first time to see what John's prisoners had made of the sheaf of dry wheat and flitch of raw bacon which the king had ordered should be left with them. Inside the dungeon the air was rank and foetid, and the youngest of the guards retched helplessly as he staggered away from the horror which confronted him.

Mother and son had not died easily, for slow starvation furnished a cruel end. Even the most robust and indifferent of the guards turned pale when he saw Matilda's teeth-marks on young William's cold, bloodless cheek and swore violently as he gave hasty orders for the emaciated bodies to be carried outside and buried as quickly as possible.

When news of the end of the defiant Matilda reached Queen Isabella, she was nursing her newly-born daughter, Joan. She listened in silence to the whispers of her women, staring at their frightened faces as they related every last detail with shocked relish.

When she finally dismissed them, she lay for a long while staring at the ceiling. She had always known John to be a sadistic and merciless man beneath his pleasant air of bonhomie which he normally showed to the world, and she had never underestimated the risk of carrying on her flirtations under his nose, but such calculated and cold-blooded savagery made a sharp tremor of fear run through her body and the palms of her hands were suddenly damp.

If John could do that to a woman simply because she had repeated a piece of unsubstantiated gossip, what might he do to one who made a cuckold of him? John had been pleased with his daughter, oddly tender as he held the tiny creature in the crook of his arm and smiled at her huge brown eyes. He had touched the child on the brow with his lips and had given Isabella a quick hug. He had been gentle enough then but, underneath his beam of pleasure, the tiger had been there, grinning hungrily as it savoured its revenge with rapt, un-wavering gratification.

With a sudden whimper of panic, Isabella, who professed to fear no living man, turned her face into the softness of her pillow and began to cry.

With the King of Scotland subdued and Ireland brought under control, John's next expedition was to Wales, and on the 8th July 1211 he marched his army across the border from Whitchurch. The situation in Wales was even more difficult than that in Ireland, with the south firmly held by marcher barons and the centre and north in the hands of the turbulent Welsh chieftains. They paid token allegiance to the English crown but no more, and since John had had some experience of Welsh affairs whilst he was Earl of Gloucester, he had known what steps to take when he came to the throne. The most powerful earl in Wales was Ranulf, Earl of Chester, who ruled like a petty king in the north and, to balance Ranulf's might, John had endowed William Marshal, Earl of Pembroke, and William de Briouze with considerable lands and wealth.

Then he had turned his attention to the Welsh princes, endeavouring to hold a balance between Gwenwynwyn of central Wales and Llywelyn ap Iorwerth of Anglesey in the north.

When Llywelyn proved too crafty to be a pawn in John's political manoeuvres the king tried a different line of approach and offered the Welshman his illegitimate daughter Joan for his wife. That had been a most successful move and ap Iorwerth had been with the king in his stand against the Scots, but the whole stability of John's delicate structure had been upset by the flight of de Briouze.

Llywelyn's latent ambitions had risen hopefully at the first sign of trouble and he was quick to offer de Briouze help in his dilemma. John had marched into Wales in May, determined to bring the tiresome Welsh princes to their knees, but he had forgotten how wily and frustrating was their method of fighting. In no time at all there was not a Welshman to be seen. All that was left were the lofty, frozen crags of Snowdonia and the prospect of starvation for the English army. John had withdrawn, but only to lick his wounds and to make better preparations for the next foray and in July he started out again, laden with ample provisions and backed by considerably more men.

Briskly the king drove his army through the Vale of Llangollen, along the River Conway to Bangor, building strong fortresses as he went, and it was not long before ap Iorwerth saw the error of his ways and sent his wife to plead with her father for mercy.

John greeted Joan with warmth. She was much like her mother, Clementina, and John had fond memories of his former mistress. He eyed Joan's slim figure with approval and was glad that she kept her head held high as she asked for quarter.

"My husband seeks an honourable settlement, your grace." Joan's voice was as clear and lilting as the mountain stream which ran down the rocks by the side of the king's camp. "He has sent me to discuss this with you."

"I dare say he has." John stroked his beard with a well-cared for hand. Even the Welsh mountains had not curbed John's passion for cleanliness although his men had cursed under their breath as they had hauled and tugged the bath-tub from one mountain side to the next. "But Llywelyn had his chance and threw it away. Now it is my turn to make terms, and whether he thinks them honourable or not he will have to accept them."

Joan's lips thinned. She had not really anticipated much softening in her father but her husband's instructions had been very precise.

"He is a prince."

"And I am a king. What of it?"

"You will not seek too much from him?"

"What is too much? His life?"

Joan's eyes widened in sudden fear.

"You would not. . . ."

"No, not his life, but he will forfeit his lands, or most of them at least, and he shall confine himself beyond the Conway where he can do no harm."

55

"These are harsh requirements." Joan's voice was low. "You do ask too much."

"I do not ask anything, I demand. And I have not yet finished."

He watched her control her anger and bite back her response. She was a fine young woman, and he almost wished he had not married her off to that savage, Llywelyn, for she might have proved a good deal more useful in some other bed. However, it was too late now, and he smiled again.

"He will pay a sum which I shall decide upon to ensure no further outbreak of rebellion and, to make quite certain that I am not disturbed again, I shall take back to England with me thirty hostages of noble birth. They shall be the sons of these reckless chieftains who have cost me good money and precious time to teach them who is their master. You will be told in due course whom I propose to take."

"No!" Joan took a step forward, her cheeks flushed with indignation. "You cannot do that. Money yes; hostages no!"

"Hostages are more valuable than money, girl, have you not learned that yet? Money can always be stolen if it is needed; sons take time to breed."

"But Llywelyn has agreed that he will resist you no longer."

"Of course, since I have him on his knees. He should have thought twice before he gave aid to William de Briouze and tried to make capital out of his defection."

"But what can I say to him?"

"That which he sent you to find out, what else? He asked for terms and I have stated them. Go back and tell him what they are." He paused for a moment. "Are you afraid of him, is that it? Do you think he will beat you because you have failed to soften my heart?"

The anger and fear was gone, and Joan's face was as cold as marble.

"No, my lord, I am not afraid, and Llywelyn will not beat me."

"How grateful you must be to me for finding you so tender a husband."

She did not answer, and John said quietly:

"You could not have expected anything else. He opposed me; did you think to find mercy?"

"He thought to find justice."

"And he will get it."

"And the hostages? You will not change your mind?"

"I seldom do, and on this occasion I certainly shall not."

"Llywelyn will not stay crushed beneath your intolerance. No matter that his lands are lost and he is held fast behind the Conway; he will rise again and with him the other princes."

"They are no friends of his. His quarrel with them is as bitter as that with me."

"Not so. In this they will unite."

"To destroy me?"

"Perhaps."

John was mocking. "Will you warn me, should he succeed in escaping from his net to do me ill? I am your father, and it is said that blood is thicker than water. Will you let me perish?"

"He is my husband. You made him so."

"That is no answer. It does not sever the natural bond between us."

For a moment they stood and gazed at each other in silence. Then Joan said slowly:

"Have I your leave to go?"

"You have. Go back to your kind and loving husband and tell him what I have said. And Joan."

She rose from her curtsey and looked at him enquiringly.

"Would you like to leave this place?" His eyes travelled round the soaring mountains rising white-tipped into the sullen skies. "You could do so if you wished."

"This is my home."

"And you will stay?"

"I shall stay, my lord."

She turned away and John watched her go regretfully. He liked her proud, confident walk and the way her body moved under her flowing gown. Clementina had walked like that, and

Joan had the same clear, flawless complexion and warm red mouth as her mother.

He sighed. Well, that was that, and he probably would not see her again, but if he had failed to lure her back to England he had at least made an end of the Welsh and their defiance.

He rose from his stool, well-pleased with the outcome of the campaign. First the Scots, then the Irish, and now the Welsh. Men would not be so ready to criticize him now for he had achieved more than his father had done; more than Richard had even tried to do, and at last he was free to think of France again and his long-delayed meeting with Philip Augustus.

He gave one last look round the bleak, unwelcoming mountain-side and with another quick sigh walked back to his tent to take a bath.

CHAPTER THREE

LLYWELYN ap Iorwerth stayed in his cage until June of the following year. Then, as Joan had predicted, he slipped across the Conway and persuaded his rivals to join him in a revolt against the English king. At first John took no notice beyond despatching Brian de Lisle, one of his able mercenary captains, to deal with what he assumed was a minor uprising. When it became obvious that one captain and his men were not going to be enough to quell the impudence of the Welshmen, John treated his court to a fine display of Angevin fury, but when this had simmered down again, he did not baulk at what had to be done.

For the past twelve months he had been preparing to meet Philip and had mustered ample men, arms and supplies for the undertaking. At Ascensiontide he had sent out writs, summoning the knights to Poitou, and with the moment of departure so near it was galling to have to turn aside. But the Welsh had to be put down once and for all and John directed the host to assemble first at Chester in August, then, when he found himself unready, ordered it to meet him at Nottingham in the second week of September.

John rode into Nottingham in fine style at the head of a cavalcade which included his own guards; mercenary captains Fawkes de Bréauté, Savaric de Mauléon, Gerard d'Athée, Martin Algais and Philip Marc; a flock of squires and servants and, last but not least, the faithful and long-suffering Petit whose job it was to ensure that every last detail of the king's comfort was attended to, that his linen was freshly laundered and spotless, and that his tunic and mantle would satisfy both his own luxurious and Sybaritic taste and impress his subjects at one and the same time.

In the courtyard of Nottingham Castle the company dismounted. Autumn was in the air and green summer had become tinged with gold and brown as the trees in the forests shed their leaves to make a tawny carpet over the earth and the gay, fragile flowers disappeared slowly from the hedgerows. It was a clear, crisp morning, and Petit sniffed appreciatively as he hopped off his mule and began to direct the complicated operation of moving John's considerable baggage into his quarters.

He gave the captains gathered about the king a quick glance. They were splendidly fierce in their closely fitted tunics of chain-mail and squarish casques and, as Fulk de Peche had pointed out, they were entirely loyal and devoted to John who had hired the swords they wore in their elaborate baldricks.

De Mauléon, a leading noble of Poitou who combined the skills of an experienced soldier with the gifts of a cultured poet, gave a sigh of relief as he pulled off his helm and ran a hand through his dark hair.

"By the Virgin, I am hungry," he said and grinned at John. "The ride has given me an appetite, my lord."

John did not return the smile. His face was grim, the sallow hue enhanced by the pallor of his lips and the dark, ugly expression in his eyes.

"Your belly will have to wait for satisfaction," he told Savaric shortly. "There is something to be done before we eat."

De Mauléon looked at him quickly for he recognized something in John's voice which he had heard before.

"Oh, sire? What is that?"

John did not answer, but turned aside to give a peremptory order to his guards who raced over the cobbles, their boots breaking the sudden silence which had fallen. Squires paused in their task of unsaddling the horses, eyes wide and breath held in; knights and nobles were watchful; the servants pale as unexpected tension broke the pleasure of the morning and held them paralysed.

Petit gestured to his helpers to be still. This was no moment to draw attention to himself by shouting at the servants for

60

their slowness, and very quietly he lowered a small chest to the ground drawing back against the protective side of the *carette* to await events. Come to think of it, the king had been a trifle out of sorts that morning, impatient when he was being dressed and irritable because his squires and grooms had failed to have his favourite mount ready for him at the precise moment of his departure. Petit shrank back a further inch or two recognizing even at that distance that the look on John's face meant trouble, for he knew each shade and degree of the king's moods and this was a frightening one.

When the guards reappeared they were not alone. Every head turned to watch them as they dragged a column of young boys across the courtyard by the chains which chafed and grated their slim wrists. Petit went cold. They were the sons of the Welsh chieftains whom John had taken as hostages a year before, and twelve months in John's prisons had robbed them of their fresh colour and melted the flesh from their bones until they stuck through their thin garments like fragile sticks.

Petit shivered. The morning was no longer beautiful. The sun was going behind a cloud and the mild breeze was assuming the sharpness of a cold wind as it whipped and fluttered the rags of the boys lined up in front of the silent king.

Finally John moved forward and contemplated them bleakly. Some of the captives were no more than children, with round frightened eyes and trembling mouths, whilst others, on the threshold of manhood, tried valiantly to sustain their courage under the threat they read in their royal gaoler's gaze.

"Well, sirs." John's voice was soft but it carried right across the yard, so deep was the silent concentration of the watchers. "You have been told, no doubt, that your fathers have risen against me."

The prisoners did not answer but the sudden panic in their eyes made John laugh coldly.

"Yes, I can see you have been told. Then you will realize that there is a debt to be paid, not only because your sires have broken their word to me, but because their rebellion has forced me to postpone my departure to France, and this I cannot

61

forgive. My whole army has been prevented from crossing the Channel to regain my lost possessions because a handful of Welsh rebels have stirred their people against me." The blue eyes flashed with sudden fire. "God's teeth, do you think I will tolerate this? If Llywelyn ap Iorwerth and his conspirators do not yet realize my determination to master them I will make clear my intent in a way they shall not mistake again. They have dared to defy me because they think me a soft fool; a fool who will not use violence lest my nightly sleep be disturbed by bad dreams."

The king took another step forward.

"I shall sleep well enough, and your fathers will learn their lesson. When I take hostages I use them if I have to, and now I have to, to bring these rebels to heel."

He snapped his fingers at the two guards who stood close to him, jerking a thumb at the shackled captives.

"Hang them."

A faint ripple of sound echoed round the courtyard. No one had spoken, but men drew in their breath in shock as they stared at the shivering boys whose faces had grown ashen at the king's order.

Only the mercenary captains were unmoved, nodding in faint approval as the king turned on his heel and joined them.

"The only way, your grace." Gerard d'Athée tugged at his beard as he surveyed the victims with dispassionate interest. "Perhaps this will teach the Welshmen that we mean business."

"It will certainly teach their sons that this is so." Fawkes de Bréauté, a small stocky man with a reputation for utter ruthlessness, was laughing. "They will appreciate the point when their heels are dangling merrily in the air, see if I am not right."

But if John's captains were sufficiently indifferent to the sacrifice of human life to make a jest of the king's order, there were many present that morning who watched what followed with something akin to horror. A few of the boys went to their death with stoic calm which many a soldier would have envied, neither resisting the rough hands which grabbed at them and pulled them over to the gibbet, nor struggling as the noose was thrust over their heads. But some of the smaller boys could not prevent a cry of terror as biting fingers fastened on their arms, dragging them inexorably and without feeling to their destruction.

Petit's face was grey as he watched the bodies swinging aloft, the sound of their last choking gasps pounding in his ears. He supposed he was a fool to have expected anything else, for John was not a man to take hostages for nothing, nor was he given to acts of mercy when he was crossed. Yet some of the sufferers had been so young that it was hard to see how even John's heart could have remained stony. Petit turned agonized eyes to the limp little creature hanging at the end of the row. He looked for all the world like a piece of old sacking hung up to dry so thin was his body beneath the torn and wretched tunic, yet no inanimate sacking ever had eyes which looked as his did. He could not have been more than seven years old, perhaps younger. Petit did not think that in John's place he could have brought himself to snuff out the tender life, but then he was not John and neither did he have the king's responsibilities nor his ability to squeeze every drop of feeling from his heart as John was able to do when the occasion demanded it.

Petit pulled himself together. The courtyard was coming to life again. The king and his captains had gone into the castle in search of food, and slowly men were beginning to move about their tasks once more, muttering restively to one another under their breath, casting furtive glances now and then at the line of corpses above their head.

When the last bag had been unloaded, Petit took careful possession of the silver jewel casket and made his way through the castle to the royal quarters to unpack, reflecting somewhat uneasily as he went that no matter the reasons or the circumstances, no one could deny that at heart John Plantagenet was really a very cruel and unforgiving man.

63

An hour later when John and his companions were tucking into a goodly spread of roasted meat well washed down with wine, the first of the messengers arrived. To begin with John waved the page away and bade him have the courier from the Scottish king await his pleasure, but when ten minutes later the page had to return to whisper of the advent of another rider, this time from Joan, Llywelyn's wife, John thrust aside his platter and ordered them to be brought before him.

"Well?"

John looked down at the two men kneeling before him, both a trifle shaken by the sight which had met their eyes on reaching Nottingham Castle, but both careful to let nothing of their revulsion show on their faces as they rose to face the king.

"What is it? You first."

John pointed to the messenger from William the Lion.

"What word does your master send to me in such haste?"

"A warning, your grace." The man rubbed the sweaty palm of his hand against the side of his tunic. There was something rasping about John's tone which rattled the courier's nerves and made his voice unsteady as he answered. "A dire warning."

John's brows met in a frown.

"A warning? Of what?"

"Danger to you, my lord, if you cross into Wales."

For a moment John stared at the man in silence. Then he said softly:

"What kind of danger? From the Welsh?"

"No, at least not at first."

"Then from whom? God's teeth, will you be done with this hesitancy! Who threatens me?"

"Your own men, sire."

"What!"

There was a quick protest from those at table which John stilled with a swift movement of his hand.

"My own men? My captains? Do you say this?"

"No, no!" The man gibbered in his terror, licking dry lips as he saw the glowering menace of Fawkes de Bréauté and the others. "Not your captains, my lord; the barons. They plan to kill you or worse. To take you captive and hand you over to the Welsh."

John's irritation was gone and his face was losing its colour. There was the horrid ring of truth about the man's words, and he had been betrayed by his nobles before. If the barons of Normandy had not deserted him at the crucial moment the duchy would still be his, and it was the possibility, indeed probability, that the English baronage were preparing to do the same thing which checked his anger and made his heart beat more rapidly.

"Go on." He was deceptively calm, for he wanted to scream aloud as fear and anger fought together in his breast. "What else?"

"They know the pope has absolved them from their allegiance to your grace, seeing that you are . . . are. . . ."

"Excommunicate? They have known that for some time and taken no heed of it."

"But now they will take advantage of the Holy Father's sentence. There is talk of deposition and the election of another king."

Despite the king's previous demand for silence the assembled captains cried aloud in protest and this time John said nothing as he slumped back in his chair.

"And you?" Finally he turned to his daughter's emissary. "What do you have to say?"

The man gave a quick bow and cleared his throat nervously.

"Lord king, the Lady Joan bade me give you similar warnings. She spoke of a blood tie and said you would understand, and then told me to say that her husband is already in league with the French king and is aware that many of your lordship's barons will not support you should you take to the field. They wait merely for you to move across the border, when they will seize and bind you fast. Also, rumour has come to us that your son, Prince Richard, has been killed; that men have plundered at Gloucester and made off with your grace's treasury, and that the queen. . . ."

He broke off, flushing apprehensively.

"The queen?" John was sharp. "What of her?"

"It is said that she has been raped and violated."

Ignoring the pandemonium which broke out at the last words, John got up and strode out of the hall, mounting the stairs to his chamber like a man in a trance. He could believe only too well that much of what the two envoys had said was true and, whilst he did not wholly trust William of Scotland, his brief encounter with his daughter gave him reason to think her word was sound.

His room was empty and he was glad of it as he flung off his mantle and went over to the window seat, staring down sightlessly at the fields beyond the castle walls where the tents of his magnates stretched for half a mile or more, fluttering aloft the standards of the greatest names in the land. John's lips tightened. Yes, they were true enough, these warnings he had received. He could feel it in his bones and in the tensing of his muscles as every nerve sent its deadly message to the mind. The disaffection had been more widespread of late and he had known it, although he had chosen to ignore it whilst he made plans to gather his army together, but now he could no longer pretend that it did not exist. It not only existed, it was growing and spreading alarmingly. Now he had to face not just the Welsh or the French; not only the pope's exasperated anger, but also the concerted rebellion of his own barons.

For a second he closed his eyes, recognizing with reluctance that he had ground men down too hardly. He would have to slacken the leading strings and bring some relief to them before the world exploded in his face. The barons would have to be divided and placated somehow; the breach with Rome would have to be healed and quickly. He could not fight all men on all fronts, not knowing whose hand held the knife which would stab him in the back.

He sat for ten minutes or so like a man in a stupor but then the paralysis left him and his mind was crystal clear and sharp as steel as he returned to the hall to give his orders.

Within an hour the expedition to Wales had been called off and the great host which the king had so painstakingly gathered together was dismissed, but not before John had demanded of every baron present a hostage to ensure his good behaviour. Gerard d'Athée was sent to take Henry, John's heir, into safe custody, whilst other captains were despatched to find the queen and put her out of harm's way. This done, John began to prepare for his return to London by easy stages.

When he learned that two leading barons, Robert FitzWalter and Eustace de Vesci had fled, the one to France the other to Scotland, any remnants of doubt as to the veracity of the tidings he had received left John, and without hesitation he seized Castle Baynard in London and Benington Castle in Hertford-shire, both belonging to FitzWalter, and ordered their instant demolition.

That done he entrusted the task of enquiring into the loyalty of his own servants and officials to Fawkes de Bréauté and turned north to de Vesci's lands to snuff out any sparks of rebellion that might still be lingering there.

It was on his return journey that he encountered Peter the Hermit. He had heard before of the fanatical creature from Pontefract who existed on dry bread and sips of water and who had spent the last few weeks proclaiming that John's reign was nearing its end. John had paid scant attention to the stories of the hermit, although many of his advisers had been alarmed at the size of the crowds who were said to be flocking to listen to the madman's words, and they had been foolish enough to arrest him and hold him in custody.

John swore at them for focusing popular attention on the recluse, but since he was passing through the town where Peter was in prison, he had him brought to his lodgings to see for himself what manner of man it was who was predicting his downfall.

The hermit was incredibly thin and gaunt, which was hardly surprising since he spurned all but the smallest amount of food, and his hair was long and matted about his shoulders, his beard a tangle below a thin, unforgiving mouth and a bold hook of a nose. John stared in distaste at the shabby, smelly creature but Peter was not in the least put out by the king's obvious

67

dislike, and his black unwinking eyes were almost triumphant as they fixed themselves on the king's.

John was torn between anger and amusement at the impudence of the man who stood before him prepared to stare him out, and making not the slightest gesture of obeisance to his monarch. Finally the amusement won, for even in the most dire of circumstances John's sense of humour was apt to get the better of him, and in the present case he found the hermit more ludicrous than dangerous.

"Well, Master Peter, I hear that you are forecasting my doom."

The hermit saw the smile and stiffened.

"You will not be laughing, John, when next Ascension day comes."

John ignored the outrageous manner of address and raised his eyebrows.

"Oh? And why not?"

"Because before that day you will cease to be king."

"By death or deposition?" John's tone was still light, but now his eyes had narrowed and he was watching the man carefully. Perhaps he was merely a harmless lunatic, perhaps not. Men said he had powers of prophecy and the thought of deposition lay uncomfortably on John's mind at that moment.

The anchorite shrugged and did not reply directly, merely repeating his words in his low, harsh voice.

"I have told you; by next Ascension day you will no longer be king of this realm."

John laughed but this time without much humour.

"You offer no proof. Why should I believe you?"

"Why should you not? You know my powers although you pretend to scoff. I see a fear in your eyes which you cannot hide. If you were not afraid, why did you send your army away?"

The king's mouth hardened.

"Watch your tongue, old man, or I'll have it torn from your head."

"That would make no difference now," returned the hermit tranquilly. "The prophecy is already made; it needs no repetition."

"Prophecy! Lies would more likely describe your ramblings."

Peter's yellowed teeth showed briefly.

"If I lie, lord king, then do with me as you will. If I speak the truth, you will have no time to worry about me."

Exasperated, but still inclined to regard the man as a charlatan rather than a serious threat, John ordered Peter to be held in Corfe Castle and went on his way, but although he joked with his companions later about the madman who scratched at his lice and refused the fresh bread which was offered to him, it seemed to Petit that John was a trifle preoccupied that night when he disrobed him, and he was careful not to disturb the king's obvious disquieting thoughts with his usual chatter as he folded John's linen in a tidy pile and crept unobtrusively to the door.

Alone in his great bed John watched the moonlight drift through the tall windows and bathe the room in an eerie glow. He no longer found the notion of the deranged Peter's prognostications amusing and the very thought of them burned in his stomach like a tight knot. It seemed that every hand was against him, from the high-born nobles who would not meet his eye, to the soft-witted fool he had now thrown into prison at Corfe. All but his mercenary captains were watching and waiting for his death, licking their lips like hungry jackals as they waited for Innocent or Philip Augustus to make an end of him.

John's head stirred restlessly against the pillow. He had heard a whisper that Philip was planning a fresh invasion of England; that he proposed to give the realm to Louis, his son. His hands clenched by his sides as he wondered bitterly how many of the barons who still protested their loyalty to him were already in touch with the French king, offering him their help and support should he set sail.

Suddenly he swore aloud and sat upright. For once in his

life he wished he had had some faith in the efficacy of prayer. He needed help now as he had never needed it before, but since he was too much of a realist to expect any response from a God whom he had so curtly rejected in the past, he padded silently to the door and went in search of the nubile serving wench with whom he had exchanged a significant glance earlier that night, and prepared to smother his worries in the soft comfort of her white arms.

It was at John's darkest hour that he received a letter from William Marshal, Earl of Pembroke, then in Ireland where he owned vast estates which had come to him with his wife, Isabella de Clare, daughter and heiress of Strongbow.

William was one of the most famous knights of the age, noble of birth and lofty of spirit, who had spent his youth winning fame and fortune with the brilliance of his military exploits. When the time came for him to lay aside his sword and to take his place at the council table of kings, he had done so readily, sighing only slightly at the pleasures which he had had to leave behind.

Henry II had placed much reliance in him, appointing him tutor and guardian to the young king, and when Richard came to the throne he too had leaned heavily on the strength and wisdom of Pembroke's advice and help.

But from the beginning of John's reign there had been trouble for William, for John trusted Pembroke no more than any other baron since he had too many lands and too much wealth to be ignored with safety. There had been a fierce quarrel when William had led the opposition to the expedition to Poitou in 1205; a bitter exchange over the French lands which the earl held of Philip Augustus; another rift when John had discovered that Pembroke had given sanctuary to William de Briouze to whom he owed fealty, with a dozen or more minor squabbles and sharp words in between the major disputes.

Nevertheless, despite the distrust and friction, William had remained loyal to John and to the house of Anjou, and on

70

hearing of the disbanding of the army at Nottingham and the messages received from Joan of Wales and William the Lion, he had sat down and dictated a letter to his secretary, offering not only a renewal of his own oath of allegiance but also promising to gain that of his fellow-magnates in Ireland into the bargain.

William meant every word which he said when he wrote of the close bonds which held him to the old king's son, but he was human enough to realize that such a timely offer on his part would dissolve any ill-feeling between himself and John, and would restore him quickly to the king's favour.

He read John correctly, for the king was overwhelming in his gratitude and praise.

"Tell the earl," he said to his own secretary, scribbling away at a table by the window, "that we thank him from our heart for his prompt and ready offer to come to us in England, yet we would not have him leave Ireland at the moment for there he can help us most. Add that we hear from the Bishop of Norwich that the earl's service and counsel is of paramount importance to him in his task of holding Ireland for us, and we would not rob him of such aid at a time like this."

John paused. The letters from Pembroke had given him renewed hope and spirit. The black cloud which had threatend to envelop him was fast receding for if Pembroke, who commanded men's respect wherever he went and could call upon so many valuable lances in time of need, still supported him there was a chance to make an end of the disastrous predicament in which he found himself.

"What else did the earl say?" He turned to his secretary. "There was the matter of peace with Rome was there not?"

The secretary nodded.

"Indeed, sire. The earl stresses the urgency of reconciliation with the Holy Father."

"Then tell him we are more than willing that such an end should be achieved. Bid him, with his advisers and our other vassals in Ireland, to draw up terms on which such peace may be made, but make it clear that these must protect our royal rights and prerogatives."

He waited for the clerk to finish writing. Then he said thoughtfully:

"Tell Pembroke also that his sons are well. Though we hold them hostage, they are treated with care and honour. Say that the elder boy needs new clothes and a fresh horse and that it will be our pleasure to furnish these. If it be the earl's wish to have his heir given into the care of John d'Erly, his own knight, we will observe and abide by such desire."

John sighed and glanced at Savaric de Mauléon who was in attendance.

"William has heard rumours of Philip's intentions, just as we have done. Philip will be quick to act as Innocent's sword and Innocent as swift to accept the offer."

"Yet the pope will not want Philip too powerful." Savaric looked up at the pacing king. "He knows Philip is no puppet to be swayed this way and that on papal strings. If he encourages the French king it is for his own purposes, not for the benefit of France."

"Let us hope our royal cousin does not see this." John was wry. "Perhaps ambition will blind him to the truth, but in any event William is right. We must prepare to send fresh envoys to Rome."

"Do you trust Pembroke, sire?"

"Oh yes. Had he not offered his renewed allegiance I might not have done so, but when William gives his word nothing will make him break it. He served my father and brother well, and perhaps I have been too quick to distrust his judgment in the past." John had a rare moment of self-criticism. "Much that he said was right, although I did not think so at the time, but now he will stand fast and many will follow him. Yes, Savaric, I owe him a debt."

"Which doubtless he realizes, my lord." De Mauléon was caustic. "Two days ago he was out of favour with your grace, his sons held prisoner. Now, he is restored and his offspring cherished guests."

"Two days ago I did not know whether he would join my enemies or come to my aid; now his intents are made clear. If he gains my ear once more it is a just reward."

"Not purchased by gold."

John's frown lifted and he gave Savaric a broad grin.

"As yours is, you mean? Never fear, my friend, I know that what you give me is beyond the price I pay to hire your sword, and you know full well the affection I have for you. No need to envy William."

De Mauléon laughed quietly.

"I do not, your grace. I am content enough."

"Then let us be done with business." The king gestured his secretary away and put a friendly hand on de Mauléon's shoulder. "Come, a game of backgammon and a measure or two of wine. We grow too serious, and some relaxation will not come amiss."

The Poitevin nodded amiably. He had never had much time for William Marshal and was fully aware that the dislike was mutual, but he had to admit that the letter from Pembroke had come at a remarkably convenient time. John had needed help; more than he, de Mauléon, and the other captains could muster for him, and for once he found himself in complete agreement with the earl, applauding the suggestion that a formula for peace with Rome was a first essential, and hoping fervently that Marshal and the Irish barons would be skilled enough to lay down terms acceptable both to the king and to the pope.

He had a mild regret that Marshal was in favour again, for the earl was a very powerful man and wholeheartedly opposed to the employment of mercenaries. However, it was unlikely that the close links between John and his captains would be broken for a while by the interference of Marshal, for he would be in Ireland with other things to attend to, and with this comforting thought in mind, Savaric de Mauléon sat down at the table opposite the king and began to play.

During the time that John had been gathering his army

together, Isabella of Angoulême had devoted the same careful attention to the collection of lovers.

She felt herself fully entitled to seek her pleasures elsewhere since it was clear that she no longer held John in thrall and that he was constantly finding his own amusements in other women's beds. In some ways she was sorry that the strong hold she had once had on her husband was gone, but on the other hand to be faithful to one man and never to taste the delights of another could be very dull.

She wished John were not so jealous. She knew he had set spies to watch her every movement, and it took much care and effort to evade the invisible net he had placed around her, yet the very fact that each new liaison brought a fresh danger added spice and excitement to a life which was otherwise wholly boring.

One morning in November Isabella sat and gazed at herself in her mirror with a contemplative eye. Childbirth had not spoiled the perfect moulding of her body nor marred the fresh beauty of her face; rather it had enhanced her attraction and given her a new maturity which she wore like a precious mantle.

She put her head on one side to observe the fall of her veil beneath the jewelled fillet and then ran a critical finger across the bodice of her gown of brocat.

"This kirtle is so old, Beatrix. I swear I have had it for a lifetime."

"Two years, madam." Lady de Gresby was comforting. "Scarcely worn at all and such a rich colour."

"But I am tired of it." The queen put the mirror down and pouted. "In three years I have had but two new gowns and those chosen by the king. He is reckless enough when it comes to spending money on his own back, but for me he will allow only a few ells of burnet and a length of green bombax, which I hate."

"It becomes you well, and only last week you had new purple sandals and a fine pair of boots."

"And that is all. Oh, how sick I am of John's parsimony. He

74

has a whole warehouse filled with brocades, tissues, gauzes, silks and sarcenets. Why should I not be allowed to choose what I want? Every last button and girdle is selected by him and I must accept them or go naked." She giggled. "Perhaps that would be a good idea, Beatrix. Shall I go naked and see what he says to that?"

Beatrix made a quick noise of disapproval.

"Madam! You know what the king would do."

"I am only joking." Isabella sighed. "I've no mind to display myself for the gratification of every man. Night is the time to disrobe and then only before a lover."

"You should be wary, your grace. I think the king suspects something. I feel there are eyes everywhere."

"And so there are," returned Isabella cheerfully, "but that is half the fun. What pleasure would there be in adultery if one's husband did not care? It helps to pass the time, finding ways and means of evading his men. Have you seen Ellis this morning?"

Lady de Gresby sighed again. Isabella was incorrigible. A natural wanton who needed men as others needed air to breathe. Even had John remained faithful, it would not have been enough for the queen and she would still have sought satisfaction elsewhere for she was incurably promiscuous. Ellis de Norham was Isabella's latest beau; a handsome young buck with a strong, well-built body and a pleasing countenance, and Beatrix had had to listen to the most minute details of their love-making, for the queen enjoyed a leisurely review of her conquests almost as much as the act of love itself.

"Yes, madam, he sent a message."

"Then why did you not tell me sooner?" Isabella turned quickly, her pencilled brows meeting in a frown. "What did he say? Is something wrong?"

"Nothing, nothing." Lady de Gresby was hasty, for Isabella could be a termagant once her fiery temper was roused. "He is in good spirits and bade me tell you he does not know how he will exist during the long hours of the day."

"Ah!" The frown was gone and the red lips curved in a

75

slow smile. "Dearest Ellis. Will he come to my chamber to-night?"

"At midnight, when the household is asleep."

"And the men the king has set to watch me?"

"The Sire de Norham has a plan to distract them. Two friends of his will help."

"That is good. Oh, Beatrix, what a long day this will be and how dull."

"The risks are still great, madam." Beatrix bit her lip. "What if the king's watchers are not deluded?"

"They will be. They are as stupid as their master in these matters and Ellis will deal with them, you will see."

Lady de Gresby said no more, for there was really nothing else to add, but she worried quietly to herself, hoping against hope that something would happen to prevent the reckless de Norham carrying out his plan. Whatever other charges might be laid at the king's door, stupidity was one which could not be sustained and she was sure that he was already suspicious. It seemed to her that he had given Isabella even more searching looks of late, and were he to discover this latest act of faithlessness he would be as swift as a rattlesnake in his revenge.

At midnight the castle was as silent as the grave. Guards nodded at their posts and the lesser members of the royal household huddled together in the great hall, finding such comfort as they could under rough blankets which covered their thinly-filled palliasses.

Ellis de Norham paused for a moment outside the queen's door to glance about him. His friends had been entirely successful in the execution of their task, and the two Poitevins who had been shadowing him for the last few days had followed the decoy like tame, well-trained dogs. He chuckled to himself. It would be some time before the guards tracked their quarry to earth and when they did, they would find two men hardly known to them, wearing garb remarkably similar to his own.

Softly he turned the iron handle of Isabella's door and crept into the room.

"Ellis?"

Isabella's whisper had a shadow of doubt in it but as he caught her to him and covered her mouth with his own, she gave a sigh of relief and relaxed against his strong chest.

"You were not followed, love?"

She raised her head after a minute to gaze fondly at his face, raising one hand to stroke his bronzed cheek.

"No, you have nothing to fear. My plan worked as I said it would."

"Then we have an hour or two together."

"I wish it could be a lifetime."

"You are greedy, sweet."

"For you, yes."

His hand was pushing aside her thin wrap, cupping one warm round breast in his strong fingers.

"Were you afraid?"

"Of course not." He was indignant, pricked that she should doubt his manhood.

"If the king should find you. . . ."

"He will not. I have told you; we are quite safe."

The wrap slid to the ground as de Norham's hands moved slowly and sensuously over her body.

"You are shivering. Are you cold?"

"Your hands are warm, and it is not the cold which makes me shiver."

He watched her lips part slightly and saw the naked desire in her eyes. It gave him a strange thrill of triumph to have the queen so completely at his mercy and he was in no hurry to satisfy the hunger she did not trouble to hide.

"Then why do you tremble?" He let his hand slide up her thigh again and laughed inwardly at her expression. "Do you fear me? Shall I go?"

"Ellis!" She opened her eyes and her fingers were urgent on his arm. "You cannot. . . ."

"I could, quite easily."

"But you would not."

He was exultant, completely sure of his mastery as he caressed one rose-pink nipple and made her shudder again in ecstasy.

"You will have to beg, Isabella. I do not give my favours lightly."

"Queens do not beg, and it is I who give the favours." Her nails were sharp as they dug frantically into him and there was a trace of tears on her lashes. "Ellis. . . ."

"You are not queen here, and you will beg. I am not like the others who fawn on you and let you trample them beneath your feet."

"I hate you!"

Suddenly she bent her head and bit his arm, her small white teeth vicious with pent-up emotion and desire.

He gave a low laugh as he freed himself and struck her hard across the face with one hand.

"Bitch! I said you were no queen here. You are just a female animal craving satisfaction, nothing more, and if you want that satisfaction you will have to crawl for it."

She gave a gasp and pounded her clenched fists against his chest but in another second he had hauled her over to the bed and flung her across it with a force which took her breath away. Then he leaned over her, keeping her shoulders pinned to the coverlet with iron hands.

"Well, madam queen, do you beg?"

She sobbed her acquiescence but he hardly heard it, for by now he himself was thoroughly roused and her flesh was soft, sweet-smelling and crying out to be taken and the time for teasing was done. They came together like two wild animals, clawing and fighting each other until their raw lust was thoroughly sated and sexual passion temporarily lulled by utter exhaustion.

Isabella's face was damp with sweat but she was smiling contentedly as she curled up against him. He was the most exciting lover she had had for many years, and although she was haughty and imperious by day she found a strange exhilaration in being treated so roughly in bed.

"You will come tomorrow night?"

"I may do."

"I beg that you will."

He turned his head and gave her a sidelong glance.

"Then perhaps I will. Now kiss me again, for I must go."

She watched him reluctantly as he left, wishing she could keep him with her all night, but her complacent and erotic dreams would have been rudely disturbed could she have known that even as Ellis de Norham slipped back to his own quarters, John's Poitevin guards were making a full report to their master.

John listened in silence to what the two men had to say, his mouth turning down at the corners in ominous lines.

"Two others you say?"

"Yes, your grace, he had help. One was dressed in the Sire de Norham's tunic and mantle, but we knew it was not he although we pretended to follow him for a while."

John said something under his breath.

"And you think they plan to meet tomorrow night? How can you be sure?"

One guard smiled knowingly. "We opened the door to the queen's chamber. Just an inch or two, of course, but it was enough."

"Did they see you?"

"Indeed not, my lord; they had no eyes for us."

"By the sinews of God I will teach that whore a lesson she will not forget." John's eyes were suffusing with a dangerous red and his cheeks were flecked with purple. "If she plans to meet her paramour tomorrow night she shall not be disappointed. He will go to her bed right enough but not, perhaps, in the way she imagines." He controlled himself with a visible effort, grinding his teeth as he looked back at his impassive guards. "This is what you will do."

The following day Isabella was at her gayest. She had thoroughly enjoyed the previous night and was looking forward anxiously to her next meeting with Ellis de Norham. Since John looked so amiable that morning she ventured to touch on the subject of her limited wardrobe and found her husband more than usually indulgent.

"But of course, my dear." John let his eyes wander slowly over her, wishing he could seize her there and then and administer the sound thrashing which she so richly deserved. "I had not realized you were so ill-clad for it seems to me that whenever I see you, you look quite enchanting."

She gave him a quick look, for he had not paid her many compliments of late, but his face was quite bland and innocent.

"Thank you, my lord, but it is some months since I had a new kirtle."

"Then you shall have two now to make up for my remissness. And perhaps some new slippers and a girdle or two, eh? Maybe even a small surprise as well."

Isabella's wariness showed this time and John laughed.

"You are puzzled, my love? Why should you be? If a man has a beautiful wife, it is incumbent upon him to clad her fitly, is it not?"

The queen hesitated a moment longer. Either John was planning to come to her bed himself, which would be vastly inconvenient at the present time, or he had found himself a new mistress and was salving his conscience with a few extra gifts.

"I fear I have neglected you lately." The king was examining the sapphire ring on his forefinger. "It is unfortunate that there have been so many urgent matters claiming my attention, but perhaps in a week or two. . . ."

Isabella gave a sigh of relief. It was another mistress after all and she gave him a bright smile.

"Of course, my lord, I fully understand the burden of responsibility which rests upon you and I am content to wait."

"I am sure you are." The deep blue eyes slid to hers for a moment. "You are a most accommodating woman, my dear, and you shall have your reward."

She murmured her thanks and slipped away, anxious to find Beatrix de Gresby to relate the happenings of the previous night, finding the day too long for comfort and the evening meal an interminable bore as course after course was served to John's guests. She fidgeted through the antics of the jesters and fools and hardly touched her food, wholly unaware that John's eyes seldom left her, and it was with a sigh of heartfelt relief that she saw the king rise and make his way from the hall followed by his companions.

She lingered for a while in the hall, pretending to talk to her women, waiting until John had had sufficient time to get to his own chamber or to that of the woman with whom he proposed to spend the night. Then she took a candlestick from Beatrix, whispering to her to get rid of the others as she mounted the stairs, her heart beating faster with delicious anticipation.

When she found her room in darkness she frowned. How stupid of Beatrix not to see that the maids had lit the other candles; she would speak sharply to her in the morning about her carelessness. She moved slowly to the bed, dipping the tip of her own candle and lighting the others in the heavy metal holders, careful not to let the hot wax drip on to her hand.

Her back was half-turned to the bed but as the room flickered to life by the light of the yellow flames something caught the corner of her eye. For a second she remained immobile, half-afraid to turn round to see what it really was that hung like dark drapes over her couch. Then, slowly, she forced herself to face the bed and look upwards.

Her mouth opened in silent disbelief and every vestige of colour fled from her cheeks as her trembling hand raised the candle to illuminate with awful clarity the three bodies which hung by their necks above the bed.

The blood was pounding in her head and she wanted to cry out, but her throat was restricted as if a hand were clutched tightly round it, and all she could do at first was to gaze in sick horror at the dead, blank eyes of Ellis de Norham which seemed to stare directly into her own. She did not know the two other men, dangling limply beside him, but even in her trance she remembered that Ellis had spoken of friends who had promised to help him.

Then the numbness broke and the holder fell from her nerveless hand as she began to scream. She tried to back away from the bed but tripped over the hem of her gown and fell headlong as the door burst open and John strode across the room followed by two of his men.

"See to that." He was short as he pointed to Isabella's tallow which had already set the straw on fire. "We do not want to burn to death."

He waited whilst the guards stamped out the blaze and then gestured them to go, turning to look down at Isabella who had thrust a hand across her mouth to quell the cries which were welling up in her throat.

"Well, madam?" He was quietly savage. "I promised you a surprise and I have kept my word. Are you satisfied with it? Does he please you? Look at him! A fine, brawny specimen, is he not? Well, why don't you look at him? You were hot enough for him, weren't you? You could not wait to get to him tonight, could you?"

He bent down and caught her by the arm, jerking her to her feet and pulling her closer to the bed.

"Don't stare at me, woman, look at him. It was de Norham you wanted, wasn't it, and now you've got him? Or is he too far above you now? Would you rather I had him cut down so you can fondle him as you fondled him last night?"

She tried to bury her face on John's shoulder but he ripped off her head-dress and twisted her hair between his fingers, forcing her head up with a brutal hand.

"No, no, my dear, don't look away. Drink your fill. Look at that broad chest of his, those sinewy arms, and strong straight legs. What pleasure you must have had with him, eh?"

"No, no!" She was moaning in his grasp, trying to escape from his spiteful hold. "Please . . . please . . . let me go."

"I shall never let you go." He forced her round to face him. "D'you hear me, you harlot? I shall never let you go. You are my wife."

"Please . . . I did not mean to. . . ."

"Yes you did." He gave her an ugly look. "You do nothing by mischance, my dear, as well I know. You meant what you did and you would have done it again tonight had your lover been in a position to join you."

He glanced up at the dead men and his laugh froze the blood in Isabella's veins.

"But he cannot satisfy you now can he, madam? He never will again."

"Please . . . please, my lord, I beg you. . . ."

He thrust her away from him, standing in front of her with his hands resting on his hips.

"Tomorrow you will be taken to Gloucester Abbey where you will stay under restraint until I give word that you are to be released. You will find no lovers there, so you will have ample time to reckon the price of your folly."

"If you would let me explain. . . ."

"I need no explanation." His lip curled. "Do you think I am a fool?"

"It is not as you think."

"It is exactly as I think, and know. I had you watched."

"Spied on you mean?" She was recovering slightly, careful to keep her eyes away from the terrible sight above her head. "You have had men spy on me as you always do."

"Watch your tongue or I'll give you a stripe or two to nurse at Gloucester."

"While you take any strumpet who catches your fancy? You are no better than I, my lord."

"Christ, you impudent slut!" He slashed the back of his hand across her mouth. "Do you dare to speak to me like that?"

She staggered but now fear was gone and she was as angry as he.

"I dare to speak the truth. Do you not care to hear it? Lecher! Libertine! Seducer!"

She fell to the ground as he lashed out at her with his fist, whimpering with pain but still cursing him under her breath as he administered the punishment.

Finally he let her go and the crimson fury died out of his eyes.

"Get up," he said coldly, "unless, of course, you want to spend the night here with them."

With difficulty she got to her feet and stumbled after him, the tears mercifully blinding her to the swaying bodies, catching her breath in painful sobs as she was led to a small ante-room along the passage and firmly locked in to await the coming of morning.

CHAPTER FOUR

At the beginning of 1213, when England had lain under the papal interdict for four and a half years and John himself had been excommunicate for almost as long, rumours began to creep over the land like dark shadows.

John listened to them with tightened lips. For many years Philip Augustus had hankered after the realm of England for his son Louis. There had been alarms and fears in 1205 and again in 1209 that he was about to set sail but these had come to naught; now the whispers of renewed French preparations were too strong to be ignored. For twelve months Philip had been mustering men, ships, arms and supplies with such vigorous determination it seemed highly improbable that he would abandon the project so near to his heart for a third time.

And Philip was not the only one whose patience was wearing thin. In Rome, Innocent III was also making ready for conclusions with the English king who had made light of the interdict, to say nothing of a considerable profit from it, and who had virtually thumbed his nose at the pontiff when the sentence of excommunication had been proclaimed.

John had no delusions about Innocent. Under his charm and kindliness, the pope was every bit as implacable as Philip Augustus and he would not hesitate to crush John unless the wayward monarch was prepared to bend to the papal will.

The king thought about Innocent a good deal and cursed quietly to himself. Born Lothar of Segni, Innocent came from a noble family, was endowed with a sharp political sense, and had an acute legal mind which probed and prodded at every last detail until all was settled to his complete satisfaction.

There was no chance that the wool could be pulled over Innocent's eyes. Innocent would demand complete capitulation and nothing less.

When it was hinted that the pope proposed to use Philip's army to depose him, John had dismissed the idea with a short laugh. Philip and Innocent had their own quarrels, and the pope would not relish the Frenchman's power increasing so vastly by the acquisition of England and Ireland. Yet when John's laugh had died away there was a germ of fear left. Perhaps they would use one another; Innocent would be quick to appreciate that if Philip invaded England, John's position would be parlous. Philip would be equally swift to see that if the pope gave even the faintest approval to his venture, it could be made to assume the aspect of a crusade or holy war against the enemies of the Church.

John ruminated on the facts of the case for some time, not least the uncomfortable memory of the small number of barons who had attended court at the previous Christmastide. Hitherto, much as they might have disliked him, they had been too afraid to turn a deaf ear to a royal summons. That year, after he had shown his fear of their treachery and abandoned the Welsh campaign because of it, they had ignored his invitations and stayed away.

There was no doubt about it. The time had come when he would have to make peace with Innocent for, if the pope's patience was really exhausted and he proposed to depose the king who had defied him for so long, John could look to no one for help in his unfortunate position.

In February John sent his envoys to Rome, offering to accept the terms of settlement which he had rejected in the previous summer, and Innocent mused on the suggestion thoughtfully.

He had been on the point of ordering John's formal deposition, since there seemed no other way to bring the wicked Englishman to heel. It was not a step he had wanted to take and certainly would not have risked issuing such a decree had he not been aware of Philip Augustus's intentions and the

86

restiveness of the English baronage which he assumed to be brought about solely by John's rejection of the Church's laws.

When the king's messengers arrived, Innocent had received them with frosty reserve. He did not trust John, or his offer, yet he was too fair-minded a man not to give the king a last chance, and too much of a diplomat to waste the opportunity of a genuine peace, and so he despatched Pandulf, the cardinal sub-deacon, charged with the task of ensuring that John really meant what he said. Negotiations had never entirely ceased during the four and a half years of the interdict, and John had kept the pot boiling merrily with his half-promises and encouraging hints whilst royal and papal servants scurried constantly between Rome and Westminster. There was to be no more of that. The pope was firm. John would surrender and accept the full demands of the Church or he would be deposed by papal decree.

Before Pandulf could reach England, word came to John that Philip's proposal to invade was serious, and if he had still not quite made up his mind how to handle the pontiff's legate when he arrived, he had no doubt at all about what to do about the militant Frenchman.

On the 3rd March he despatched from New Temple letters patent to the bailiffs of every coastal town and to all sheriffs throughout the realm, bidding them to assemble ships, men and arms to defend England. His orders were concise and detailed and any mists of fear and hesitation which had temporarily clouded his mind were swept away as he threw himself wholeheartedly into the task of calling his people together to resist their enemies.

Preparations went on apace. Arms and food were collected in great quantities and packed into long wooden carts; men refurbished their armour, sharpened their weapons and bade farewell to their families. Whatever feelings the people of England might have had for John, they responded to his call without a moment's doubt, for this was not some wild dream of the king's for regaining his lost lands on the continent in which they had no interest or concern. This was the defence of their own homes and possessions and John's voice had a true Angevin ring as he summoned men to Barham Down near Canterbury to await the coming of the invader.

By May a vast host was assembled and it was while John was surveying it with some satisfaction that two Templars arrived at Dover with the request that John should talk with Pandulf, the pope's legate and familiar.

On the 13th May John received the cardinal sub-deacon with full honours. He had by now made up his mind what had to be done, for it was quite clear that he could not fight on two fronts, and when the elaborate preliminaries and courtesies were over, he took Pandulf to his own tent to discuss Innocent's latest requirements.

"Well?" John's eyes were bright as he looked at the gaunt, forbidding face of the pope's ambassador. "It would seem that the time has come when our quarrel must end."

Pandulf frowned. He was still not sure whether the king really intended to capitulate. The size of the muster beyond the tent was very considerable and perhaps sufficient to encourage John to dicker and prevaricate yet again.

"For the sake of your soul's salvation, your grace, I pray that this is so. There is not much time left."

"Before Philip invades?"

"Not only that. There are other dangers."

"Ah yes, our immortal soul." John could not resist a last mockery. "But that is a hardy thing and it has survived a goodly time already without the comforts of the Church."

Pandulf drew himself up to his full height.

"Sire, if you have no intention of. . . ."

John raised his hand quickly and his tone altered, for he had seen the real anger in Pandulf's eyes.

"No, no. Our intents are serious. What are the pope's terms?"

"As they have always been. The acceptance of Archbishop Langton as primate; the reinstatement of the exiled English bishops; forgiveness for Eustace de Vesci and Robert FitzWalter, and full compensation to the Church and clergy for their losses. Do you accept this?"

John shrugged." We have no other choice."

"That is scarcely good enough," returned Pandulf sharply. "The Holy Father will expect absolute contrition. This is not a matter of expediency, your grace."

The king looked at Pandulf sombrely. It was clear that he would have to abandon his flippancy and convince the legate of his sincerity in order to save his skin, and John was nothing if not a good showman.

"Father, we are truly contrite."

Pandulf looked at John suspiciously but the deep blue eyes met his own frankly, and when he thought he saw a trace of tears in them he thawed slightly.

"As if you were on your death-bed, my son? Your penitence should be of that order."

"It is, we swear it."

"And you will submit to the Church and to the Holy Father and make your peace with God?"

"We will."

"And you will make full restitution for the property which you have confiscated?"

"We will so do, as soon as we are absolved from the unhappy state in which we find ourselves, and meanwhile we will furnish our clergy with eight thousand pounds so that they shall not suffer embarrassment until their goods are returned to them."

"This you will order by charter?"

"It is already prepared."

Pandulf gave a deep sigh. "You are wise, for you trod very near to the brink of disaster."

"We have an army to protect us."

Pandulf's light grey eyes fixed on John's.

"Have you, my son?"

John's sallow cheeks paled.

"We do not understand you."

Pandulf folded his thin hands neatly together over his scarlet habit and cleared his throat.

"Philip Augustus has many friends and allies."

"We would not deny it."

"Some of them are here, amongst your army."

The colour had fled completely from the king's face and his breath was a rattle in his throat.

"What! What is this you say?"

It was the legate's turn to lift a comforting hand.

"No need to fear now, your grace, provided I can convince the pope of your sincerity. I fear, of course, that he has learned to doubt the quality of your promises, but even so perhaps I can persuade him to. . . ."

"What is this you say?" John's voice was harsh. "Are you saying that in our own army we harbour traitors?"

Pandulf's faint smile was almost pitying.

"It would not be for the first time, would it? I hear that when you planned to take an expedition into Wales, some similar plot was uncovered."

"Plot!" John choked the word out. "Do you claim that there is another conspiracy against us?"

"It is said that many of the nobles have already written to Philip Augustus offering their fealty to him, should he invade."

"But that cannot be! Look beyond the tent. What do you see?"

"An army, my lord. A great host."

"And are the barons not there? Are they not assembled with their knights, ready and waiting for our command?"

Pandulf's gaze grew more compassionate.

"They are assembled certainly, but for what purpose I do not know nor would I venture to guess. Perhaps they would fight Philip, perhaps not. They might welcome him, who can tell? But for the moment you have nothing to fear, for the pope has forbidden Philip to invade your realm until you have had time to make your peace with the Church. If Innocent believes me, Philip will not sail at all."

"Philip does not wait upon Innocent's word." John slumped into a chair and looked up at Pandulf. "It is for himself he would seize our kingdom, not for the papacy."

"Perhaps, yet he would not dare to invade against papal prohibition."

"And then we should never know."

"Know what, your grace?"

"Whether our barons would have stood with us or against us." John's mouth was bitter. "Come, Father, we have work to do."

And without further ado John rose to his feet and led Pandulf out into the sunshine where, before the face of his whole host and in the presence of the assembled earls and barons, John went down on his knees before the cardinal sub-deacon and offered his humble submission and apologies for past transgressions and his earnest promise to fulfil the stringent demands of Innocent which would win him forgiveness and absolution.

That night when the camp was asleep, John sat huddled on his mattress hugging his mantle about him as if it were mid-winter. It was not a cold May; indeed the sun had been fierce upon him as he knelt before Pandulf earlier that day. The chill was within himself and the icy trickle down his spine was a message sent by the brain to warn the body of its peril.

Petit had left candles burning on a rough wooden table in the centre of the tent and there was a plentiful supply of wine near at hand, but for once John had no taste for the juice of the grape for his mind was on other things.

He had tried not to believe the cardinal sub-deacon. He had wanted to shout in his face that he was lying about the barons' intentions and to deny hotly that any one of them would send letters to Philip offering him aid and homage, but he had not not been able to do so. Pandulf's words had had an authentic note of truth about them and he had been quick to point out that the barons' doubtful loyalty had already caused one campaign to come to an abrupt end. De Vesci and FitzWalter had many friends across the Channel and who was to know what tales they had told since they had fled from England and from royal retribution.

For a moment John's head drooped until it rested on his locked hands. What was it that made his barons turn from him thus? He knew they hated the mercenaries whom he had taken into his pay but, if they themselves had been prepared to serve him loyally, he would have had no need of such men in the first place. They claimed he taxed them too heavily, but they had made no attempt to consider why this was necessary and had simply blamed him for gross extravagance. They had accused him of violating their wives and daughters. John gave a sigh. Well, perhaps that charge had some validity, although the women themselves were not always unwilling or blameless.

It was Normandy and the Welsh Marches all over again. A great army was encamped outside his tent, yet he could not really trust the nobility which led it. He could not be certain, should Philip land, that they would not turn to him and abandon their lawful sovereign.

He raised his head. This was no time for feeling sorry for himself for something more drastic was needed to secure his position. Pandulf had received his public submission with benign gravity, but in private he had warned that Innocent might still be suspicious of John's promises.

He turned sharply as a shadow fell across the opening of the tent but before he could reach for his sword, Petit slipped inside and was making a sketchy bow to his master.

"What is it?" John relaxed but his eyes were still wary. "Is something wrong?"

"No, sire, at least I hope not."

"Speak clearly." John was short, for he was not best pleased at having his train of thought interrupted and was prepared to deal harshly with his servant if his mission was a trivial one. "I have no time for riddles at this hour of night."

Petit was unconcerned. John might be impatient now but he would have raged like a bull if he had been kept in ignorance of what was happening outside.

"The Earl of Essex, your grace."

"Mandeville? What of him?"

"He meets with the Earls of Oxford and Hereford in secret."

John was instantly attentive, like a hunting dog with its nose quivering as it caught the first scent of its quarry.

"Secretly? How?"

"They rode off together, to the meadow beyond Friar's Wood."

"And they are still there?"

"As far as I know."

"Who is with them?" John's mouth was a hard, straight line. "Do you know if any others followed?"

"Norfolk, I think. Henry de Braybrook and Simon de Pattishall."

The king let his breath go in a quick hiss.

"Pandulf was right then. He was not merely trying to frighten me or to force my hand. He spoke the truth when he said that my own men would turn against me."

"I cannot be sure of the purpose of the meeting," began Petit when John gave a snarl of anger.

"No, you cannot, and neither can I, yet I would wager my crown as to its reason, and my mind is made up. It is clear now what I must do."

Petit cocked his head on one side and waited. It was obvious that John had more to say and Petit had been the recipient of many a confidence from his master, for John was in many ways a lonely man with few to whom he could talk freely.

"Will you hear my plan, eh, Petit?" The anger was gone and suddenly the king was chuckling almost light-heartedly. "Would you know what is in my mind?"

"If it be your will, lord king."

"It is, for you are a creature of some wit and you shall tell me what you think of the scheme I have for ending both Philip's dreams and my barons' plottings." He paused for a moment, pulling his cloak about him again. "I have submitted to Innocent's emissary, yet the pope may still not believe that I am truly sorry."

"And are you, your grace?" asked Petit innocently.

"You know full well that I am not, but the pope must be convinced that I am. His letters to me have been as cold as ice, edged with frost, and condemnation leaps suspiciously from every line. Thus, he must be won over to my cause in such a way that I shall forever have the papal sword at my side;

forever be assured that his support is mine; forever certain that when he speaks it is in my favour. How can I ensure this?"

Petit looked at John in silence. It was clear that the king had already thought of a way, but it was too choice a morsel to be blurted out in a hurry. John was savouring it with relish, expecting doubts and bewilderment from Petit, and Petit did not disappoint him.

"I cannot think. You have sworn before all men to give your full submission. You could swear it yet again, I suppose, or have it written down by your scribes and confirmed by the Great Seal."

"Which Innocent would question as he has questioned my word before."

"Then I confess myself baffled." Petit scratched his head. "What else is there to do?"

John gave another snigger.

"You cannot think? Oh come, Petit, it is not that difficult. What would make Innocent fly to England's defence no matter who attacked her? What would make him thunder of the pains of hell against Philip if he should set sail against us? God Almighty man, can you not see?"

Petit shook his head blankly. He had played up to John's game, but in fact he could see no way by which such papal fidelity could be secured and it was with genuine interest that he waited for the unfolding of the king's solution.

"You are a dolt after all." John winked at his servant and rubbed his hands in satisfaction. "The answer is plain enough; as plain as the nose on your face. I will give England to the pope."

Petit's jaw dropped. "Give . . . give England to the pope!"

"Of course. It is so beautifully simple. I will resign my crown to Innocent and pay him homage as my suzerain. England shall become his, and I will hold it of him as a feudal fief. Can you not see, Petit?" The king was rocking backwards and forwards, convulsed with laughter. "I, John, by the grace of God, King of England and Lord of Ireland, will from this time forward be truly faithful to God, to the Church of Rome, blessed Saint

Peter, and to my liege-lord, Pope Innocent III and his Catholic successors."

"But, your grace!"

"But, but! There are no buts! Innocent will jump with joy. He already has overlordship of Sicily, Poland, Sweden, Denmark, Portugal and Aragon, but he has nothing so precious or so mighty as the kingdom of England."

"But the barons. . . ."

"Perdition to the barons." John's teeth bared. "But I doubt that they will quarrel with what I do, for they will think to wrest some benefit from the situation for themselves. See if I am not right; they will agree. They have no mind to go to war with Philip if this can be avoided, and whatever Essex and his friends are up to this night, they are wasting their time and would have done well to rest quietly in their beds. Soon I shall be too strong for their mischief. If I must submit to Innocent, then I will do so with my whole heart and thereby gain his undying friendship. He shall keep me safe from the French and from my own magnates alike. Call my secretaries to me. This is no time to rest."

As the king had predicted, the nobles favoured John's proposal, looking at him with unusual respect as they applauded the astuteness of his suggestion, seeming to ignore for the moment that John, having enjoyed baronial support in the long struggle with the pope, was now abandoning any pretence of defending lay rights in ecclesiastical appointments, a subject very near and dear to the barons' hearts. They were more immediately concerned with the unpleasant thought of a French invasion, and they stood in a circle round John as he prostrated himself before Pandulf again on the eve of the Ascension and offered his kingdom to Innocent as a papal fief, smiling and cheering as Pandulf gave John his blessing and returned England and Ireland into John's hands for his safe keeping.

And whilst Pandulf began his journey back to Rome to break the splendid news to the pontiff, John had the trouble-maker of Pontefract taken from his prison in Corfe Castle and brought to Wareham. Although there were many who claimed that

Peter had been right in his predictions, since the king had now relinquished his realm into the hands of the pope, John had the hermit tied to the tail of a horse and dragged ignominiously through the streets of the town and finally hanged by his neck in the market place before the gaze of the awestruck townsfolk.

Then John returned to Westminster to make plans for the reception of Archbishop Langton and for a further expedition to Poitou, a project which had never for one moment left his mind and one that was now charged with new and exciting hope as he basked in the novelty of Innocent's warm and unqualified approval.

When Philip Augustus of France heard the news of John's submission to the pope and the nature of his enemy's manoeuvre, he raised his clenched fists to heaven and let out a string of oaths which rattled round his chamber like a peal of thunder, making his ministers and attendants quake nervously in their shoes.

Philip was a corpulent man like his grandfather, Louis VI. He wore his silks and satins with a commanding air and was never afraid to spend money to ensure that all men understood the nature of the monarchy as represented in his person. A virulent fever which had attacked him whilst on crusade in the Holy Land had robbed him of his hair and scored his square-cut face with deep lines, making him appear older than his years and certainly a good deal more mature than his rival, John, a mere two years his junior.

Philip was a new kind of king. Ascending the throne at the tender age of fifteen he had been plunged immediately into the fury and frenzy of war and international politics, soon learning to hold his own against men of the calibre of Henry Plantagenet and Pope Innocent III. He had surveyed the state or France with a bleak eye, angry and resentful at the wide territories possessed by the Angevins and the small, almost insignificant, holdings of the French crown. He had seen at once that if France were to be a great power, as he was fully determined she should be, the Angevin empire would have to be crushed and from the first moment the crown had been placed on his head all his energies had been bent on winning back the lands which he felt to be his by right.

Not even the most able of his clerks had been competent enough to teach Philip Augustus to read or write Latin, for he was no scholar, but nevertheless his mind was shrewd, alert, practical and unswerving in its purpose and he was capable of instigating the most elaborate of plans and of seeing them through to complete success by personal attention to the most minute of details.

He had spared sufficient time from his primary task to deal with internal affairs, and had brought about the most remarkable changes and improvements in the judicial and fiscal systems of the kingdom, fostering and encouraging trade and industry, even finding the odd moment to order the beautification of his capital city of Paris by paving its muddy streets and laying out colourful gardens to delight the eye.

His servants found him severe but scrupulously fair. He had no fawning favourites or mignons cluttering up his court, and if a man succeeded in winning the king's approval it was because he was hardworking, efficient and completely loyal to his master's cause.

At first Philip had met with no success in his self-imposed task of undermining Angevin power, for Henry II had been more than a match for him, and he had done little better in opposition to Coeur de Lion for whom he had developed a strong personal hatred, but John had proved more promising material. Philip had taken a malicious delight in setting the young weakling against his father and elder brother, slyly coaxing, and whispering sedition in John's ear, fanning the flames of rebellion when they appeared to be growing dim.

When John had become king, Philip's spirits had risen. Wresting Normandy from Henry or Richard was one thing; taking it from the irresponsible and feckless John was quite another and he had smiled scornfully when the English king had quarrelled with the nobles of his southern French territories thus playing straight into the hands of their waiting suzerain.

He had always wanted Normandy, acutely conscious of its vital importance to France, and now that the duchy was his he was biding his time until the opportunity should arise for further encroachments into John's continental domains.

He had toyed with the idea of invading England on two previous occasions, regretfully abandoning his plans when he could see that the season was not right for such a move, but twelve months ago the chances had seemed more propitious and he had thrown himself zestfully into the task of building up a great fleet backed by an even stronger army which was to cross the Narrow Seas and grasp the English plum for his heir, Louis. Louis would hold England as a French appendage, strictly controlled by the terms of the agreement which Philip had discussed with his son in council at Soisson in April of that year, and with John defeated there would be no further danger of the tiresome Plantagenet returning to France to try once again to win back his losses.

It was natural, therefore, that when he was told of John's skilful manipulation of the situation he should shake with rage at the set-back to his plans, and when he had finished with his heartfelt and highly-coloured oaths, he turned to his chamberlain, Estout de Chatillon, and said curtly:

"And what is this message the cardinal sub-deacon has sent to us?"

De Chatillon offered up a quick prayer to God, for Philip's face was far from encouraging.

"Sire, the cardinal has bid me tell you it is the Holy Father's command that you shall dismiss your army and fleet and return to Paris in peace. He reminds you that England is no longer enemy territory but a papal fief, and should you seek to conquer it you would be moving against the Holy Church itself."

"Good God, does Pandulf expect us to throw away a whole year's preparations? Are we to waste the sixty-thousand pounds we have spent on ships and arms and supplies? What of the weapons we have accumulated? The men, ready and waiting for the word to sail, what of them? Are we to dismiss them? Is this what Rome asks? Pah! It is impossible. You may tell the legate that we have no intention of heeding such demands. The invasion will go on as planned."

Estout exchanged a quick look with his fellow-councillors who had begun to mutter amongst themselves. He could see it was not going to be an easy task to convince the king of what must be done.

"My lord," ventured Ruald de Dinan, the seneschal, nervously. "I pray you to pause for reflection. If your grace were to sail against England now you would be declared excommunicate."

"We have been excommunicate before," returned the king tartly. "That is an old weapon with which to frighten us and one which Innocent has used too often to gain his ends. That damned Angevin is lying. Does his Holiness not realize this?"

"I doubt it." De Chatillon looked as worried as his companions. "He believes John's contrition is genuine."

"Then he is a fool," declared Philip shortly and ignored the gasp of consternation from those about him. "John is neither contrite nor genuine. It is a trick."

"But a clever one."

De Chatillon said it half to himself but Philip heard the comment and scowled anew.

"Very clever, but it will not stop us. We shall sail as planned. In the name of Our Saviour, are we to be used as the plaything of papal policy? It was not long since that the pope was offering us his support in what we proposed."

"Well . . . hardly support, sire."

"Hardly discouragement either." Philip ground his teeth. "Christ, we even released that harridan, Ingeborge, from her prison and became reconciled with her and you, my lords, are well aware how distasteful she is to us. Yet for the sake of our success and to appease the pope we were willing to make such sacrifice and take her to our bed again."

He gave a slight shudder whilst the company paused to consider the lengths to which the king had been prepared to go to sweeten Innocent. Philip had loathed Ingeborge from the first moment of their marriage and had soon put her away in favour of the beautiful Agnes of Meran, thus bringing the pope's wrath down on his head in the shape of a decree of excommunication. When Agnes had died some years later in childbirth the papal sentence had been lifted, but Philip had felt very smug as he finally obeyed the pontiff and took back his legal wife, although the very sight of her still made his hackles rise.

"Have I endured these nights lying beside her, smelling her foul breath and feeling her sweating body close to mine for nothing? And John will be enjoying every moment of this." Philip began to pace the room, his eyes flashing with anger. "Can you not picture him rocking with mirth as he thinks of us poised on the other side of the Channel with the pope's hand grasped on our neck to hold us back? Can you imagine the pleasure it will give him to know that even taking Ingeborge back was not enough? He knows how we detest that woman and he has a coarse and mischievous sense of humour. He will split his sides with laughter when he thinks of this. Can you not see how he will gloat over our discomfiture? No, no! We will not give him such satisfaction. Pope or no pope, we shall go on."

But of course Philip could not go on. When the first flush of rage had died down and calmer counsels prevailed, not even Philip Augustus dared to send his fleet against a papal fief and, since he had to have some outlet for his pent-up fury, he turned instead to deal with Count Ferrand of Flanders.

Ferrand had been in league with John for some time, although hitherto he had tried to keep his negotiations secret and had left open diplomatic channels with Philip. As one of the great feudatories of France, Ferrand had been expected to bring his men and arms to the muster at Gravelines and when he failed to do so, Philip declared him contumacious and set about teaching him a lesson. If he could no longer invade England, since he had been deprived of any shred of an excuse and bereft of his powerful ally at one stroke, he could at least bring his own vassals to heel. It had by then come to his knowledge that Ferrand had been instrumental in fostering the coalition of the Lowland princes against France and it was with a savage smile that he ordered his ships to set sail with all speed to the Swine, whilst he himself raced into Flanders at the head of his army.

Ferrand, aghast at the fate about to overtake him, sent hasty messages to John whose host was still assembled at Canterbury. Delighted to have the chance of attacking Philip, John quickly ordered the Earl of Salisbury and the Counts of Holland and Boulogne to take five hundred ships laden with horse, foot and provisions and go to the assistance of his unfortunate ally.

Longspée and his companions had a fair wind and soon reached the Swine. They had intended to drop anchor there and to land for a few hours, but when the great harbour of Damme came into view they stared in open-mouthed astonishment at the sight which met their eyes.

The harbour was alive with ships. Hardly a patch of the sparkling blue water was visible, so many vessels rode at anchor, rocking gently under the bright morning sunlight.

There were war galleys as long and lean as hungry wolves, furnished with two rows of oars like sharp teeth; swift dromonds bearing arms and military machines; esneccas, large, round and built to convey men and horses into battle; busses to carry stores, and the small, swift colombels and salties for scouting purposes.

Their bemused gaze moved on to the beach where more ships had been dragged up from the water, a veritable forest of masts and sails standing like sentinels on watch.

Finally Longspée said softly:

"Ships I see, my lords, but where are the seamen?"

William of Holland, travelling with Salisbury, screwed up his eyes in the hard light.

"I see none. It is like a graveyard. There are no voices, no sailors on the decks, none at work on the rigging."

"No." Longspée gave a broad grin. "No, you are right. There will be some, of course, for they would not leave the fleet completely unguarded."

"But where are the rest?" Holland looked bewildered. "I do not understand."

"I do." Salisbury's voice was almost dreamy. "They are out

101

marauding. They did not expect us and so they have taken the opportunity of pouncing on the prosperous towns here about."

The count's frown cleared. "Then, my lord, we can. . . ."

"Indeed we can," returned Longspée cheerfully and jumped down from the high forecastle to shout his orders.

The few unfortunates who had been left to watch the fleet were soon overcome and Salisbury and his men quickly selected three hundred ships which they filled with as many stores as the holds could carry, and then sent them on their way to England.

That done, the earl gave the word to fire the remainder of the vessels, watching with admiration the splendid blaze which swept across the harbour and licked with ravenous orange tongue at the wooden quays. When they were tired of contemplating their handiwork, the English settled down to a good meal of fresh meat and choice wine, stolen from the French ships, and then bedded down to snatch a few hours sleep.

On the following day Count Ferrand arrived and when he had expressed his great delight at Salisbury's success, the company mounted up and made for Damme. This expedition was short-lived, however, for Philip was already on his way and Longspée and his party had to turn tail and run for their lives as the French king came storming up to survey the remains of his shattered fleet.

Philip was white with passion. John's ruse to gain papal protection had been a bitter enough pill to swallow but as he stood on the shore and gazed at the charred hulks of his ships, watching the water spew up fragments of burnt timber on the beach, his eyes glowed with such fury that those who accompanied him took a hasty step backwards out of range of his twitching hands.

At long last he turned away from the reflection of his defeat and gave orders for the remainder of the vessels to be destroyed. The invasion of England was now a thing of the past, and to leave even the smallest craft seaworthy was to invite another visit from the dashing, impudent Salisbury and the pestilent counts who had allied themselves to John.

"Burn them," he said to his captains in an expressionless voice as he began to walk away from the harbour. "It is clear that on this occasion God does not favour us, but there will be other times and other places. This time the dice were loaded in John's favour; next time they will roll for us."

And with that he stalked over to his waiting horse and rode away as if the devil himself were after him, not turning back once to dwell on the humiliating sight which had driven iron into his very soul and which had ended the enterprise so near and dear to his heart.

CHAPTER FIVE

WITH the threat of invasion gone, John became a new man. He had twisted the pope round his little finger and was now enjoying a spate of effusive letters from the pontiff couched in terms which made him crow with delight as he read passages aloud to Petit in the seclusion of his chamber.

"D'you hear this, Petit? 'Lo! You now hold your kingdom by a more exalted and surer title than before, for the kingdom is become a royal priesthood.' What do you make of that, eh?"

"Most gratifying." Petit shook the folds out of a scarlet dalmatica and hung it carefully on the wooden pegs at the far side of the room. "It has a good ring about it—a royal priesthood."

"Yes, Innocent knows how to round out words, I'll say that for him. And heed this. 'Come then, exalted prince, fulfil the promises given and confirm the concessions offered!' " The smile faded for a moment. "He'll not let me forget those you may be sure."

"It was to be expected, your grace."

"Aye, and it's cheap at the price." The king's smirk returned. "I'd have paid twice as much could I have seen Philip's face when he heard the news. Ah well! It is satisfying enough as it is."

"Will the price be high, lord king?"

John shrugged. "High enough, though the pope has let it be known that since I have confessed my sins so frankly and submitted so completely to his mercy, he'll use that mercy freely when the assessments are made. God's teeth! What humbug!"

He stretched out full length on the bed and stuck out a foot for Petit to pull off the stocking.

"I've a thought or two about that myself. The monasteries will be clamouring for compensation. Already their representatives are howling at my door and when the pope's envoy arrives they'll worry at him like dogs to get what they want."

"Whom does his Holiness send?"

"Nicholas, cardinal-bishop of Tusculum." John wiggled his bare toes against the softness of the satin bedcover. "An angel of salvation and peace, so Innocent says."

"He will heed the monks when they beg him for succour."

"Unless I've gained a quittance from them for my debts." The oblique eyes turned for a moment to contemplate his servant. "Nicholas does not arrive until the autumn. Much can happen between now and then. When I've done with them, these snivelling minster-men will be glad to acknowledge that I owe them nothing."

He rose to his feet to enable Petit to loose the ties of his tunic.

"But there are more important matters afoot than these. My army is still awaiting my orders and there is no doubt what these will be."

"Yes, my lord."

The king jeered. "You have no notion what I plan, Petit, have you?"

Petit rubbed his bald head and grinned.

"Were I your grace, I'd be for France, to hit Philip Augustus as he tried to strike at us."

"Splendid! You have your wits about you after all, and you are right. Salisbury shall go to Flanders with ample men and money to stiffen Ferrand. They can worry Philip's flank, whilst I sail to Poitou to bite at him from the south. Is my bath ready?"

"Aye, and also the new robe you ordered. It is a fine piece of work, stitched with pearls and silver thread."

"You think the queen will find it becoming on me?"

"How could she do otherwise, your grace?"

"Fetch her, Petit. Have her await me."

Petit bowed as John went off to his garderobe and to the hot scented tub which William the bathman had prepared. Petit pulled his lower lip thoughtfully. He wondered how long the reconciliation between John and his queen would last. Isabella's father had died not long before and her mother had hastened to England to put herself under her son-in-law's protection. Since Isabella had now inherited the rich and fertile Angoumois, John had found it in his heart to forgive her for her previous infidelities and for the past few weeks had virtuously foresworn the company of other women in his bed.

As he trotted off to Isabella to give her the king's message Petit was shaking his head. He doubted very much whether either of them intended to remain faithful to the other for very long, and their present outward billing and cooing could only be of very short duration. Already he had noticed that Isabella's attention was straying to a handsome Flemish count, and it would only be a matter of time before some fresh-faced wench caught the king's fancy.

When John returned to his room, naked and glowing beneath his newly-fashioned robe, Isabella was already in bed, the thin linen sheet pulled tightly about the perfect outlines of her breasts.

John took a deep breath. She was still a most beautiful creature, immoral though she might be. Her dark hair was soft and perfumed and her sloe eyes were watching him in a way which made his muscles tighten pleasurably.

"Well, madam?" He kicked off his slippers and perched on the side of the bed. "What do you think of my new gown?"

Her red lips parted fractionally, moist and inviting over small pearly teeth.

"Most becoming, my lord. I swear you would outvie me any day."

"Do you still complain that I keep you in rags?" He was content to tease her. "God, only the other day I gave you a new kirtle."

"But of poor material. Nothing so fine as this."

106

She sat up, still keeping the sheet about her as she stroked the sleeve of John's robe with her long fingers, making the action a blatant sexual invitation.

"You're never satisfied." He grunted but he was not really annoyed for at the moment her closeness was intoxicating him. He had forgotten how seductive Isabella could be, and was glad that he had had enough sense to recall her from Gloucester. It would have been a shameful waste to keep a body as divinely shaped as Isabella's mouldering away in a cold, remote abbey.

"I'll give you another." His voice was growing a trifle husky as her fingers tightened. "You shall have two if you want them."

"Of silk?"

"If you wish."

"With gems such as these to trim them?"

"If it pleases you."

"It would please me."

"Then you shall have them, but first you'll earn them."

Her eyes widened in mock bewilderment.

"Earn them? But how? How could I do anything to warrant such a reward?"

"You're a saucy vixen, d'you know that?" His hand reached out for the sheet. "I've missed you."

"And I you, but it was not my will that we parted."

"It was your fault, and the less said about that the better." His fleeting frown vanished as slowly he stripped the sheet away. "Christ! Yes, I had forgotten what a comely strumpet you were."

She pouted, but her eyes were satisfied as she saw the hot desire in John's gaze. Lovers were all very well but now and then it was necessary to remind John of what she could offer, for to lose all influence with him would have been high folly. She lay back languorously against the bank of pillows and held out her arms.

"Then perhaps it is my duty to remind you, my lord. Will you not let me show you again what pleasures we can have together?"

John nodded, hardly paying attention to her words as he slid from his wrap. He was only conscious of the purity of her flesh which had a magical sheen by candlelight and of the delicious contours of her body now freed from the muffling folds of the sheet. Although they had made love more than once since her return he now felt as stimulated and eager as if this were the first time he would possess her, and with a quick satisfied sigh he pulled her into his arms. As their bodies met in mutual hunger, their mouths greedy on one another's, all thoughts of his easy victory over Philip and Pope Innocent fled from John's mind as he turned his attention to the more immediate business of mastering the breathlessly excited woman writhing beneath him.

John ordered his host to Porchester at the end of June, but although the first part of his plan was put into operation by the departure of Longspée to Flanders, the king found himself once again confronted by the truculence of the barons who refused to accompany him to Poitou, making the excuse that they could not do so whilst he was still excommunicate.

John said some harsh things under his breath about the men who had not hesitated to follow him, excommunicate or not, to conquer William the Lion of Scotland and later had marched with him to the Welsh border, to say nothing of the numerous occasions when they had gathered at court to eat and drink copiously at his expense, despite the papal ban.

But now was not the time to quarrel openly with them and John swallowed his wrath and waited for July when Stephen Langton and four of the exiled bishops landed at Dover.

On the 20th July John went to Winchester to greet them. He was determined to play to the full the role he had assumed, that of a penitent son of the Church, and he rode out to meet the primate on the green hill which overlooked the city on the eastern side.

Langton watched the king approach and his heart was beating faster. It was the first time that he had seen John, the man who had refused to accept him for so long, but now that his moment of triumph had come he felt oddly empty and drained. Stephen Langton was a tall, spare man nearing the age of fifty, with greying hair and light blue eyes under straggling brows. His face had a quiet serenity which none of the difficulties of the last few years had touched, and his smile was kindly and warm, his voice low-pitched and soft.

He knew that his task would not be an easy one for, although John had submitted so completely, the archbishop was not so simple as to imagine that the Plantagenet leopard would change its spots entirely. He did not doubt that John meant what he said; he merely suspected that the king would be unable to live up to the high ideals he had expressed so freely to the papal legate. Stephen had had a long time to think about John and his kingdom, and already had made certain plans should the king begin to slip back into his old habits. He was intelligent enough to realize that his own rather pedantic views on the tyranny of monarchs and the inalienable rights of every living creature would have to be moulded and adapted to the situation he found in England, but he was quite prepared to bend with the wind to achieve his ends, for if he was a scholar and school-man, he was also a practical understanding human being who accepted that no world was ever perfect, least of all a world contained within the court of a king.

When John reached him they stood and looked at one another in silence; the short stocky king, dressed in his finest robes, wearing glittering gems on his carefully tended fingers, and the tall, lean primate, austere and almost chilly in his spotless vestments. When John prostrated himself full length at the archbishop's feet, Stephen gave a faint sigh of relief.

Perhaps it would not be too bad after all. The fears he had felt in the ship as it tossed its way to Dover were probably the result of his own lack of faith and the doubting of the Almighty's wisdom, and it was with humble hands that Stephen raised John to his feet and begged him not to weep.

"Come, sire," he said gently. "No need for tears on such a day as this. Now comes the time of rejoicing."

John permitted the primate to take his hand, ostentatiously

brushing the moisture from his eyes as he followed obediently to the door of the cathedral where the clergy were already chanting their psalms.

In the first moment of their meeting John had read the measure of Langton and inside he was fuming quietly. There was a stubborn kind of strength in the primate which would not be easy to overcome, and if there was any honesty at all in John's tears it was brought about by the knowledge that once again he would have to fight a hard battle to get what he wanted. Langton would prove as troublesome to him as Becket had been to Henry, and John cursed silently to himself as he prepared to renew the oaths made at his coronation and to give his sacred word that he would restore to the Church all that had been taken from it during the interdict.

The archbishop listened intently as the king made his promises, one hand resting on the gospels. John gave his solemn word to honour and defend the rights of the Church, for which he had hitherto shown nothing but contempt; to bring into usage once more the good laws of his ancestors, particularly those of the sainted Edward the Confessor; to make away with bad laws; to give justice to every man in accordance with the right and proper judgments of the royal court; to render unto each man the rights due to him.

To John these were mere words, a trifle more elaborate and fulsome than the coronation oath he had taken so lightly many years before and which he had no intention of honouring in the future, but to Stephen the promises represented something so vital that he was prepared to die in their defence.

It was the difference between what the Angevins promised and what they carried out in practice which Langton was determined to abolish. Henry II and Richard had both ignored the justice of their courts when it suited them, acting arbitrarily and in accordance with their own will and decree; John had been no better. Most of the complaints of the barons had stemmed in the beginning from the fact that what they regarded as their rights were smothered by royal whim. They had grumbled because Henry would not recognize their claim to be heard by properly constituted courts; the Lusignans, hot with chagrin, had turned to Philip Augustus because John had refused them the judgment of their peers and offered them battle by his professional champions instead.

Perhaps at the beginning of his reign Henry had been right to make his will absolute, for he had faced the chaos and anarchy left by the disastrous reign of Stephen, but when the time had come when he could have slackened his grip with safety, he had failed to do so. Indeed, he had tightened it further, and so had Richard.

Langton nodded slightly as John's voice died into silence. Whether the king meant to keep his promises or not remained to be seen; that he, Langton, intended that John should do so was beyond question. Every free man was entitled to be shielded from the will of a tyrant, even if that tyrant happened to wear a crown. The oaths John had now taken, and which the archbishop was determined should be enforced, would give just such a protection, and in future the justice of the king's court would stand like a solid bulwark between a royal despot and the least and most humble of his subjects who could not otherwise defend themselves.

With the disability of excommunication lifted from his shoulders, John hurried back to the coast to make ready to sail, only to find that the magnates had thought of new reasons why they could not accompany him to Poitou.

For a whole day he listened to the explanations of his peers and knights. First, they told him they had used all their resources to equip their men to defend England and could find no more money for a French expedition. If John wished them to go with him, the treasury would have to finance them. When John refused indignantly, reminding them that their service was due to him under the terms of feudal tenure, they denied this with equal heat and claimed that he could not call upon them to serve outside the realm.

In a rage John embarked with his household knights, hoping that when they saw him sail away the barons would be shamed into following him, but they watched him go with complete indifference, exchanging a ribald joke or two about his chances of success with so small an army at his command.

The king went as far as Jersey before turning back. Not a single mast or sail was to be seen on the horizon and once again his precious hopes had been dashed to the ground by the disloyalty and ingratitude of the barons. He did not believe for one moment that any one of them was penniless, and he stoutly refuted their claim that the tenure of their land did not require their service beyond England's shores. His father and brother had demanded such service and had got it without argument. He was smarting with wrath and almost choked with tears as he returned to port to find the nobles had ridden off to their homes without a further thought for the fate of their sovereign.

"By the tears of God I'll make them pay for this." John struck the arm of his chair and made the wood groan complainingly. "They have made me a gazing stock and I will have their blood in compensation."

Petit looked at John sadly. He too had been angered by the attitude of the lords, wondering if they would have refused Henry or Richard, knowing in his heart that they would not have dared to do so. Yet he thought the king had been foolish to make the gesture of setting off alone. That had indeed made him a gazing stock and had underlined the whole bitterness of the rift between the crown and the baronage in a way which could no longer be disguised.

"Will you take some wine, sire?"

Petit knew it was a feeble offering to make to a man whose heart was bursting with torn pride and galling, impotent anger, but he knew no other way to help his master in his hour of greatest need.

John's blank eyes turned to his servant.

"Wine? Is that all you can offer me when I need swords? Can you give me nothing better when I need fidelity and true hearts? Oh Christ, Petit, why do they turn away from me time and time again? They would have gone if it had been Richard leading them, yet what did he have that I cannot offer them?"

Petit was silent. There was no answer to make to such a question, for the truth would have destroyed John, and so he merely shook his head and proffered the goblet again with a hand which shook slightly.

"Very well." The king grimaced. "Wine it shall be but not a sip or two. We will drink it until our senses are so fuddled that we can no longer be tormented by dark memories. We will swim and wallow in its depths until nothing holds any meaning for us. But then. . . ." The blue eyes were very cold. "Then, Petit, when we are sober again we will take steps to punish these men who have offered us such unjust affront. We will go north and make an end of their insolence once and for all. If they will not fight with us in Poitou they shall fight against us on their own doorstep, and we will make them bleed in their chambers and groan in agony on the cobbles of their court-yards."

He took the jewelled cup and drained it quickly, wiping a hand across his mouth and smiling unpleasantly.

"Come, man, do not stand there dreaming. Fill it up again for we have a mountain of sorrows to drown before we take our revenge. Fill it quickly and to the brim, for we have much to forget."

While John was making his way north to give his barons there a taste of the absolute power which he claimed to be his by divine right of kingship, Stephen Langton was in council at St. Paul's devising ways and means of curbing that very power which had kept him in exile for long years and which was bringing to breaking point the patience of the assembled nobles who sat and listened in dutiful silence to his sermon.

When this was done and Langton's last exhortations had died down, he drew the barons about him and considered them thoughtfully. He had no illusions about them. They were greedy, land-hungry, power-seeking and ruthless, every bit as tyrannical as John, but with less opportunity to exercise their despotism than the monarch whom they were slowly but surely beginning to hate in deadly earnest.

Langton thought it was strange that John, able and competent in so many ways, should have failed completely in his task of keeping his baronage loyal. He had shown himself every bit as efficient as his father but his administration and politics had the whiff of expediency about them; he had demonstrated at Mirebeau that he could more than match the military skill of his brother, but he had none of Richard's open-hearted boldness and unswerving resolution. His nobles claimed that their dislike of John was based on his refusal to recognize their rights and his habit of laying the weight of unjust and crippling taxes upon them, but Henry and Richard had done precisely the same thing without arousing such open antagonism. No, it was John himself. Given many natural gifts he had used them like a low-born intriguer instead of a great king and men were aware of the failings without understanding their real nature.

When the archbishop looked down at the sea of upturned faces about him he was conscious of the great burden of responsibility which rested on his shoulders. It would not take much for these men, eager and anxious for action, to recreate the anarchy of Stephen's reign as they fought for selfish motives and personal interests. But if only they could be made to seek their ends by lawful means; means which would give succour to those less fortunate than themselves, then they could be fashioned into a strong arm to protect the weak and a sharp sword to clip the wings of John's unfettered power.

Langton had not wasted his years of exile. He had had plenty of time to consider how to control John without destroying the dignity of the crown; how to satisfy the barons and at the same time to force them to recognize their responsibilities to their own knights and tenants.

There was a stir of interest when he began to speak; began to tell them of the charter of King Henry I which, he said, had recently been discovered. No one bothered to contradict the primate or to point out that the charter had been available all the time if anyone had taken the trouble to look for it. They were far too interested in the promises made by the long-dead king, for the charter of the Conqueror's son touched very closely upon the grievances which they nursed corrosively to their hearts.

Henry had promised that the Church should be free, and followed that by an expansive but vague undertaking to remove all the evil and wicked abuses practised by William Rufus. He would not, he had agreed, force the rightful heir of any tenant-in-chief to buy his inheritance at a crippling price but would allow him to take that which was his on payment of a modest and lawful relief. He would not demand vast tracts of land in exchange for royal consent to the marriage of the daughter or sister of an earl or baron; he would not retain for the crown the property of an heiress upon her marriage, using the excuse of wardship to milk her estates and thus leave her husband cheated of his dues. He would give widows their dowries; he would allow the mother or other close relative of a child-heir the rights of guardianship and would not bestow these upon his favourites in order that they could enrich themselves at the heir's expense.

Langton was careful to stress that Henry's promises had been accompanied by a demand that the barons should act in like manner towards their own tenants, for him this was a vital part of his reforms, but the barons listening with bated breath to the archbishop paid no heed to this, for they were waiting expectantly for further revelations of Henry's oath.

Rufus had been in the habit of confiscating the property of a man who died intestate; Henry had promised that the dead man's wife or heirs should be allowed to deal with his goods and wealth. He had agreed to ask no more than moderate bail in cases of foreiture; not to punish those who offended him in accordance with his own unrestricted will but in a way which measured justly with their trespasses, and lastly he had given his word that knights holding land by military tenure should not be forced to pay amercements and other contributions, but should be free to equip themselves with horses and arms in order that they should be able to serve the king when he called upon them to defend their country.

The barons were delighted with what they heard and when

Langton had finished speaking they broke into loud cheers, declaring that John had fulfilled none of Henry's promises and swore vehemently to fight to the death for the privileges which Beauclerc had set down in the charter for his people.

Langton did not for one moment doubt that their enthusiasm was dictated by the chance of personal freedom and gain, and he was fully aware that they were not in the least interested in the problems of their own knights and tenants, but at least he had caught their ear and had aroused them to making some common declaration of intent. With the aid of such men as William Marshal he could mould the present selfish cries to something stronger and more far-reaching, and with a gratified light in his eye he rose again to offer them his aid in their task of reaching a just settlement with the king.

But the archbishop's satisfaction was short-lived, for no sooner had he left the council chamber than he was confronted by a messenger who told him of John's journey north and of his expressed intention of punishing those who had failed to accompany him to Poitou.

Stephen's lips compressed. It had not taken John long to forget the oath that he had made at Winchester. The tears and humble submission had soon been set aside as the king's true nature bubbled to the surface again in a flood of fury.

Quickly Langton set out to follow John, coming upon him at Northampton on the 28th August.

John was not best pleased to see the archbishop, for he had a very good idea what he had come for, but he greeted the primate civilly enough as he offered him refreshment after his journey.

"Thank you, no." Langton was short and to the point. "I have no time for such things. I have come to ask your grace the reason for your journey."

John's eyes smouldered. He had been right to keep this tiresome churchman out of his realm for so long. He had always suspected that Langton would prove a thorn in his flesh and now it was obvious that he had been correct in his assessment of the situation.

116

"That is our affair."

"Hardly. It must concern us all if your grace intends to take vengeance against those barons who refused to sail with you."

"And why should we not do so?" The king rounded on Langton and his face was white with anger. "Are we to submit tamely to their insolence and disobedience? We called them to war, as we have the right to do, and they ignored the summons. Now they shall pay for that."

"But not at your hand," returned Langton swiftly, "for if you punish them without due process of law, you break your oath given to me at Winchester. If they have committed offences, let those offences be heard in your court by all men, and let judgment be made upon the wrong-doers in accordance with the justice of this realm."

"We shall do no such thing. The right is ours and we shall exercise it. Take heed, archbishop, for you dabble in affairs which are not your concern. Content yourself with your prayers and the righting of wrongs within the Church, for God knows there are enough abuses within it to keep you busy. Leave us to attend to lay matters, for these are none of your business."

"They are every man's business." Langton's own face was slightly paler but he did not back down. "It is for all of us to see that each man's rights are protected, be he the most powerful of your magnates or the most humble of your freemen. You gave such promises at your coronation and repeated them to me at Winchester. Have you not learnt yet that you cannot rule without regard to the law?"

"How dare you!" John was beside himself. "Do you presume to stand there and tell us what we may and may not do? We are the law. Our word is absolute and we shall do what seems best to us. Take heed that your meddling does not land you in trouble, for our patience wears thin at your impudence."

"Your word is not the law." Now Langton was as angry as John, but he had better control over himself. "Will you not see this before it is too late? The law is written clear, and you are subject to it as are the barons you now seek to punish. Let their peers judge them; that is their right."

"They have no rights," screamed John and sent his fist crashing down on the table in front of him. "Don't rant to us of justice, archbishop, for we dispense that in our own way and will take no tuition or interference from you in the matter. Go on your way and leave us to go ours. Get out of our sight before we do that for which we will later suffer the pangs of regret."

And with that John stamped out of his tent, but Langton was not done. When John set out for Nottingham on the following morning, still highly incensed, he found to his annoyance that Langton was close behind him, once again taxing him with his folly and making a few threats of his own.

"If you take your army north, sire, I shall excommunicate every last man who rides with you."

"You would not dare."

"Indeed I would."

"It is beyond your power."

"It most certainly is not."

The red light died out of the king's eyes and he stared dubiously at the archbishop, seeing the militant, implacable gleam in Langton's gaze and the rock-hard thrust of his bony jaw.

"If I tell your men what I will do should they follow you, do you think they would go?" Langton saw the hesitation in the king and pressed his advantage. "Would you have them reject you publicly?"

John slumped down in a chair, his chin sunk in the palm of his hand. Langton had touched a very sore spot with his last question, and even as bitter resentment curdled in his stomach, John knew he would have to give in. He could not risk another humiliating defeat and he had no doubt that Langton was right when he said the army would not follow were the threat of excommunication to be brandished over its head. It would be the same old pattern all over again; humbling, nerve-breaking, and wholly shattering in its effect.

He looked up dully, his bluster quite deflated.

"What would you have us do?"

Langton let the faintest sigh escape him. He knew it had

been a near thing, but he had been determined not to let John win for the issue was too important.

"Simple enough, your grace. Bring the barons to judgment and let them be heard."

"And Poitou?"

"The season is not ripe."

"Will it ever be?" John said it half to himself. "We have been patient."

The archbishop looked at the king and shook his head. John was obsessed with his desire to win back the lands he had so casually thrown away some years before. Langton was aware of the strengthening of the alliance with the princes of the Low Countries, but was equally conscious of the enhanced might of the French king. Furthermore, England was out of sympathy with John's ambitions, and the baronage saw no reason or profit in the expedition for which John had worked unceasingly for the last few years. The time for such conquests had passed away, but John could not see it. He was out of touch with the heartbeat of his own people; blind to the fact that the days of Angevin greatness on the continent had long since gone.

When Stephen had offered John a few meaningless words of comfort and sympathy and had gone on his way, John continued his journey to the north, making no attempt to wreak vengeance on the recalcitrant barons, but simply parading his army about the countryside in a manner which half-hinted at the violence within his heart.

In the end he did no more about the barons who had refused to accompany him to Poitou and the subject of their judgment in court was never mentioned again. Instead, the autumn of that year was given over to pacification and reconciliation, with John and the barons reaching some kind of temporary and watchful truce, whilst the pope's 'angel of peace', Nicholas of Tusculum, arrived in England to help to smooth the ruffled tempers of the king's subjects and to fill a number of bishoprics and abbacies with men carefully selected by the curia in Rome.

Langton was the first to wax indignant at this latter task of the pope's envoy, for he considered it no business of Innocent's to pluck the richest plums for his own favoured men, but John ignored the complaints of those who felt they should have some voice in the appointments, since he had no intention of quarrelling with the pope over the matter. He had bought Innocent's protection at a very high cost and he was not going to jeopardize it by siding either with the churchmen in their wrath or with the lay patrons in their dissatisfaction.

John was far more interested in continuing his plans for the spring offensive against Philip Augustus, and during the last few months of the year turned his attention to the building up of the fleet at Portsmouth, entrusting the details of the task to William de Wrotham, Archdeacon of Taunton, sending emissaries to his nephew, the Emperor Otto, and nurturing the support of such men as the Dukes of Brabant and Limburg and the Counts of Flanders, Holland and Boulogne who were to provide one pincer of his attack upon the French.

Langton and Nicholas of Tusculum worked hard for a settlement despite their differences as to the manner in which ecclesiastical vacancies should be filled, for Langton was wholly dedicated to fostering agreement and co-operation between John and the baronage, whilst Nicholas had been charged by Innocent to ensure that the English nobility fully recognized that its king had seen the error of his ways and had made his peace with Holy Church and that there was no further need for their suspicions or disloyalties in the future. The pope had assumed that the ill-feeling between the king and his barons had been brought about entirely by John's fall from grace, his excommunication and the prolonged disagreement with the papacy, a view which had been strengthened by the clamant, if wholly false, assurances of Robert FitzWalter and Eustace de Vesci.

Totally unaware of the true situation which existed in England, Innocent was deaf to the rumours of strife and discontent which still churned beneath the surface of the tenuous tranquillity in his island fief. John, on the other hand, only too well aware of the truth of the matter, affected not to notice the disquiet. He was passionately determined to sail to France in the spring and still clung to the hope that in the end many of the sullen barons, despite their present animosity, would be prepared to see reason and to accompany him in his venture.

Normally quick-tempered and impatient, John also knew how to hold his wrath in check when the issue was serious enough, and he spoke to his noblemen with soft tongue as he bided his time and waited for the moment when he could teach them a richly deserved lesson.

Once they had served their purpose he would deal with them fast enough. Every last complaint and black look had been noted and stored away as carefully as the chancery documents were filed and docketed. As soon as they had helped him to deal with Philip Augustus they could quickly be brought to heel. When he was master of Europe, they would learn to watch their manners and to stop their nonsensical gibbering about charters and rights.

And so John smiled sourly to himself as he put aside the urge to take immediate action against men such as de Vesci and FitzWalter, settling down in comparative calm to await the coming of the spring.

But before spring could come, winter had to be endured. A cold, hard season with rivers and lakes frozen to iron and the branches of every tree laden with glittering snow beneath grey, sullen skies.

That year the Christmas court was to be held at Windsor and on a cheerless morning in late December, Miles Carlingford, son and cherished heir of Earl Hamelin of Renfell, rode his sturdy piebald horse along the slippery track which led to the castle, his small retinue of knights and servants puffing and cursing at the disagreeable weather as they plodded after him.

Miles was twenty-four years old, but ten years of battle experience had given him a hard, steely look which even the richness of his fur-lined mantle and heavily embroidered tunic

121

could not entirely disguise. Tall, lean and spare, his shoulders were broad, his legs long and muscular beneath brightly coloured hose and high boots of expensive leather. Under the hood of his cloak his black hair had the sheen of satin, clubbed at the neck and cut bluntly across his brow. His clear blue eyes were cool and watchful, his nose thin and patrician, his mouth firm with no hint of weakness about the well-cut lips, his chin markedly determined.

When he moved it was with an easy, unconscious grace, every muscle and nerve co-ordinating with such perfect precision that a clumsy gesture was an impossibility, yet despite his elegance there was no mistaking his quality. He was a soldier and he looked it. A warrior who, for a brief season, had laid aside his chain-mail and helm in favour of silks and brocades, but whose strong gloved hand strayed unthinkingly now and then to the hilt of the sword he wore at his side.

When the castle came into view Miles drew his mount to a halt and paused to contemplate the massive pile as it glowered menacingly across the river valley below. The Conqueror had chosen the site, but it had been John's father who had been responsible for the present splendid structure, ordering his workmen to haul the great blocks of stone up the steep incline and sending to Cumberland for the best lead available to cover the roofs. It was an impressive sight, with its huge tower and range of buildings which ran for half a mile or more, and although neither Henry nor Richard had spent much time at Windsor it was a favourite haunt of John's and he was proud of the facilities and comforts which his castle could offer to his guests.

Conscious of the restiveness of his men and of the icy blast which whistled about him, Miles signalled the party on and was soon dismounting in the courtyard where chaos reigned as squires and grooms helped their masters from their saddles, and where the king's household bustled noisily about the task of preparing for the swarm of visitors which was expected for the festivities.

The kitchen buildings at one side of the inner ward were

thronged with royal bakers, poulterers, fruiterers, cooks and confectioners. The voice of the Usher of the Spithouse rose raucously above that of the Keeper of the Dishes and vied with the shouts of the Master Steward of the Larder as each tried to make himself heard in the deafening pandemonium.

In the great hall dozens of clerks, secretaries, chaplains and pages scurried about their duties, threading their way nimbly through the press of nobles who were making their way to John to offer him their greeting and homage.

John received them with a bland smile, noting carefully those for whom he could risk some trust and those whose intents were all too clear in the coldness of their stares. But good behaviour was the order of the day and even the most bellicose and dissatisfied of the lords bent the knee humbly before the king that morning and then moved on to make way for his companions.

When it was Miles's turn, the coolness of John's manner vanished as he leaned forward in his chair to greet Carlingford with genuine delight and a few words of warm welcome.

That night, the eve of Christmas, John reserved a place at his left hand for Miles, an honour which did not go unnoticed amongst those who gathered about the royal table to indulge themselves heartily at the sovereign's expense.

John eyed Miles with affection. It was so rare an experience for him to feel completely at ease with an Englishman of Carlingford's rank that he savoured it pleasurably for a moment as he sipped his wine and watched Miles carefully dissect a chicken's leg with his deceptively slender fingers. Earl Hamelin was one of the few of the greater barons for whom John had neither suspicion nor distrust. Whenever he called for knight service Hamelin was amongst the first to respond, and he had sent his son to Barham Down with fifty of his hand-picked knights and a hundred apologies that he had not been able to be present himself.

"We were sorry to hear that your father had broken his leg," said John after a moment. "Doubtless the Lady Clemence is finding his temper somewhat short."

Miles looked up and smiled, his habitual reserve gone for a brief second.

"A trifle, but then my mother is well used to dealing with such circumstances."

"A most remarkable woman. You are fortunate, for she is as beautiful as she is witty. You are very like her."

Carlingford's grin widened.

"In my wit or beauty, sire?"

"You have her looks right enough and, it would appear, a fair share of her wit as well. You should marry."

Carlingford nodded. "I intend to. There is a girl. . . ."

"Not any girl, Miles. You must have a great heiress."

"It is not necessary. My father is rich enough. The amount of dues and taxes which he pays your grace must assure you of that."

John acknowledged the dig with a hoot of laughter.

"Maybe, but I've a mind to show your father something of my gratitude. I have not been blind to his fidelity and now there is a way in which I can repay him."

"Oh?"

Miles was cautious but John went on unheedingly.

"Yes. Have you heard of the Lady Juliana Ducarel?"

"Ducarel? The name seems familiar yet. . . ."

"Her father, Gervase Ducarel, died three months ago. He, like Hamelin, was a rich man, possessed of much land particularly in East Anglia. Two months after his death his wife killed herself, and Juliana, their daughter, is now my ward."

"Gervase Ducarel. Yes, I remember now. I had heard of his death although I did not know he had a daughter. She is his only child?"

"Yes, his heiress. She shall be your wife."

Miles stiffened slightly and he took a long draught of wine before replying for he needed time to discipline his words.

"Your grace is most generous but, as I have said, an heiress is not necessary. Also, the girl I mentioned. . . ."

"Forget her." John waved the notion away with a quick movement of his hand. "Or, if that is impossible, make her your

124

mistress if you've a mind for it. But I've set my heart on this marriage, for it will serve a treble purpose."

Miles took a deep breath. It was clear that it would not be too easy a task to shift this idea from John's mind and his own objections would have to be delicately lodged if they were not to cause a rift between his father and the king.

"What treble purpose is this, sire?"

"A token of my affection for your father, a reward for you, and a demonstration that I do not give every high-born heiress to my foreign mercenaries as my barons claim that I do. They shall see now how false their accusations are, for you will wed Juliana Ducarel by midsummer."

"But. . . ."

"I will hear no buts." John was still jovial but his voice was very firm. "Come, boy, fill Sir Miles's goblet for him." He snapped his fingers at a hovering page. "Enough of buts, for if you persist with them I shall began to think you lag behind your father in his regard for me."

Carlingford's blue eyes met John's for a long moment. The suddenness of the king's proposal had caught Miles off-balance. He wanted to snap his refusal in John's face but the king's warning had been very clear. Miles was to have no choice in the matter. It was a gesture of goodwill and friendship to the earl and he, Miles, merely the instrument and channel through which the king's favour was to flow. It was useless to protest and to plead his growing affection for Galiena de St. Lis, whose home was a convenient mile or so away from his own. A waste of breath to shout that he wanted nothing to do with Juliana Ducarel despite her wealth and her father's vast lands. Pointless to argue that a man had the right to choose his own wife in his own good time.

Miles turned his head for a second and let his eye move round the table. He wondered what some of the assembled barons would have to say about it when they heard. The Earl of Essex, FitzWalter, de Huntingfield, de Braybrook, Simon de Pattishall, FitzPaien, Roger Bigod the Earl of Norfolk and Saer de Quincy, Earl of Winchester.

John was right when he said that they resented the way in which wealthy heiresses were given away to the king's hired captains but he was wrong in thinking that a marriage between Juliana Ducarel and Earl Hamelin's son would bring them any pleasure.

The leaders of the baronial opposition had long tried to seduce Earl Hamelin from his loyalty to the king and had failed utterly to make even so much as a dent in his attitude. They resented Hamelin's rough tongue and the blunt, uncompromising words he used to paint his savage portrait of their treachery. It was beyond question that when the king's intentions were made public there would be a fresh outbreak of resentful mutterings in their councils.

He turned back to John. He would have to accept the situation and show some measure of gratitude. He would have to resign himself to the inevitable and face the unwelcome and heart-wrenching task of explaining his reasons to Galiena, whose sweet smile and gentleness had aroused an unusually strong streak of protectiveness in him.

"Forgive me, your grace. I would not have you think me insensible of the honour you pay me and my father. It was simply that I had not thought. . . ."

"No, no, of course not. I understand." The king was quick to accept Miles's apology, deliberately overlooking the slight frown which still marred Carlingford's brow. "I fully understand. You had not expected any recognition of your services and I respect you for your modesty. But you will be fully satisfied, I can assure you. She is a lovely creature, so I am told."

Miles had a momentary vision of Galiena's heart-shaped face and wide violet eyes and winced.

"Then I am doubly fortunate."

"You shall marry when our work is done. Do you come yourself to France in the spring?"

"Of course." This was safer ground and Miles's disquiet was gone. Anything might happen between now and next summer. The Ducarel girl might sicken and die of the plague, or she might run away and marry another if she had the courage to defy the king, or she might even be driven to take the veil. "When do you go?"

"As early in the new year as I can. I have waited long enough."

It was the king's turn to make a survey of the table.

"Which of them will come with me I wonder." His mouth turned down at the corners. "Look at them! Stuffing their bellies with my food and gulping down my finest wine, but who amongst them will honour their obligations and sail with me to La Rochelle?"

"Some, sire."

"It is to be hoped so, but even if they should fail me, I shall still go. The princes are ready and I will hire enough *routiers* to fill up the gaps in my ranks. I shall manage."

As John turned to answer a question from Longspée at his right hand, Miles picked up his goblet and stared at it unseeingly, glad that the king's attention had shifted to another for a while and that he was free for a few moments to gather his scattered wits.

Of course his father would be delighted by the news, touched that John had thought of so practical a way of expressing his affection. Hamelin was aware of his son's feelings for Galiena but had scant patience with them, for Galiena came of a minor family with neither the lustre of a noble name nor land and money to bring to her husband. The fact that Hamelin already had a sizeable fortune himself would not stop him rejoicing in the circumstances which added the Ducarel lands to those of his own family and which poured the contents of the dead Gervase's coffers into the Carlingford money-bags. No, Hamelin would be very happy indeed, there was no doubt about that.

"Why so stern, Sir Miles?"

Carlingford jerked to attention as the queen called to him across the table, smiling ruefully at her teasing expression.

"Too much wine perhaps, madam."

"That I doubt. You were deep in unpleasant thoughts. This

is no time for such ponderings. Shall I come and sit beside you to give you cheer?"

Miles shot John a quick look, but the king was still engrossed in his discussion with his half-brother.

"I pray that you will not," said Miles hastily, "for were you to do so, I should be robbed of the vision of loveliness which faces me across the table. If you were beside me, I should not see your grace so well."

Isabella smothered her mirth. She had seen Miles's swift glance in her husband's direction and despite the polished compliment had understood young Carlingford's dismay at her suggestion. She thought Earl Hamelin's son a remarkably handsome creature. He was not simply a strong, well-built body with a beautiful face like poor Ellis had been. There was something much deeper and more complex about him, as if he were withholding some secret part of himself, never showing exactly what he was thinking, nor letting emotion override his senses. A man powerful and wholly unyielding of whom a closer study would provide endless fascination.

The thin face with its high-bridged nose was at once arrogant and attractive but she did wonder at times whether anything ever warmed the cold eyes to life and softened the hard line of his mouth. She wondered also what he would be like in bed, for Isabella tended to measure all men by such a yardstick, and felt herself tremble slightly at the thrilling thought of being held naked in Carlingford's arms. Ellis had pretended to be masterful and she had fostered the pretence for it had amused and excited her but she had always known that de Norham's dominance was a hollow thing which she could have crushed in a second had she wished to do so. Miles Carlingford would not need to pretend, and since she had been listening intently to John's conversation with him, she found herself resenting the good fortune of the girl whose father had been sufficiently rich to make her such a catch on the marriage market.

"Then I will stay here." Her smile returned. "But later, my lord, you shall sit with me while we listen to the mummers and who knows what may come of that?"

Miles opened his mouth to make some excuse but was spared the effort as John turned back to seek his views on the number of horses which would be required for the spring expedition. When the meal was over and John's guests began to mingle together in the great hall, Carlingford made good his escape and, despite the bitterness of the night, ventured into the courtyard warmly wrapped in his heavy cloak.

He welcomed the wild, whipping snowflakes for they were clean and wholesome in their icy caress; the wind which stung his cheeks a stringent relief from Isabella's poisonous breath. He almost felt sorry for John and prayed that whatever other faults his bride-to-be might have they would not be those of the exquisite voluptuary who shared the king's bed and betrayed him with monotonous regularity.

For a while he strode about in the darkness, half-blinded by the curtain of white, rubbing his gloved hands together to dispel the biting chill. Then, when he calculated that Isabella's attention would be concentrated on some other man, he made his way back into the hot, noisy hall, joining a group of his friends by the fire to drown his new-found worries and problems in a gallon or two of good strong Gascon wine.

CHAPTER SIX

On Candlemas Day 1214 John finally sailed from Portsmouth to La Rochelle. It was the fulfilment of his ambitions and his heart was high as he embarked with Isabella, his younger son Richard, and Eleanor, sister of the dead Arthur of Brittany.

Very few of the great earls and barons came themselves in response to his call, nor did they send their knights as John claimed they were bound to do by feudal law. It was, indeed, an open question as to whether they would agree even to pay the fine and scutage which the king demanded in lieu of service, for their discontent and resistance was growing stronger with each day that passed.

But if John had few nobles with him he certainly had a vast host of low-born mercenaries, ample treasure for the purchase of more service should this prove necessary, and his dazzling collection of gems and precious stones. The smouldering resentment he felt for his barons was temporarily lulled by the fact that his long-awaited journey was at last possible, and he was too much the politician to quarrel openly with those who remained behind lest, in the last resort, he had to call upon them once again for aid and reinforcements.

In the previous autumn Geoffrey FitzPeter, the justiciar, had died and John waited until he was on the point of departure before appointing Peter des Roches, Bishop of Winchester, as FitzPeter's successor. This done, he confidently consigned his kingdom to Almighty God, the pope, the Holy Roman Church, and Nicholas of Tusculum, and then went on his way. It was true the situation in England was far from satisfactory but John had no time to worry about it at that moment. His realm was now a papal fief, and Innocent knew how to look after his own;

Stephen Langton and William Marshal were there to give advice should it be needed, although John had frowned doubtfully over Marshal's attitude. Marshal, whilst sending his knights to serve the king, had refused to take part in the campaign himself since he still held French lands of Philip and could not bring himself to go against his other overlord.

As John was making his way to La Rochelle, William Longspée set off for Flanders, taking with him hand-picked English fighters, an army of mercenaries, and heavy money-bags to finance the allied princes who were to strike at France through Flanders and the north-east, whilst at precisely the same time John would attack from the south through Poitiers.

However well-prepared Philip might be, the two-pronged onslaught would prove too much for his resources and John was happily complacent as he landed at La Rochelle, a safe starting point because of its close trading relations with England.

There John waited whilst a number of barons from Aquitaine came riding in to offer him fealty. It was not affection for John which sent them scurrying to La Rochelle but the certain knowledge that life would be a good deal easier for them under the suzerainty of a king ruling from his island realm of England than under the closer and more searching eye of the unbending, ambitious Philip Augustus.

For the next few weeks John engaged himself in a roundabout journey, designed to confuse Philip who was waiting on the Poitevin border to discover John's intentions, and to test the strength of the opposition or support in the counties of the south. The king quickly put out feelers to the Lusignans, the barons of Perigord and to the viscounts of Limoges and Turenne, and then, moderately satisfied with the result, continued his wandering perambulations.

By March John was prepared to move further away from his base, marching his army down the Charente and through Isabella's province of Angoulême to the Limousin, receiving homage as he went, and leaving trusted officials behind him to watch his interests. When April came the king was ready to ride into Gascony to satisfy himself that no trouble would come from that quarter, fully recognizing, however, that until he had made a final peace with the smouldering Lusignans he could not safely turn his back on the south to deal with Philip. To bring about the much-desired reconciliation John offered his daughter, Joan, to young Hugh de Lusignan, a move which brought a sharp reaction from the French king who in turn made tentative overtures to John, hinting that one of his sons might make a better spouse for John's legitimate daughter, a suggestion which was contemptuously ignored.

To ensure that the Lusignans would not break off their negotiations with him, John rode out to attack their main strongholds, and by the end of May the three brothers had seen the folly of their continued resistance and had paid homage to John as their overlord.

With this difficulty out of the way John got down to the real issue, and in June made his first stab in the direction of the French army, then turning quickly north-west across the Loire where he captured Ancennis lying on the border of Brittany and Anjou. His enemies received the news of his movements with perplexity. Did he intend to encircle Angers? Was he preparing to come up upon it from the rear? What was the true purpose of his extraordinary tactics? Their questions were soon answered for John did a sudden volte-face and raced back across the border of Brittany, seizing the port of Nantes where he took Philip's cousin, Peter of Dreux, prisoner.

Hastily the people of Angers opened its doors to John, for his continued success had struck the chill of fear into their hearts, and John was triumphantly back in the ancient city of his house by the middle of June.

It was then that the blow fell. The one weak spot in John's grasp on Anjou was the fact that William des Roches, Philip's seneschal in that area, still held fast to his newly-constructed fortress at Roches-au-Moine not far from Angers. John could see clearly the need to reduce this pocket of resistance and settled down firmly to besiege the castle.

But John was not the only one interested in the fate of des

Roches' stronghold. Louis, Philip's son, was also watching the situation with concern, realizing that if the castle fell to the English, John's stranglehold on Anjou would be complete. After hesitating for some time Louis finally made up his mind to ride to the defence of des Roches' keep and when John heard that the enemy was on its way his eyes gleamed with satisfaction. His army was slightly larger than Louis's and Louis was not his father. The moment was ripe for conclusions. His progress had been most satisfactory so far. City after city had opened its doors to him. Rebels had been brought to heel. The Poitevin barons had been forced to accept him by superiority of arms and a marriage-tie. Now, at last, the time had come when his successes must be capped with action in the field and his rewarding progress sealed with a well-won battle.

When John heard that the Poitevin barons were refusing to fight, his face grew ashen.

"What!" It was a tortured whisper as his blazing eyes turned to the unfortunate captain who had been detailed to break the bad news. "What is this you say?"

"They have said they will not take the field in open fight against the French king.

"Who speaks for them?" John could feel the blood pumping violently in his heart and his mind was racing with the enormity of the news. "Who says this?"

"Amery of Thouars, sire."

"That renegade! God, I should not have trusted him, for this is not the first time he has betrayed me. Bring him here. Quickly! Quickly!"

His voice rose dangerously and the captain hurried off before the Angevin fury overflowed like boiling oil, but when he returned with the bland and insolent viscount, John was calm again.

"What is this we hear, my lord?" John was remarkably composed as he let his eye wander over the elaborate accoutrements of his shifty ally. "We cannot believe what we have been told is really true."

"It is true enough." The viscount was disposed to be off-hand

and he did not trouble to disguise the fact that he was bored with the whole proceedings and anxious to be away. "We have done as you have asked until now, but we are not minded to fight Philip and nor, sire, do we think you are serious in your intent."

John's mouth was an ugly line.

"What does that mean?"

"Simply what it says. We do not think you mean to fight. You have shown no inclination to do so so far and the French are mocking you for your dilatoriness. It is an empty boast, nothing more."

"The season has not been ripe until now." Still John kept an iron grip on his temper despite the fact that he wanted to scream in the face of the impertinent, craven Poitevin. "To have courted battle before now would have meant destruction, but now we can deal with Louis's army."

"You may be able to do so, if you feel yourself sufficiently strong of stomach, but we shall not even try. We are returning to Poitou with our troops. You will have to make good your vain promises without us."

"Get him out of here." John could hold back the rage no longer and he began to scream as the floodgates of his passion broke under the torrent of anguish and despair. "Get him out of my sight before I kill him with my own hand. Let him go, if he will. He and those other traitorous, cowardly creatures who blow in the wind like broken reeds. Get them out! Get them out!"

He took a sudden step forward and Amery, his boldness disappearing with remarkable rapidity, turned and fled whilst John staggered back to his chair and sank on his knees, burying his head in his hands as tears poured down his cheeks.

Almost within sight of his goal. So close to a successful and conclusive engagement against Philip's son, with his own allies in the north ready to pour across the Breton border to sink their teeth into the Frenchman's tail. So near to the thing for which he had hungered for so long and for which he had worked unceasingly since the loss of Normandy. Now it was destroyed.

The pieces of his precious plan lay in his trembling hands as he shook like a man with a fever. He would have to turn away. Without the Poitevin forces behind him, he dare not ride out to meet Louis; dare not even stay in Angers or venture so much as a short foray into the quicksands which lay ahead of him. There was only one course to pursue; a fast and humiliating retreat to the safety of La Rochelle.

Slowly John raised his head, his vision still blurred by his tears. What malignant strands of fate had wound themselves about his cradle at birth? What devil had decreed such bitter ends for him? Why could he not hold men's hearts secure as Richard had done? Why, with so much within his grasp, had disaster struck again in the same time-worn pattern which had haunted him from the first moment when the crown had been placed on his head?

Drearily he pulled himself to his feet, moving like an old man to the opening of the tent to give his orders. The life was squeezed out of him and he was a dry husk, milked of spirit and drained of hope.

"We return to La Rochelle," he said hoarsely as his captains came rushing up to him. "Make preparations with all speed for there is no time to lose. We fall back on La Rochelle."

And whilst his men raced away to obey his command, John went into the tent again and fell upon the narrow bed set up in one corner for him, turning his face away from the light as slowly his heart began to break.

Whilst John was recovering at La Rochelle and trying to disguise his agony in the despatches he sent to England, the allies in the north were beginning to brace themselves for action.

Miles Carlingford, who had sailed with Longspée, had been alarmed and critical at the length of time the earl had been roaming about Flanders, doing little more than keeping a watchful eye open for stray French troops. Salisbury already had first-class English detachments under his command, with plenty of Flemings under Hugh de Boves to back him. The counts of Boulogne and Holland were there with their men and so was Ferrand of Flanders. Miles shook his head. The delay was too long. They should be moving now if John's plan for the double attack on France were to succeed, but Salisbury had had orders to wait for the Emperor Otto and was helpless to remedy the dire situation which was developing.

In the third week of July the Emperor Otto joined the allies at Vivelles to the south of Brussels, embracing the Rhineland princes beneath his bold banner of the dragon and golden eagle.

The delay which had worried Miles so much had given Philip Augustus all the time he had needed to study the situation, and when he recognized the full strength of the alliance against him he promptly called out not only the feudal host but also the commoners from the towns and villages who were swift to answer his order for troops to defend their land of France.

As soon as his army was ready, Philip marched into Flanders hoping to drive a wedge between the Germans, the Lorrainers and Longspée, but he had left his move a trifle too late and when he found that the allies were already in Valenciennes he turned back from Tournai and prepared to meet them in pitched battle. Looking around for a suitable spot for conclusions with the emperor and Salisbury, Philip's eye fell on a wide sweeping plain beyond the village of Bouvines, and there he settled down to await the coming of his enemies.

The allies arrived in the vicinity of Bouvines on Sunday morning the 27th July. It was already suffocatingly hot despite the early hour, and beneath the gambesons of padded leather and heavy hauberks of chain-mail the knights were sweating profusely as they waited for their commanders to conclude their conference.

"I say we should not fight today." Renaud of Boulogne wiped the perspiration from his forehead where his yellow chair clung in damp ringlets. "It is the Sabbath and we should court disaster were we to stain the Lord's day with blood and killing."

"I agree." The Emperor Otto was resplendent in silvered mail, the hood pulled tightly about his shapely head. "The count is right, my lords; I have never yet won a victory on a Sunday."

Hugh of Boves said something under his breath. He dared not aim his scorn at Otto but no such consideration held him back from making his views plainly known to the Count of Boulogne.

"God, what difference does the day make, or the hour for that matter? We are here and so is Philip. Are we to sit and twiddle our thumbs until tomorrow?"

"So short a delay will make no odds," replied Renaud coldly, for he could see the contempt in his companion. "We shall have a better chance of success if we wait."

"A better chance too of being overrun by Philip." Hugh snorted in disgust. "Have you not heard the proverb, my lord, that it is dangerous to delay when things are ready? Well! Things are ready; they will never be more so."

"Are you so impatient to die?"

Hugh's red face grew duskier still.

"No, by the arm of God I am not, yet I would not tarry and thus give Philip the chance of winning this encounter. Do you not realize how much rides on this passage of arms? King John has put all his trust in us, and he has paid us well to fight for him. Will you take his silver and then turn tail and flee when the enemy is within sight?"

"You know quite well that I shall not run." Renaud's hand was clenched tightly about the hilt of his sword. "Save your spleen and accusations for those who deserve them, for I do not."

"My lords, my lords!" Otto was soothing. "This will not do. Come, we must not quarrel amongst ourselves for our enemy lies yonder and it is he who must feel the weight of our wrath. Like Count Renaud here, I doubt the wisdom of fighting today, yet if others share Sir Hugh's impatience I will not hang back. What say you, William?"

Salisbury shrugged. "I confess I wish it were any day but Sunday, yet Hugh is right when he says that all is ready. If Philip should decide to take the initiative, we would have lost the advantage."

"And you, Ferrand?"

"I'm for getting within a sword's length of his men, sir. We have waited long enough."

"And you, Miles?" The emperor gave Carlingford a friendly look. He had taken an immediate fancy to the young Englishman and was laying secret plans to lure him back to Germany to serve in the imperial guard when the fracas with the French was over. "What say you?"

Miles gave the Count of Boulogne a quick, apologetic glance.

"I would fight now, your grace, without delay. It is weakening to the men to linger idly in this heat, and spirits will have flagged by morning. I think we should advance."

"It would seem, Renaud, that we are outnumbered." The emperor gave a faint laugh. "Pray God the warning in my fingertips plays me false, and I would not have Sir Hugh or any other man lay cowardice at my door. So be it, we will fight today."

The decision taken, the allies divided their men into three battles, with the right commanded by Ferrand of Flanders, Salisbury and the Count of Boulogne; the left by the emperor; the centre by William of Holland and Hugh of Boves, and when the chaplain had said prayers and given absolution to the men, the army mounted up and rode off to the field where Philip awaited them.

When the first clash came Philip Augustus was lying on the grass under the pleasant shade of a leafy tree conversing idly with Enguerrand de Coucy, the Count de Saint Pol, the Count of Sancerre and Guillaume des Barres. He had already destroyed the bridge across the River Marcq which lay at his back, so that none of his troops should be tempted to retreat, and he was calmly confident as he gave his last-minute instructions.

As the noise of fighting broke through the tranquillity, Philip rose quickly, stopping long enough to say a prayer or two in the chapel nearby before fastening on his armour and calling to his squires for his mount.

He sat astride his charger looking every inch a king, his sword already in his hand as he raised his voice to shout to his men.

"To arms! Warriors, to arms!"

He did not wait to watch his knights mount for he had no doubt at all that they would follow him with alacrity, and he rushed off to the plain at such speed that his banner-bearer, Gallon de Montigni, had to spur his horse on savagely in order that the bright red oriflamme of St. Denis should flutter protectively over the king's head when he entered the field.

Guerin, the Bishop-elect of Senlis, entrusted with the arrangement and disposition of the *batailles*, had placed them craftily and in such a way that the French had the sun behind them whilst its full blistering rays fell straight into the allies' eyes as they advanced. It was so hot and dry that as the great destriers' hooves pounded the ground beneath the weight of their steel-clad masters the dust rose like a fog, choking in the throat and blinding to the vision, whilst the sun, now at its fiercest, burned and scorched as the initial assault began.

The allies' right wing was the first to move, charging so boldly that it broke through the ranks of the French scattering them haphazardly as Renaud of Boulogne stormed his way towards Philip and unhorsed him. Philip cursed aloud as he fell to the ground, raising his head to see the unnerving sight of Renaud's naked steel slicing down towards him. A second later the terrifying vision was gone as Pierre Tristan, one of the king's bodyguards, flung himself on top of his master and took the vicious sword thrust through his own side.

Philip rolled his dying servant away, muttering a quick benison as he rose to his feet. The slight delay occasioned by the incident had given his men time to re-form their ranks and charge against the Count of Boulogne, whilst Philip mounted again and threw himself into a desperate effort to force the enemy to retreat.

Driven back by Philip, Renaud's company found itself trapped between the French in front and the allied centre behind it, and in the confusion which followed Renaud came upon Hugh of Boves and swore at him roundly.

"So much for your battle, my lord! Did I not say it would be a disaster? You accused me of cowardice because I wished to wait for a more propitious day, but now we shall see whether it is you or I who will run away first. For my part, I shall stay to fight, or die, if God wills it so."

Hugh had no time to answer for he was immediately beset on three sides by Philip's men, and the pall of dust had quickly blotted out the sight of the Count of Boulogne as he turned aside to attack a group of French knights.

The Flemings on the left of the allied force had already been scattered by the French and Count Ferrand taken prisoner, and when Thomas of St. Valéry swung his cavalry round from the French left wing, the Emperor Otto had his horse killed beneath him for the third time. Otto had fought with superb courage that day, shouting and urging his men on, exhorting them not to lose heart as he struck out again and again with his blood-stained sword, but when his imperial troops were put to flight by the vehemence of another French attack, the emperor was faced with the unpalatable choice of running or falling into Philip's hands. The decision was not hard to make and when one of his vassals dismounted and offered his lord a chance to escape, Otto swung into the high saddle with a swift word of thanks and hastily made off for Valenciennes.

As the long, hot afternoon wore on it became painfully clear that the allies were losing the struggle. The confusion of the battlefield showed no clear and decisive military manoeuvres as it degenerated into a series of mêlées in which personal prowess became more important than tactics, and the skill and experience of Philip's aristocracy slowly but inexorably overrode the blunter and cruder methods of his enemies.

Salisbury, fighting like one possessed, was finally clubbed from his horse by the Bishop of Beauvais, and Renaud of Boulogne captured by the war-like Bishop-elect of Senlis. The Duke of Brabant, whose behaviour both before the battle had commenced and during its weary progress had caused Salisbury to question his loyalty, took to his heels and fled, his abrupt departure sending hundreds of his followers flying after him in panic.

It was when he heard that Salisbury had fallen that Miles

Carlingford realized the battle was lost. He had fought unceasingly since noon and had proved remarkably successful in close combat with the French knights, but he was too much of a soldier not to realize what was happening. As he held his horse still by the edge of the field and gazed at what remained of the fighting his heart sank. John had pinned all his hopes upon this last and vital encounter with Philip and now it was lost. All the years of waiting, planning and scheming were squandered within the space of a few hours and there would never again be another chance for John.

Philip had done more than defeat the allies. He had doused once and for all the flame of John's ambitions and made safe the kingdom of France against attack from the English.

The dust was settling now and Miles could see what was left of John's forces. A mere seven hundred or so Brabantines were still on the field, bravely refusing to turn around and run but, even as Miles watched, Philip gave the order for their slaughter and Carlingford shut his eyes, sickened by the sight of the élite French cavalry cutting the helpless mercenaries to pieces.

There was nothing left to wait for. It was over, and all that remained were the tears and recriminations. Carlingford turned his horse's head away and drove in his spurs as he made for Valenciennes and safety.

When Philip's horsemen had finished their gruesome task, the king himself rode on to the plain with the Count of Saint Pol.

"It is well," he observed to the count. "Our enemies are broken before us."

"Thanks be to God and to your skill, sire." Saint Pol wiped the blood from his cheek and nodded gratefully. "It is indeed the day of your triumph."

"Not ours alone." Philip was smiling. "Nor yet of our brave knights and nobles. Here today is the victory of the commoners of our kingdom of France. The men of Ile-de-France; the burghers of Orléanais; the peasants of Champagne and Burgundy; the humble villagers from Picardy. Mark my words, my lord, from this day forward these victors of ours shall speak with one proud voice, acclaiming themselves true Frenchmen. They have made our kingdom strong and have wrought our crown of steel. The imperial banner lies beneath our feet; John is defeated; our realm is safe."

The count was silent for a moment, conscious of the emotion in Philip's voice and reluctant to break the spell which seemed to hold the king in thrall. Then Philip said quietly:

"Bury the nobles."

"Yes, sire, and what of the prisoners?"

Philip turned his head. "Some we will ransom when the time comes. John will pay heavily for Salisbury."

"And Ferrand of Flanders and Renaud of Boulogne?"

Philip's eyes grew frigid. "No ransom for them. They were our vassals and they fought against us. Take them in chains and they shall rot in our dungeons until it is our pleasure to let them go. They shall grow old and withered in fetters and learn what reward treachery brings to those who practise it."

"Count Ferrand is wounded, your grace."

"He deserves to be. Make a litter for him, but manacle him just the same. He shall savour humiliation and defeat for what he did."

"The emperor escaped."

"It was our intention that he should. He would have been an embarrassment in our hands, and he is no longer of importance. He risked his throne and now he has lost it as surely as John has lost his chance to regain Normandy. Come, sir, we have seen enough. Now it is time to give thanks to God for his mercy and grace."

And with that Philip turned away from the carnage and rode back to camp, there to count his losses and to assess his gains, exultant and triumphant at his most splendid victory, whilst the survivors on the allied side sent hasty messengers to John to tell him of the tragedy.

When he had heard the news John gave a shuddering sigh.

"A sad tale," he said to Petit later when the emissaries had gone and his captains had retired to their own quarters. "A sorry end for me, Petit."

Petit nodded and sniffed miserably.

"If you had been there, sire, it would have been different."

John gave a wan smile.

"How so? What could I have done that Salisbury did not do?"

"I do not rightly know, seeing I was not there to judge the temper of the battle, yet I know that if you had been there in person we should have had the victory."

The king shrugged. "Who can say now? They fought with courage, of that I am sure."

"But not perhaps with wisdom. If you had been there to lead them and to direct them. . . ."

"But I was not, and so we shall never know what might have been."

And after that he would say no more, remaining quietly and despondently at La Rochelle until the autumn. Philip made no attempt to attack him again, nor to use the army of his son Louis to seek further successes in Poitou or Aquitaine. He had done what he had set out to do: he had secured the north and the kingdom of France was impregnable. Aquitaine was a dream for the future, and in any event Innocent had now sent his cardinals to make peace between the two kings, for he was anxious that their war-like intents should be turned against the infidel instead of against one another, and by September a truce had been settled which was to last until 1220, by which each sovereign was to keep the territory in his hands at the time the treaty was signed.

There was nothing left to keep John in France after that. The goal for which he had stretched out his hand was now beyond his reach and, when he had made the necessary arrangements for the ransoming of prisoners in Philip's hands, John took ship to England, arriving at Dartmouth in the middle of October.

He had expected to come back a conqueror; to have the rebel barons kneeling at his feet seeking his pardon. Instead, he had been beaten to his knees by faithless men, incompetent strategy, and the same bad fortune which had always dogged his footsteps.

With his head held high, John came ashore his eyes gleaming belligerently. If the English barons had been with him in France his victory would have been certain, but they had stayed at home instead and left him to fight his war alone. Very well: the choice had been theirs but now they would pay for their decision, and even before he left Dartmouth he was busy with new and ruthless plans for collecting the fines and scutages due from his hostile vassals who had left him to fall to Philip's sword and robbed him of his precious and long-cherished dream.

On a bleak day in November when night was nudging day's elbow and hastening it off with dark shadows and thick curls of grey mist, the servants at Juliana Ducarel's castle at Rockingham were lighting every torch and candle they could lay hands on, glancing nervously over their shoulders as they scuttled along stone corridors and through the great hall which echoed eerily like an empty tomb. Already they were saying that the castle was haunted. They whispered together that the silence was not natural; that if one held one's breath, one could hear a footstep or two where no one trod. They claimed they had heard the sound of a woman crying in the chamber which had belonged to the Lady Passerose but, when the bolder of them had ventured in, there had been nothing but silence to greet them. No female servant would walk alone at night for, they said, they could feel someone or something following them, and now and then the perfume which Passerose had used seemed to envelope them in a sickly cloud, sending them screaming to their companions for comfort and reassurance.

They were convinced that she was still there. Although they had watched in stricken awe as their mistress's body had been taken from her bower for burial, they accepted without question that her spirit had returned to the place where she had lived in happiness with her husband and without whom she had not been able to face the long years ahead.

Her chamber had not been touched since her death. The expensive gowns and wraps still hung on their perches; the carved chests were full of delicate shifts and hose; the table by the window still bore the small intimate reminders of her existence as if she would be returning at any moment to pick up the ivory comb or small silver scissors and to finger the gold chaplets, rings and bracelets in the enamel box by the polished mirror.

Juliana Ducarel watched her maid, Sibile, light the last of the candles by her side and saw the shaking of the woman's hands. At nineteen Juliana's beauty was breathtaking but strangely cold. The exquisite moulding of her cheek and jaw-bone and the perfect arch of her brows over clear grey eyes had an almost timeless quality, as if she had never been young and would never grow old, whilst her mouth, lovely in its lines and seductive in its colour, seldom smiled to lighten the almost frozen immobility of her face. Her gown of heavy brocade was covered by an embroidered surcoat, softly lined with fur to ward off the chill, and her silky hair, ash-blonde in hue, was invisible beneath a fine silk veil topped by a fillet of crisp linen.

She said nothing as Sibile bobbed a nervous curtsy and went quickly from the room, sighing as she looked back into the depths of the fire and stretched out a hand to its blessed warmth. She knew why Sibile was so frightened; why all who dwelt under her roof were growing oddly pale and terrified. Why they jumped at the slightest sound and huddled together at night like sheep waiting for some dread and inevitable fate to overcome them.

She could not find it in her heart to scold them for their folly, nor could she bring herself to offer them the bracing reassurance which would have blown their terrors away with brisk and rousing commonsense. The tragedy was still too near to her and only by holding herself in with rigid discipline could she prevent wild hysteria gaining the upper hand and stop the scalding tears which burned behind her eyes flowing down her pale cheeks. Only under the icy reserve which she had adopted could she go on living, surviving the crushing blow which fate had dealt her beneath a frigid mantle which had frozen her youth and killed all the joy and laughter within her. And she understood what her women meant when they spoke of

145

whispers and footsteps, for she thought she had heard them too.

She had often stood alone in Passerose's bower, stroking the softness of her mother's mantle or holding her jewelled scent-bottle against her cheek, wondering what she would see if she were bold enough to glance over her shoulder into dim corners where the light of the candles did not reach.

Sometimes she found it hard to believe that it had happened at all. She had adored her father, worshipping his strength and vitality, basking in his handsomeness and gaiety, at her happiest when he was there to tease and pet her and to make her feel wanted and important. She had loved her mother too, although that love had been tinged with an unconscious envy for she had always accepted with a curious adult perception that Gervase and Passerose had lived for one another and for no other purpose. Other people moved through their world and they had welcomed them. They had smiled and laughed and offered their affection to those for whom they cared, but Juliana had known instinctively and without doubt that she, and everyone else who had come within their orbit, were as mere shadows and only in one another did life and love truly exist. She knew that even as they had stroked her hair and kissed her cheek they were waiting for the moment when the pretence of living could end and they could withdraw to their own chamber where reality began.

When she had first heard the news of her father's death she had cried bitterly, sobbing her grief into her pillow as she tried to shut out the blankness of the future, but Passerose had not cried at all. She could remember clearly the expression on her mother's face as her husband's captains came to tell her of the manner of his end. She had listened in silence, not a tear blurring the purity of her sapphire eyes as she nodded and dismissed them with a quiet word of thanks. Juliana had not understood how she could be so calm. How she could go about her everyday tasks as if nothing had happened, looking almost happy and contented. She found herself beginning to hate her mother for not caring that the god-like being who had been

146

the centre of their world had died and left them alone, shunning Passerose's company as she sought the comfort and sympathy of her maids. She had not known about the messages which Passerose had written to the king and, even if she had been aware of the letters which had been despatched from Rockingham, it would have meant nothing to her for her own tearing grief filled her every moment, and it was not until one evening three months after Gervase's death that she had begun to understand.

She had not seen her mother all day, and when the evening meal was prepared she had gone to Passerose's chamber and tapped lightly on the door. After a while she had ventured to open the door, cautiously lest her mother was sleeping, but as she crossed the floor she could see the great bed was empty, its embroidered coverlet smooth and neat over the thick mattress and fur rugs. She had looked about her quickly; at the spindle lying idle by the hearth; the table which held the cosmetics and trinkets; the seat by the window where Passerose had loved to sit and watch for Gervase's return. Then she had begun to be afraid and she had trembled as she pushed open the door to the garderobe where her mother's bath-tub stood by one wall, flanked by the tall metal ewers which the maids used to fill with piping hot water and scented oils.

Then she had seen Passerose, and her world had come crashing down upon her. She had heard herself screaming but had been powerless to stop the frantic cries as she stared at her mother's body impaled on the point of the sword which Gervase had worn on his hip with such pride. She had seen the redness of the blood which stained the stone floor and had leaned back against the wall in reeling faintness until the servants had rushed in to support her and draw her away from the sight of Lady Ducarel's cold white face with the blissful smile of happiness touching the corners of the ashen lips.

It was then that she had realized the truth of the matter. That Passerose had said good-bye to life on the day on which Gervase had died and had waited only long enough to put her affairs in order and to beg the king to care for her daughter

147

before leaving an empty world for the longed-for reunion with her husband.

Juliana jerked to attention as the door opened again, thrusting the vision of her dead mother into the secret recesses of her mind as Melisenda de Gressi came quietly to the fireside and took a stool on the opposite side of the hearth.

Melisenda was a distant cousin, an elfin seventeen-year old with huge brown eyes, a small tilted nose and a smile which warmed and comforted its beholder like a blessing. She had arrived a week or two after Passerose's death and Juliana had been glad of her company, although even with Melisenda she had not been able to thaw sufficiently to talk of her loss. Yet somehow Melisenda understood, making no demands and offering no superficial sympathy, settling down in Juliana's household as if she had been there all her life.

Now she looked at Juliana lovingly, wishing that she could melt the agonizing misery which held her cousin in its grip, but making no attempt to intrude as she said softly:

"The servants are laying the cloths in the hall. It is nearly time for the meal. Shall we have ours here by the fire?"

Juliana sighed once more. It was always a trifle uncanny to come back to such mundane things as meals when she had been so wrapped up in dreams of the past, and what had gone before seemed to her far more real than the present, but she nodded and made a valiant effort at a smile.

"Yes, I would like that. Did you see the two men who arrived here this morning?"

"Oh yes. We have had so few visitors of late that the whole castle was agog with curiosity to know whom they might be. They came riding out of the mist like two spectres and . . . oh!" Melisenda's face was stricken as she put a tardy hand over her mouth. "Oh, Juliana, I did not mean to. . . ."

"I know." It was Juliana's turn to offer comfort. "And you are right. I saw them canter into the courtyard, appearing suddenly as if they had come from another world, and so they have in a way."

Melisenda looked doubtful. She could have bitten her tongue

148

off for her carelessness, for references to ghosts and apparitions were wholly out of place in the castle of mourning, yet Juliana had not winced and there was a new and indefinable air about her that day which Melisenda had not seen since she had arrived.

"What way, love?"

"They come from the king."

Melisenda's eyes grew round. "From the king! Oh, how exciting!"

Juliana's smile deepened fractionally and for the first time in weeks it seemed to Melisenda that her cousin was really looking at her and seeing her as a person, rather than as part of the drab background to her sorrow.

"Do you find it dull here? I have been selfish and kept you with me when you should have been in a happier place."

"No, no!" Melisenda was quite definite. "It is not dull at all, and I have no wish to be elsewhere."

"But you will be soon, for the king has bidden me to court."

"And I am to go with you?"

"Of course. I shall take you and a few of my women, knights and servants. The king would not expect Gervase Ducarel's daughter to arrive like a pauper." Juliana's chin tilted. "We shall appear at court as my father would have wished us to do. Tomorrow we must put the sewing women to work for we shall need new gowns and shifts and mantles."

"Oh, Juliana!"

A small, unusual chuckle escaped Juliana.

"And you shall choose the silks and brocades yourself, and your surcoat shall be trimmed with vair and thread of gold."

"Oh!"

Juliana's smile faded and Melisenda saw her cousin's face harden again.

"But that is not all. The king has said that I must marry."

"Marry? So soon?"

"It was inevitable. I am his ward; my father was a rich man. It is well-known that John is not slow to use assets such as I am."

"And your husband? Does his grace say whom it is to be?"

149

"Yes. It is Miles Carlingford, Earl Hamelin's son."

"Carlingford?"

They were both silent for a moment as they contemplated the unnerving prospect. Miles Carlingford's reputation as a soldier was common knowledge and Melisenda shuddered. It was right, of course, that Juliana should marry and, indeed, a worthy husband might well break down the prison walls which she had built about herself since her parents' death, but Carlingford! John placed much reliance upon him, so rumour went, and thus he would be a ruthless man, not afraid to sink to any depths to serve his master. He would be hard and rough and brutal as Captain Guibert de Bray, whom John had sent to guard Juliana and her castle; a man of thick, muscular stature with a red face and great coarse hands. De Bray was a good-natured enough creature, for he had not bothered Juliana much since his arrival, but he was crude in his words, dirty in his person and rawly basic in his appetites. He was typical of John's captains and if Carlingford, for all his noble birth, was even remotely like de Bray, Juliana would be driven to the very edge of insanity.

"Does the king say why he chose him?" asked Melisenda finally. "Earl Hamelin is a very wealthy man and his son should not need...."

"A rich wife? No, John does not give his reasons, nor would I be permitted to ask. Doubtless I am a kind of reward to his favourite."

"Are you afraid, Juliana?"

"I cannot let myself be. I will not show the king or Carlingford that they can make Gervase's daughter cringe. Even had my father lived, I should have had to wed and though he spoilt me shamefully, he would not have sought my opinion as to my spouse. Women are not granted such privileges, sweet, for they are mere pawns in the game of power which their masters play."

"But a man like Carlingford! Even I have heard tell that he can kill a man with a single blow and they say he shows no flicker of emotion as he does so."

"I shall ignore him. His grace can command me to marry his

high-born captain; he cannot force me to show him affection, and I shall not do so."

Melisenda looked unhappier still.

"But there will be times when such indifference may be . . . difficult."

"In bed?" Juliana was blunt. "You are wrong. He may take my body but I shall not give my true self to him. No one can force me to do that, not even a man as well-versed in sieges as Carlingford. He may become possessed of my lands, my money and steal from me my virginity. He shall not take my soul, I will see to that."

She looked at her cousin and saw the tears well up behind the dark eyes.

"Melisenda, I forbid you to cry, and we will not skulk here in my chamber pecking our food like two frightened sparrows. We will go down to the hall, for it is time we reminded ourselves of what it is like to live with others. We must grow used once more to their laughter and chatter and noise, for there will be plenty of it at court."

Melisenda sniffed dubiously but her face brightened. The message from the king had not been particularly welcome, but at least it had had the effect of bringing her cousin back from the limbo in which she had dwelt for too long, and the militant gleam in Juliana's eye was a solid reassurance after the dead, blank looks of the last few months.

When they reached the hall the meal was already in progress and the babble of voices died into silence as the Lady Ducarel made her way calmly and collectedly past the stares of her knights, their ladies and the members of the military garrison which John had sent to protect her.

Guibert de Bray dropped the succulent leg of chicken which he had been demolishing with his strong white teeth and got to his feet, his eyebrows rising in silent surprise.

He had found his task at Rockingham remarkably easy and a good deal more enjoyable than many of the commissions which John had imposed upon him in the past. He had scarcely seen the girl whom he had been sent to care for, for she had

151

kept to her bower, presumably overcome by grief, and certainly none of her men had shown any inclination to challenge his somewhat slack hold on the castle. Thus, he had had plenty of time for hunting in the surrounding woods and been able to fill his belly with the good food and wine provided by his charge's servants, whilst at night there had been more than enough nubile wenches ready and willing to giggle their way into his bed to provide him with satisfaction of another kind.

"Madam." He wiped his greasy fingers surreptitiously on his tunic and reddened slightly. The Ducarel girl was only a slip of a thing but she had an air about her which made him come to attention as he helped her to her chair, shuffling uneasily as sedately she arranged the folds of her gown and looked up at him with a cool, appraising stare.

"Sit down, Captain de Bray. I would not have your meal spoiled because of me. Eat your fill: it would be a pity to let so much food go to waste."

He sat down abruptly, but when he returned to the chicken he found that it tasted like straw in his mouth and he quickly abandoned it in favour of his wine.

"You have heard that I am to go to court?" asked Juliana after a moment, her gaze travelling slowly from the untidy thatch of his reddish hair to the corpulent stomach resting awkwardly against the edge of the table. "Are you to accompany me?"

De Bray twisted in his seat. She was making him feel oddly ill at ease, like a clumsy intruder who had no right to be sitting by her side and partaking of the many dishes spread over the board. He wished she would stop eyeing him in that uncomfortably dissecting fashion which made him sweat with embarrassment and colour up like some callow youth.

"No." His confusion made him brusque. "I stay here, but you will be given ample men to guard you on your journey."

"I don't doubt it." Her smile was honey-sweet but the words bit like acid. "I am too precious to lose, now that his grace has found a use for me."

"I know nothing of that," he returned roughly. "What the king does is his own business."

"Of course; who could deny it? And I have the comfort of knowing that this castle will be well-cared for whilst I am gone, for soon you will have to account for every last stick of furniture and for each sheep which grazes in my fields out yonder."

He burned with anger, wishing he could clout her to silence with his fist, but even as he searched for an answer to make her hold her tongue, her brittle sharpness vanished and she said slowly:

"Do you know Miles Carlingford?"

"I know of him." He glanced at her suspiciously. "Why do you ask?"

"Is it not natural that I should enquire what manner of man the king has chosen for me, or had you not heard that I am to wed him?"

She was still looking at him with those clear, disconcerting eyes but now he thought she looked apprehensive and his irritation faded as he said gruffly:

"Aye, I had heard."

"But have you ever seen him?"

"Carlingford? No, not I, but I have heard tell of him times enough."

"What things have you heard?"

He scratched his head thoughtfully. "Well now, that's hard to say."

"It should not be so. Is he a good captain?"

"Indeed he is. A rare fighter, so they say, whose men will follow him anywhere." De Bray was on surer ground now. "He has the courage of a lion and no man has ever seen him retreat so much as an inch. The king favours him greatly."

"So it would seem." She was dry. "And is he loyal to John?"

"Loyal!" His mouth gaped. "Madam, be careful what you say!"

"I meant no offence." A faint smile lurked round her mouth. Not all of the king's barons are loyal are they? Some will not fight for him, and they make demands upon him which he finds extremely irksome."

His small bloodshot eyes narrowed. "You seem well-informed, madam, for one who lives closeted within her bower."

"I did not always live so. My father spoke to me of these matters."

"Then he should have told you that Earl Hamelin's son was the king's man. If he gave you to understand differently. . . ."

"We did not even speak of the earl's son. I had no reason at that time to ask about him."

De Bray grunted and suddenly found himself trying to reassure the girl who only a few minutes before had been rubbing his self-esteem raw.

"You'll do well enough." He was not used to comforting women and it was difficult for him to find the right words. "You're favoured that his grace should choose such a man for you. He's a fine soldier."

"Do fine soldiers make fine husbands, captain?" Juliana put her head on one side. "Can you answer me that?"

"I cannot and that's the truth of it, but you'll be safe enough."

After that de Bray would say no more, and Juliana was left to ponder on the question by herself as she sipped her wine and looked round at the assembled company, now engrossed in their meal and light-hearted chatter once again. She had been bold enough in her assertions to Melisenda, too proud to show the fear which sent her heart racing, making her finger-tips tingle with dread whenever she thought about John's message, and it was not until she was back in her own chamber that she realized that for two whole hours she had not even thought of her parents' tragedy. It was vastly strange, for all her attention had been fixed on her own uncertain future, and there was a frown on her smooth brow as her maids hurried forward to disrobe her and prepare her for the long night ahead.

154

CHAPTER SEVEN

A T the beginning of November Miles Carlingford arrived at his father's home at Renfell. He rode the last few miles in quiet contentment, uncaring that the day was cold or that a damp and discouraging drizzle was misting the landscape. He had been born at Renfell and he loved every acre of it; every gentle slope and each sturdy tree was a reminder of a happy childhood when he had learned to run and ride and hold a sword in his small determined hand under the careful guidance of his father's knights. It was good to be home for a while, for such interludes were rare now, and his heart was light and buoyant as he clattered into the courtyard to be greeted by the smiling welcome of the earl's squires and grooms.

He knew them all by name: knew their wives and their children, understood their problems, and held them high in his affection. Although he was anxious to be off to the castle where his mother, Clemence, and the earl awaited him, he showed none of his impatience as he stopped to talk for a while to the men clustered round him, offering a word of condolence to one, quick congratulations on the birth of a son to another, a smile of encouragement to a third.

Finally he was free to go, striding out quickly and taking the stairs three at a time, thrusting open the door of the room where Earl Hamelin sat by the fire with his leg propped up on a long stool, the Lady Clemence on the opposite side of the hearth stitching a fine seam in a shirt of saffron linen.

"Miles!" Clemence rose to her feet in a rustle of silks, her small hands held out eagerly as her son crossed the floor to hug her firmly in his arms. "Miles, dearest Miles!"

He kissed her soundly on both cheeks, holding her away

from him for a moment so that he could search the well-loved lines of her face, feeling an unexpected lump in his throat as he saw the warmth of her smile.

Clemence was a tiny creature, delicately formed and exquisitely graceful, with a complexion of cream and roses and eyes the colour of a summer sky. Beneath her snowy wimple and fillet her hair was the colour of pale ash, but neither that nor the lines which touched the corners of her mouth and eyes succeeded in making her look old. She was so wonderfully alive it seemed that time could not touch her and when she laughed she had all the gaiety of a young girl in her first innocence.

He held her a moment longer, then kissed her again, turning to his father to clasp Hamelin's hand between his own strong slim fingers.

Earl Hamelin, in his early fifties, was a tall, burly man with hair of iron-grey and a luxuriant beard curling crisply beneath his firm mouth. His nose was as bold as his son's, his eyes the same piercing blue, his face weather-beaten and tanned by the roughness of the wind and the glare of the relentless sun.

There was no need for Hamelin and Miles to use words. The touch of their hands and the long look they exchanged was enough, for the affection they had for each other was deep and unbreakable, but when the brief moment of emotion was past, Miles straightened up and said with a slight laugh.

"I am sorry to see, sir, that your leg is not healed. The king is grieved by your suffering."

"By God's bloody wounds he is not as grieved as I am." The earl was addicted to colourful speech at the best of times and his prolonged captivity in his chamber had done nothing to improve his temper which tended to be fiery. "I am like a captive bear, tethered to a pole, baited and tormented by those who should know better."

He shot his wife a censorious look and Clemence laughed gently as she came to his side and laid one hand on his brow.

"Your father is angry with me because I make him take the medicaments the physicians have ordered for him, and he does well to liken himself to a bear for he growls just as fiercely."

"Medicaments! Hell's pains, woman, what good will they do? It is my leg which is ailing not my belly. The physicians are a pack of fools, for not one of them has been able to set the bone straight. They are like a gaggle of squawking geese with their stupid draughts and clucking disapproval."

"They do not squawk, my love," said Clemence and grimaced at Miles. "They merely bid you to use your commonsense which you will not do, and they reproached you because you attempted to go hunting when they had told you to remain still. No wonder the bone will not set. How can it, when you are forever getting to your feet?"

"I cannot lie here for ever." Hamelin's indignation was growing hotter. "Am I some feeble woman that I have to be chained to a chair? I have work to do."

"There are plenty here who can do your work for you and that is but an excuse. You want to go hawking and chase the fallow deer and go off and fight for the king. You are merely jealous because others enjoy these things whilst you have to forego such pleasures for a while. And if only you would accept what the doctors say, you would soon be healed again."

"Woman, hold your tongue, you are every bit as tiresome as they are. I swear that I shall. . . ."

"You will what, dear love?"

Hamelin looked into his wife's innocent azure eyes and was lost. Miles grinned as he watched the wrath die away and the familiar besotted look which the earl reserved for Clemence take its place. They were as deeply in love as on the day they had married and the diminutive Clemence had never lost the ability to wind her husband round her tiny finger and hold him fast.

"Well, I . . . I . . . ."

She planted a feather-light kiss on his forehead and gave Miles a conspiratorial wink, turning quickly as the door opened again to admit a young man with hair of copper brightness curled about his well-shaped head who bounded over to Miles and caught him vigorously by the shoulders.

"Miles! God, I am glad to see you again. It is an age since we met. Does all go well with you?"

Miles nodded and clasped his cousin's hand.

"Yes, all is well with me, but I did not know you were here, Doun."

"Your father has complained so much since you arrived that I swear I have had no chance to tell you." Clemence sat herself down in her chair again and picked up her sewing. "Doun is staying with us for a few days before he turns south. He has grown very beautiful, do you not think so?"

"Really, Clemence!"

Hamelin began to scowl again but Doun was unmoved for he was used to his aunt's gentle mockery.

"Of course I am beautiful; I always was. Don't you agree, Miles?"

Carlingford considered his cousin carefully. He had not seen him for three years or more and Nature had spent the time well. The thin young boy whom he remembered had broadened into a handsome man whose slim flanks were complemented by wide shoulders and strong sinewy legs. Miles looked approvingly at the bright hazel eyes under straight brows, the blunt nose and chiselled lips, and nodded.

"You'll break a heart or two I've no doubt. Is that how you have been spending your time?"

Doun's smile faded. "Indeed no. There have been other matters of more importance to claim my attention.'

"But the expedition to Poitou was not amongst them." Miles rubbed a reflective finger along his jaw. "I had expected to see you at Barham Down."

Doun FitzAnthony gave a terse laugh as he shot Miles a derisive look.

"You cannot mean that."

"Why not? It was your duty."

"I deny it. Feudal law does not require foreign service."

158

"Then feudal law has undergone a remarkable change since I was instructed in the obligations it imposed." Miles's voice hardened. "Who taught you such nonsense? De Vesci? Fitz-Walter?"

"They are not the only ones who think as I do. There are many who support my view."

"Your view!" Earl Hamelin snorted. "You impudent young puppy. Your duty lies with the king."

"But not in everything which he does, my lord." Doun did not back down under the earl's wrath. "He has no right to ask us to fight in France."

"No right! Christ, boy, you talk of the king."

"I do not overlook the fact; none of us do. But we are no longer prepared to bend to John's selfish will. Now we require him to rule in accordance with the ancient laws and customs of this realm, restoring to us our privileges and rights."

"And those are?" Miles's tone was silky but the light in his eye was cold. "What rights do you claim that John has taken from you?"

"You know well enough. I do not need to list them for you. Whilst you have been away, discontent has surged to the surface. Men are rising in anger against des Roches' rule, for he has imposed ruthlessly the new scutage for which the king asked last May. He is nothing more than a bandit and a foreigner what is more. Can the king not see how men hate these Poitevins and Flemings with whom he surrounds himself? Why cannot he understand the resentment aroused by the favour he shows them? He places all his reliance in them but will not trust his own barons."

"And who can blame him?" Clemence paused to look at the tiny pleat she was stitching. "I wonder if that is too narrow; perhaps it should be a trifle wider. If I were John I would not trust my barons either, at least not those who had refused to support me. Would you like some wine, Doun?"

FitzAnthony looked baffled. Although he could cope with her teasing, his aunt's habit of leaping from one subject to another with bewildering rapidity never ceased to bemuse him, and he always had the feeling at the end of a conversation with her that he had, in some indefinable and subtle way, lost a vital argument.

"Madam, I. . . ."

"I will pour some for you." Clemence smiled brightly and rose to her feet. "Do go on, dearest. Tell Miles how you feel, for I am sure he is most interested."

Miles gave his mother a quick look. Clemence had reduced Doun, the aggressive warrior and champion of the barons' rights, to a small tongue-tied boy. He was constantly amazed by his mother, for under her apparent vague insouciance, Clemence was as sharp as the stab of a sword and terrifyingly shrewd in her judgments.

"Whatever you may think," said Doun finally, "the Bishop of Winchester has failed to reap his master's harvest. He has got precious few dues out of Norfolk and Suffolk and none at all from Essex, Hertfordshire, Lancashire or Yorkshire."

"If you expect us to applaud the stand they have taken you will be sadly disappointed," said Miles shortly. "Those who refused to sail with John owe him scutage and they should pay it."

"They do not owe it and they will not pay it." FitzAnthony took his wine with a brief word of thanks. "Eustace de Vesci is now openly defying John's officials."

"Eustace de Vesci is a despicable traitor," returned Hamelin angrily. "In the name of God, Doun, do not pattern yourself on such a man as he. He thinks of nothing but his own interests and neither he nor the others who follow FitzWalter will impose their will on the king."

"And why not, uncle? The pope did so successfully, as did Philip Augustus. The king has been overcome twice. Why not a third time?"

"By his own barons? Are you mad!" The earl struggled to get up and was defeated by the pain in his leg and a cautionary look from Clemence. "Do you dare to stand there and tell me that you would ally yourself with such men as these? You, my own flesh and blood!"

"I do, sir, and so will many more like me. If you had any sense you would join us, and you too, Miles."

"I have no intention of lending my name to your folly," said Miles bleakly. "My father is right. De Vesci and FitzWalter are nothing more than greedy rogues. What they seek is neither lawful nor just."

"It is easy for you to condemn them, but you have not suffered under John as we have done. You have not paid a crippling fine as I had to do when I came into my inheritance last year. You have not been faced with the claim for scutage of three marks."

"No, I have not, but then I was not afraid to fight for the king. He has not asked those who went with him for knights' fees."

"I was not afraid!" Doun flushed. "It was a matter of principle which held me back."

"Principle! Pah! FitWalter does not know the meaning of the word. He has gulled young fools like you into believing he speaks of a great truth, but all he is doing is inciting a rebellion against his sovereign." Hamelin gritted his teeth. "Don't prate to us of principles, boy. At least be honest enough to recognize what you are doing."

"Oh I am sure he does, my lord." Clemence gave her nephew a dazzling smile. "John and FitzWalter both make demands on men, but John's bite the harder because he has the right to make them. It is always much easier to be nibbled by a cause which has such a resounding ring as FitzWalter's."

"Madam, you do not understand," began Doun, when Clemence laughed again.

"You would be surprised, love, how well I do understand."

"If you want a cause, you would do better to heed Archbishop Langton and William Marshal." Hamelin had sunk back in his chair and was eyeing Doun darkly. "If there are things to be remedied, they are the men to show the way."

"If there are things! God save us, my lord, can there be any question of that? The realm is thoroughly corrupt and so is John's administration. The law waits upon the king's word, and justice is sold to the highest bidder. Loyalty to the king is one thing. Stubborn blindness to the harm he is doing is another. We are being ground under the heel of Angevin greed. The fines, the exactions, the fees we have to pay. Widows and heirs are sold like cattle to the king's friends, the merchants are faced with crippling tolls. Our rivers are blocked by royal weirs; towns may not build bridges unless they pay for the privilege; corn and wheat is taken for the king's use. Free men are arrested at John's word without cause, outlawed or exiled for trivial offences. Must I go on? Are the abuses not clear enough?"

"Then seek help from Langton and Marshal," repeated Hamelin sharply. "Do not disgrace your proud name by lending it to that mob of common criminals."

"They are not criminals. Why can you not see this? They are men whose birth is as noble as ours. They have given John every chance."

"They have given him none at all. He was condemned even before he took the throne. I say again, Doun, be done with them. If you thirst for reforms seek them in Langton's wisdom not in FitzWalter's sword-thrust, for the archbishop's vision is wider than Sir Robert's."

"It is too late." FitzAnthony's lips were tight and his eyes stormy. "Men like de Vesci, Richard Percy, Robert de Ros, the Earl of Clare and Roger Bigod of Norfolk are tired of waiting. We are not cut-throats but men of honour demanding no more than our just entitlement."

"And so you will fan treason in the kingdom to gain your ends?"

"There is no treason. We seek only to make John obey the laws of the realm and to recognize us as his rightful advisers."

"I am sure the king would be delighted to have your advice, Doun. It has probably never occurred to him that you would have any to give and so he has never thought to seek it. Have some more wine, child, you look quite flushed and when you were small that was always a sign that you were sickening for some illness." Clemence patted the bench beside her. "Come, sit here by me. Have you heard that Miles is to marry?"

162

Doun obeyed reluctantly. He had by no means finished with the subject but he knew it was hopeless to argue with his aunt and so he swung round petulantly to obey her, stumbling heavily against Hamelin in the process.

The earl let out a bellow like a wounded bull, clutching at his injured leg and emitting a string of oaths which took the last vestige of colour from Doun's face.

"Sir, I do beg your forgiveness. I . . . I . . . ."

"He is not hurt." Clemence squeezed her nephew's hand. "It is good for him to have a sound reason to swear now and then. It is fate he is really cursing, not you. Now, did you know that Miles was to wed?"

Doun tore his eyes away from his uncle's purple face and nodded.

"Yes, I had heard. The Lady Juliana Ducarel, is it not? They say she is as beautiful as she is rich. You are most fortunate, Miles."

"Am I?" Miles poured his father another goblet of wine and gave it to him with a sympathetic glance. "I do not account myself so. I have no desire to marry at present and I certainly hoped to choose my own wife."

"That pretty child, Galiena. You recall her, Doun?"

"Galiena de Gifford? A skinny brat who was forever following Miles and me about."

"She is not skinny now. In fact she is an enchanting creature. How sorry I am for her."

"Why?" Miles was curt. "What is wrong? Has something happened to her?"

"Only that she cannot marry you, and that is quite enough to break her heart."

"Madam, really. . . ."

"Miles, it is true. She will be devastated by the news. You will have to ride over yourself and tell her, for it would not be seemly for her to find out from somebody else."

"You think it more fitting that I should break her heart in person? I am of a mind to refuse this ward of John's."

"You cannot do that." Hamelin had recovered himself,

163

encouraged by a generous swallow of wine, but now he raised his head abruptly and gave his son a hard look. "There can be no question of that. The king has honoured us greatly by this offer. You cannot spurn it, and in any event the de Gifford girl is not good enough for you. It must be the Lady Ducarel."

"Why? We do not need her money."

"That is not the point." Hamelin was beginning to splutter with anger again. "This is not a matter of money."

"Indeed it is." Doun gave his cousin a sardonic smile. "This is just how John pays his debts. Because Miles followed faithfully to France when his grace beckoned to him, he is to be rewarded by a damsel whose coffers are well-lined with gold."

"Did you wish to marry her yourself?" asked Miles softly and Doun shot him a quick look.

"No, why should I? I do not know the girl and I do not need her money either."

"Then hold your tongue, or I'll come over there and cut it off with the point of your own sword."

"You may try, cousin." Doun was on his feet in an instant, stung by the cool contempt in Miles's voice. "But I am not the youth you put down so easily in years gone by."

"Sit down!" shouted Hamelin furiously. "And be quiet, both of you. I will have no fighting in here for the next thing I know you will have fallen on my leg again. You have no sense, either of you. Miles has no choice in this matter, that is clear, and you, Doun, would do well to keep silent for you have talked enough nonsense for one day. Am I never to have any peace in my own home?"

Miles and Doun exchanged a long look, and then Doun began to laugh.

"Forgive me, I am at fault. It is no business of mine what fate and the king have designed for Miles, and I will not torment him a moment longer for he will need all his strength and patience to deal with his new bride. I hear tell that she is somewhat odd."

"Odd? In what way?"

"Have you not been told?" Doun was all innocence. "Why,

she seldom stirs from her chamber, so they say, and all her servants are terrified for they believe the castle in which she dwells is possessed by the spirit of Gervase Ducarel's wife."

"Rubbish!" The earl glared at FitzAnthony again. "Doun, I have warned you. . . ."

"Sir, I am done. It is, as I have said, no affair of mine, and I am content to leave Miles to his lovely, rich and haunted bride." He stretched his arms above his head and yawned. "I'm for a ride while the light lasts. Will you come, Miles?"

Carlingford shook off his irritation and nodded, bending to kiss his mother and to lay a gentle hand on her cheek.

"You will not forget to ride over to Haverling, love?"

"I will not forget, but later."

Hamelin watched his son cross the room and when the door closed behind him he said quietly:

"Pray God that Doun will not persuade the boy against his better judgment."

"He will not. Miles is every bit as pig-headed as you. It will take more than Doun to make him change his mind."

"It is an ugly situation though. I would not admit it before Doun, but the numbers of the disaffected are growing. Every day more join FitzWalter's party, and John is playing into their hands with his insistence that the new scutage be paid to the last penny."

"And now he plays from a position of weakness." Clemence's work was left unheeded for the moment. "Had he won the encounter at Bouvines they would not have dared to challenge him. Now they are bolder. John no longer overawes them."

"Sometimes I fear for him."

"For John?" She chuckled. "Love, there is no need. He is an Angevin with all his father's determination and a good deal of his brother's courage."

"Let us hope that will be enough."

"It will be, never fear. Now it is time for your medicine."

Hamelin looked at her for a moment with a wicked gleam in his eye.

"To the devil with my medicine, woman. Thrust it down the

165

throats of FitzWalter and de Vesci if you will, but not down mine. Come here this instant and give me a kiss."

Blushing rosily, Clemence tripped lightly across the floor and let herself be enfolded in her husband's strong arms, all thoughts of the physicians' unwanted cures fleeing from her mind as delightedly she gave herself up to Hamelin's enthusiastic caress.

That evening Miles Carlingford rode over to Haverling to see Galiena de Gifford. She lived in a disused hunting lodge on Earl Hamelin's estate with a vague, elderly aunt and two servants. Her parents had been dead for many years and, since they had had nothing to leave their only child, it had fallen to the earl to make provision for her and to ensure that she lacked none of the essentials of life.

The lodge was small, but Clemence had seen to it that it was comfortably furnished, and every week one of the stewards from the castle would ride over with fresh meat and grain, and now then Clemence would send a length or two of silk with a bundle of ribbons and some trimmings of fur or braid so that Galiena and her aunt could provide decent clothing for themselves.

There had been no official understanding between Carlingford and Galiena. They had simply known one another since childhood and were fond of each other, but of late Miles had thought more and more about Galiena and her gentle grace and although he knew the earl would frown upon the suggestion of marriage with one of such humble status, he had been prepared to risk his father's stormy objections in so good a cause.

Now there could be no question of a marriage between them. John had dealt the idea a death-blow with his offer of the Ducarel heiress and although he had made his protests Miles knew that in the final analysis there could be no escape for him.

Galiena came to the door to meet him, for there was no formality in her household and the two servants were advanced in years, with more than enough to cope with in the kitchens and gardens beyond, where Galiena grew fruit, vegetables and herbs for the table.

"My lord." Her face lit up as she stood aside to let him enter. "How good to see you. I had thought you still in France. The Lady Clemence sent word to me that you had followed the king."

"So I did."

He smiled down at her, admiring anew the colour of her eyes and the delicate flush which touched her cheeks making them look for all the world like a newly-opened rose. Her gown of yellow material was clearly not new but it was well-fitting and spotless, tied about the waist with a neatly-worked girdle, the goffered fillet on the crown of her head pale saffron in hue.

"May I get you food, sir? I have some most excellent veal, thanks to Lady Clemence, or there is a capon if you would prefer it."

"Neither, thank you. My mother has fed me well, as if she believed I should not eat again for at least a week."

They laughed together for a moment and then Miles grew serious.

"I came to tell you something, Galiena."

"Yes, my lord."

She waited obediently, not hurrying him as he picked his words carefully.

"You will learn of the news soon enough I know, but it is right that you should hear it first from me."

The violet eyes darkened warily and he took a deep breath.

"I do not know how to begin. It is difficult, for I am conceited enough to think that what I have to say may hurt you, and you know that this I would never want to do."

"I know." She clasped her hands in front of her, very still as she braced herself for what was to come.

"But then again, there has been nothing between us which . . . that is to say . . . we have not. . . ."

He broke off and cursed himself for his inarticulate ineptitude. Always so ready and able to give sharp decisive orders on the battlefield or to turn a graceful compliment to a high-born woman at court, he could not find the few simple phrases which were necessary to tell Galiena that he would not see her again.

Then Galiena said quietly: "You are to marry?"

He looked at her quickly. "You have been told already?"

"No, but I guessed the reason when you found it so hard to tell me."

"I am a fool and most clumsy."

"You are not. Neither foolish nor clumsy. It was difficult for you for, as you say, there was nothing between us yet you have a kind heart."

He grimaced. "Kind heart or not, I have made a poor showing here tonight."

"It is not important."

"None of it?"

"Sir?"

"You know well what I mean, Galiena. Is it not important to you that I must marry?"

She tried to stop herself trembling, for Miles was suffering enough and he must not see the pain in her which would add to his own unhappiness.

"Of course, but doubtless it is your duty."

"It is the king's will."

"Then there is no more to be said."

"Nothing? You do not even ask whom she is?"

"It is not for me to do so."

"No curiosity?"

"That is a luxury I cannot afford."

"Oh God, Galiena, don't . . . don't!" He caught her in his arms and his mouth was hungry on hers. "Did I mean no more to you than that? I know that I have not been able to visit you very often but, when I did come, it seemed to me that we had much to say to each other in a way in which words did not matter. Was I so wrong? Tell me, Galiena, tell me! Was I wrong?"

He saw the drops of sorrow on her face and closed his eyes for a second, holding her close to him and murmuring softly in her ear. Then he gave a shuddering sigh.

"Thank you for that. If you had sent me away without your

tears I should have been a lesser man. Dear love, if I could . . . if I had been able to. . . ."

She put her finger-tips on his lips.

"But you were not able to, Miles, and it cannot be helped. And if it had not been the king who had come between us it would have been the earl, for he would never have let you wed me. You know that as well as I do. Oh, I have dreamed a thousand dreams of having you in my arms in our marriage bed but when daylight came again I knew they were mere fantasies. It could never have been, dearest; not for us."

"I think tonight that I truly hate life and could wish it over for me."

"No, you must not say that. You have so much to live for; so many things to do. Miles, promise me you will never say such a thing again."

"I promise." He took her face between his hands. "Dear Galiena, how sweet you are and how much I shall miss because I cannot have you."

"Not as your wife, at least."

He frowned quickly. "I do not understand you."

"Yes you do; you understand me well. We cannot marry, yet here and now I could be yours."

"And dishonour you? Take you like a harlot for a night's pleasure? Is that what you mean? Is that what you think my love is worth?"

"I know the value of your love. Do not be angry, and do not draw away from me. Listen to me and do not close your mind to my words."

Reluctantly he held her close again but his frown did not lift. "I am listening."

"You came to tell me that we should not see each other again, did you not? That after tonight I could not look forward to those rare and precious moments when you come here to Haverling to see me. I think I have always known that such a day as this would come, for it was clear enough that you would marry soon and I should lose you. Miles, I can bear the loss if I have a true remembrance of our love to comfort me. I know

169

that you want me for I can see it in your eyes. You may deny it all you will, but I know that you long for me as I long for you. Why should we both be starved of what we both need so much at this moment?"

"Galiena, you do not understand. If I take you now I rob you of your innocence and your future. What man will look at you thereafter? And if there be a child. . . ."

". . . which pray God there will be."

"Galiena!"

"Sweet love, have I shocked you? So much for my innocence, although what you truly meant was my ignorance. But I do not want to be ignorant and I shall not marry. How could I now? Come to my chamber with me."

"Your aunt. . . ."

"Is away, visiting friends in the village."

"The servants. . . ."

"Are about their tasks and then they will settle down to sleep in the stables."

"But Galiena. . . ."

"Must I disrobe myself to whet your appetite? Must I strip myself naked and force myself upon you?"

"If you were to do so I think I should take you here and now, for I need no goad to my desire. Dearest, it is not lack of love or interest which holds me back. God knows I want you, but honour dictates. . . ."

"A fig for your honour! Why do men never understand that women have no time for such pretences? And why should you stand so nicely on a point of courtesy when there cannot be a man of your acquaintance who has not had at least a dozen mistresses."

"My father has not."

"He has never needed one. The Lady Clemence is a being set apart. Who would look at another if she were his wife?"

"Yet. . . ."

Galiena pulled herself from his hold and tore the veil and fillet from her head so that her shining hair tumbled in a careless cascade down her back.

"Galiena, stop it! Stop it!"

She paid him no heed, shrugging the gown from her shoulders and letting it slip to a pool of silk at her feet. He stared at her, his face white and grim as the shift dropped to her waist, his jaw clenched in a hard line as he watched the gentle rise and fall of her breast.

"Do I not please you?" Her eyes were very bright and there was a patch of high colour on each cheek. "Can you refuse me now and make a fool and worse of me? Miles, dear Miles."

With one swift movement he bent and picked up her gown, wrapping it hastily around her and stepping backwards as if the touch of her flesh had burned his hand.

"I am stronger than you think," he said in a low voice and felt his heart tear open at the expression in her eyes. "I will not be swayed by temptation, although I ache with every fibre of my being to make you mine. It would be wrong for you, and I will not do it. Hate me if you will, but I care too much for you to make a whore of you."

"Then go." Suddenly her voice was dull and lifeless and she did not look at him again. "Go quickly. At least do that for me. Go now, before I am utterly destroyed."

He turned on his heel and raced out of the hunting lodge, leaping into the saddle and driving in his spurs with such force that his mount plunged off into the night like a thing possessed.

He did not turn back to look at the lodge. He could not even bear to think of it and of Galiena standing there in front of the fire, the yellow glow painting streaks of gold on her bare satiny skin. He did not quite understand why he had refused her despite his protestation of honour, for his longing for her had been almost overwhelming, and it was clear that he had now done her a greater injury than if he had raped her on the sweet-smelling straw which had lain beneath their feet. He tried to drown the agony of her eyes in the excess of speed with which he thundered back to Renfell but he knew that it would take a hundred days and nights before the vision of her suffering was blotted from his sight, and he cursed aloud as he galloped the final reckless mile towards the castle.

He could not have hurt her more if he had taken his whip to her, for no physical pain could match her present torment. He flung himself from the saddle and gave his exhausted horse over to the grooms, swearing again as he strode through the great wooden doors and poured himself a generous measure of wine, staring blindly down into its dark depths.

Well, it was done. Crudely and in a way that would leave ugly scars which would be slow to heal, but it was done. She would hate him now, and perhaps it was just as well that she should. Yet were it not for the damnable Ducarel wench he could have had Galiena. Had the softness of her body for his own and the love and warmth which she had offered him so desperately.

"God, how I shall dislike this woman," he said aloud to the empty chamber when his wine was finished. "What a debt she owes me and how cruelly I shall make her pay it."

And with that he slammed the goblet down on the table as he made for the stairs and the cold loneliness of his bed.

Miles Carlingford was not the only one who was angry. At Bury St. Edmund's, whence the court had travelled early in November, John was storming about his apartment, his face livid with rage, his mouth distorted with the curses which poured forth like a string of ugly blows.

"Damnation to their souls! May worms eat their foul carcasses and devils prick their skulls with a thousand knives."

As he sent a stool spinning into the corner with a well-aimed kick Petit took a cautious step backwards, rubbing the smooth baldness of his pate nervously, but Isabella, comfortably ensconced by the side of the fire, merely helped herself to another sugared titbit from her comfit box and yawned.

John's anger was not directed at her, and so she had no particular interest in it and, furthermore, she had heard her husband's tirades against the barons so often of late that she was becoming heartily bored with them.

"Do you know what these men now maintain?" John rounded suddenly on Petit. "Do you know what they are saying?"

"Yes . . . yes . . . your grace, at least . . . at least I think so."
John ignored Petit's stammered answer as he clenched his
fists into tight, threatening knots.

"They dare to claim that I have no right to call upon them
for military service in what they choose to call a foreign war
and thus, even though they skulked in England when I went
forth to challenge the French, they now deny me scutage."

"I had heard, sire." Some response was called for, but Petit
could not conjure up the quality of comfort which John needed,
and he swallowed unhappily, tugging at his collar as the king
glared at him. "I knew that they had refused to meet the dues
demanded by Bishop des Roches."

"And so they have, or at least a good many of them have
done so." John's eyes were like flints. "They rendered such
service to my father and to Richard, my brother. Why then do
they refuse it to me?"

"I cannot say."

"Nor yet can I. And since they claim my summons was unlawful, they garnish their insolence by saying that as this is so, no
scutage is due either. Christ's blood, I should have their heads
not their money! It is my right to call for knight service beyond
these shores when need arises and thus, were I of a mind to it,
I could also claim forfeiture of their estates since they have
broken the contract between us. Know you, Petit, these men
seek the best of both worlds. On one hand they whine and
gibber about their rights and privileges which they say I have
taken from them, eager and greedy to suck every last drop of
advantage from the feudal bargain which gives them their lands
and castles. On the other, they would shake off the responsibilities which such privileges bring. They curse me for seeking
so much; they should go down on their knees and thank the
Almighty that I ask so little."

Petit nodded. The initial fear which John's towering rage had
engendered in him was fast fading. The king showed no further
signs of physical violence and underneath the wrath Petit could
see the longing for reassurance, carefully hidden, but there
nevertheless. John should have been able to look to his nobles

for such support, but he trusted so few of them. He could have turned to his hired captains who served him loyally but he had not done so. He was unburdening himself to his favoured body-servant and the last shreds of nervousness fled as Petit felt pride surge through him.

"They are a scurvy lot," he declared roundly and his thin face was red with indignation. "A mongrel brood whose helms grow too tight for their swollen heads. And they are led by one who should know better, seeing how you have favoured him in the past."

"FitzWalter?"

"Aye. It is no secret that he is amongst the richest in the land. How did he gain such wealth? Did your grace not give him special privileges for his ships which carry wine? Does he not owe you much for this favour and many others? Yet this is not the first time that he has betrayed you."

John's face was assuming its normal colour. The worst of his spleen was done and Petit's words were oddly soothing on the ear.

"How so?"

"Did he not surrender Vaudreuil in Normandy to Philip Augustus without so much as drawing his sword? He and Saer de Quincy who shared the task of holding it for your grace. They were craven then, and showed no better valour when you called on them to accompany you to Poitou."

"That's true enough." John gave a terse laugh. "Yet Sir Robert would soon make an end of you if he heard you call him a coward. But you're right, Petit, they've no stomach for a fight, and they sicken me with their excuses."

"So they should, sire. Robert FitzWalter is no better than a common malefactor for all his rich vestments and silvered mail."

"He's always hated me." John gave a sudden sigh and sat down opposite the queen. "Hated me and my father and brother before me, for he says our rule has robbed the barons of their rightful power. It was he who spoke of the good laws of Edward the Confessor and urged the others to press for their return. The laws of Edward!" His lip curled. "There is not one

174

amongst them who could name those laws, for they were not written in the Rolls and there are none left now who could tell us what they were."

"It is the good laws of Henry I they look to now." Petit moved a step or two nearer to the king's chair. "They have done with the saintly Edward, for the archbishop has pointed out to them the charter which exists setting out Henry's promises to his people."

"To his barons, you mean." John looked up to meet Petit's faded eyes. "They are not interested in anyone but themselves. Langton may prate of the rights of all freemen, but de Vesci and FitzWalter care not a jot for them. They think only of their own interests. I am not so blind that I cannot see what such a charter would do. God's teeth, it would set my kingdom on its ear and make a mockery of my sovereignty. I will never agree; never! Do you know what it would mean? When a man died, his heir, if he were of age, could take his inheritance on payment of the old relief; if he were not of age, he could claim what was his when the time came without payment of a fine. They would have the guardians of the lands of a minor hemmed in by rules, so that only a pittance could be taken from the estate, yet it would be the task of those guardians to husband the land, the houses, the ponds and the mills, keeping them in good order, taking only sufficient money from the inheritance for such an undertaking. They would have me agree that heirs be married without disparagement and, what is more, to inform the close relations of the heir of my intent. What impertinence!"

"Indeed, sire, and you would be the poorer."

"Vastly so." John's grin had no humour in it. "And there is worse. They would have it that no scutage be payable without the common counsel of the realm, save should my person need ransoming or my eldest son become knight, and even then they would limit such aid, the villains."

"Insolence, your grace, but Archbishop Langton also says that such matters must be observed by the barons in dealing with their own men."

"So he says, but FitzWalter has no intention of heeding that.

175

They say that common pleas shall not follow our court but be held in a named place: there are clauses which limit amercements and those which require me to take from the rivers my fishtraps. I am to fix one measure for wine throughout the kingdom, another for ale, another for corn. No freeman shall be taken and imprisoned, nor outlawed nor molested, nor shall I send against him, except by the lawful judgment of his peers and by the law of the land. The law of the land! Do you see the design emerge, Petit? They would make a cipher of me if they could."

"Indeed, and I hear tell that by such charter men would be free to leave the kingdom at will and return with equal freedom."

"Yes, save in times of war, and then there are items as to forests which would leave me so bereft of woodlands that I would scarce have sufficient for my hunting." The king's mouth turned down at the corners. "There is worse. They would have inserted in this infamous document a promise that I will send from this realm those men who have served me loyally and with courage. Engelard de Cigoné; Geoffrey de Martigny and his brothers; Philip Marc, and many others. I am to rid myself of all my Flemish knights and serjeants; my foreign bowmen and my mercenaries, leaving myself naked and undefended against my native enemies. I am to remit all unjust fines; makes recompense to the Welsh; return to Alexander of Scotland his sisters and those of his men whom I hold hostage. Finally, when these and many other promises are forced from me, I am to put my seal to a charter which permits these turbulent barons to choose twenty-five of their number to ensure that the new laws are carefully maintained. They will be set to watch me like a cat watches a mouse, and should I falter so much as one step they, together with the community of this land, shall have power to distrain me and take my lands and possessions from me unless I rectify and put right that which they claim is at fault."

"You will not consider it, my lord!"

"Not for a moment. Why should I bend to the will of these jackals?"

"The archbishop and the Earl of Pembroke favour such a charter." Isabella gave John a slow, feline smile. "They and such men as Salisbury, the Earls of Chester, Warenne and Cornwall think it has some merit."

"What do you know of such things?"

"I listen to men when they talk."

"Do you indeed? I am surprised you have the time or the inclination."

Isabella gave a soft laugh.

"You would not have me ignorant, my lord, surely? The archbishop says such reforms are necessary, for your grace's rule is too harsh and hangs like a heavy yoke about the necks of free men."

"The archbishop would do well to mind his own business, and so would you. These matters do not concern you."

"The archbishop says they concern us all." Isabella was unmoved by John's sharpness. "He will support the barons, but not so that they may line their pockets. He seeks justice and good laws for all your subjects.

"Then he will seek in vain," snapped John. "Be advised, madam. Stick to your embroidery and leave affairs of state to me."

Isabella shrugged but said no more, watching from under slumberous lids as Petit fetched wine for the king and hovered about his master like a protective mother-hen. Isabella thought John's reliance on a body-servant slightly ridiculous, impatient that her husband should pour out his troubles and innermost thoughts to a low-born menial, but whilst he could turn to Petit she was at least spared the effort of offering consolation herself and could give her mind to other and more interesting developments.

Not a week ago a new face had come to court. A broad-shouldered, good-looking knight with hair the colour of pure gold. His name was Guarine de Fulcon and at the very moment of their meeting they had exchanged a significant and meaningful glance as he had bowed over her hand.

They had waited a full two days, doing no more during that

177

time than casting a quick look at one another now and then, but Isabella had felt herself wonderfully and hopefully alive as she watched Guarine's tall figure moving amongst those assembled at St. Edmund's. On the third day she had contrived a meeting with him, late at night and in the coldness of an ill-lit corridor. John had been abed and she had neither known nor cared whether he slept alone, for he had not sought her favours for over a month, yet the fact that he had been within a few yards of where she first felt the touch of Guarine's lips on hers added the spice of danger to the satisfying of her rabid appetite.

Even as she and de Fulcon had lain on her bed, huddled intimately beneath the warmth of the soft covers, there had been the nerve-tingling possibility that the door would open suddenly and John would stand there before her, bellowing his rage and demanding painful retribution.

But John had not come and the night had passed, if not peacefully, at least in a manner which filled her with a glow of happy contentment.

She began to take more care than usual with her dress, fussing endlessly as her women touched her cheeks with a hint of rouge and perfumed her temples and wrists. She had her seamstresses fashion new shifts from the delicate materials which she had persuaded John to disgorge from his tightly-locked chests, and she had even won a pair of jewelled slippers from him when she had beaten him in a game of backgammon.

She began to smile to herself, all thoughts of John's fury and the silly charter over which men wrangled interminably gone from her mind as she made plans for that night. Beatrix had told her that John had found a shapely village girl whose task it was to help scrub the tables in the kitchens. He had not cared that her hands were red and rough or that her skin was innocent of powder and rouge. His experienced eye had noted the quality of her hips and lingered over the thrust of her bosom and that had been enough for him.

With John thus engaged it would be simple enough, with Lady de Gresby's help, to get Guarine smuggled into her chamber so that they could spend another fulfilling night together, rousing each other to hot excitement as eager hands explored thigh and breast and desire mounted to a screaming frenzy.

John watched Isabella over the rim of his goblet. He knew that faraway, dreamy smile of hers and understood only too well what it meant as his teeth ground together. One day he would make an end of her whoring. He had not yet discovered the identity of the man she now had in her toils but it would not be long before he knew and then he would make short work of him. And as for Isabella. He glowered at her silently. She was as dazzlingly beautiful as ever and she could still arouse a jealousy in him which he could not control despite his efforts. He would have liked to have torn the kirtle from her back and whipped her until she screamed for mercy, forcing from her thereafter what she was preparing to offer so willingly to her new lover. Then a tempting thought occurred to him and his teeth were no longer clenched in anger but bared in an ironic smile as he said mildly:

"I swear, Isabella, that you grow more lovely with every day that passes. I shall not know how to contain my impatience until supper is done and I am free to come to you."

He felt the laughter well up inside himself as her jaw dropped and consternation flashed nakedly in her eyes, almost hugging himself with glee as she tried to control her dismay.

"Yes, sweet, I see that it is the same for you, but never fret. Night will come in the end and we shall have our time together."

He got up quickly, giving her a last malevolent grin as he walked from the room, leaving Isabella with tears of frustration trembling on her lashes as the vision of Guarine de Fulcon's splendidly built body faded abruptly from her mind and the prospect of a blissful night of love crashed in small fragments about her.

CHAPTER EIGHT

On the following day John was in a savage humour. The malicious joke he had played on Isabella had turned its sour talons on him, for when he had made his way to her room he had found her shrill, ill-tempered and spoiling for a quarrel.

She had not been disappointed either, for beneath John's jest had been genuine anger and they had shouted insults at each other, hurling spiteful abuse across the chamber like shafts of lighting. In the end the king had thrown his wife to the bed and taken her by force, but he had derived no pleasure at all from the exercise. Isabella had grown as cold as ice in his arms and finally he had flung her away from him in disgust.

Now he sat and glared at those about him, ignoring the queen, tight-lipped and silent by his side, brooding peevishly on his failure to discover the name of her latest paramour.

When Juliana Ducarel arrived he rose to greet her, his brow clearing as he saw the perfection of her beauty. He spared a glance for the small girl by her side, pausing for a second to admire her great brown eyes and thawing slightly under the warmth of her smile. Then he looked back at Juliana's set face and said almost gently:

"We grieve for you, madam, in your loss. Your father served us loyally and we shall be the poorer without him."

Juliana inclined her head. John was not quite what she had expected. He was fatter than she had imagined, his balding head making him older than she had thought him to be, but he was also more human and less remote than she had feared and her heart slowed down to a normal beat as she rose from her curtsy.

"I am grateful, your grace."

"And you shall be more grateful still, for we have found a handsome lord to be your husband."

She chilled at once, her fine brows meeting quickly in a frown.

"The thought does not please you?"

"I had hoped not to marry yet."

"In the name of heaven, why not?" John was genuinely surprised as his eyes travelled slowly from the top of her goffered fillet to the tips of her silk slippers in a way which made her blush. "A comely wench like you? Of course you must wed. Who's to care for your father's lands now he is gone?"

"I am your ward, sire. It is your responsibility."

John gave a guffaw of laughter.

"Ah, a saucy madam too. Well, I like a woman with spirit; not one who is forever moaning and weeping." He gave Isabella a contemptuous look. "But have you not heard men say how we plunder and rob the estates of our wards? Have you not listened to the gossip which condemns us as a felon and would have a sealed charter to stay our hand?"

"I know nothing of such things, but my father trusted you and so do I."

"Well said, girl, well said." John gave an approving beam. "But our promise is made now and in the spring you'll be wed to young Carlingford as we have decreed."

"If you command it, sire." Juliana met his eyes unflinchingly. "It is not my wish, and I would be spared it, but I will obey you."

"Aye, that you will." John was fingering his beard and now there was something besides interest and approval in his eye. She really was a most shapely creature. Oddly withdrawn, but perhaps that was natural enough seeing how fate had robbed her of her parents in such a manner. But if she could be warmed to life again. That full red mouth was not made to straighten in a hard line. It was designed to be hot and moist against a man's lips, and those grey eyes which now looked like the sea

181

on a winter's day should be bright with passion and desire. He cleared his throat. "You'll not find it so distasteful, that I promise you. Come now, who is this you bring with you?"

"My cousin, sire. Melisenda de Gressi."

"You are welcome at court Mistress Melisenda."

Melisenda gave the king a wide smile as her eyes danced with pleasure.

"I am glad to be here, your grace. I had not thought to find a place so full of colour and life."

"It has been quiet at Rockingham since my parents died." Juliana was defensive. "I fear the Lady Melisenda has grown tired of silence."

"No, no!" Melisenda was quick to deny it and her small hand stretched out to touch Juliana's arm. "It is not that, sire, not at all. I would not have wished to be anywhere else but with my cousin, yet here it is so . . . so splendid that my breath is quite taken away."

"Then drink your fill." John's former ill-temper had mysteriously vanished and he felt somehow renewed and recharged with energy at the sight of his two delectable visitors. "You shall take supper with us tonight and watch our fools about their antics. You shall drink heady wine and dance until the hour is late. We will make you forget your shadows, that we promise you."

And John was as good as his word. Melisenda sat at table that evening entranced by the vision of the king's guests in their colourful robes, dazzled by the glitter of their jewels and wholly caught up in their sophisticated conversation and light banter as they sipped at their wine and partook of dishes of such richness and variety that her eyes grew round with wonder at the sight of them.

She was so intent on watching the jesters in their red and yellow motley, so bemused by the efforts of the court musicians, so absorbed in all that was going on about her that she did not notice Juliana slip from the hall on the pretext of fatigue and a badly aching head.

Juliana was glad to reach the stillness of the chamber which had been prepared for her; thankful to remove the fillet which was beginning to feel as heavy as an iron helm; relieved to be able to free herself from the enveloping wimple and veil and to release her startlingly fair hair from its prison. She did not even care that there were no maids to help her remove the long gown of dark red brocade, although the ties were tiresome and her fingers grew clumsier as she struggled with them. She simply wished to be alone; away from the deafening noise below and away from the penetrating gaze of the king which had seldom left her since the meal had begun.

She could not understand why he should stare at her so. His unwinking attention had made her feel uncomfortable and ill at ease and she had half-expected him to forbid her to leave the hall when she pleaded for his indulgence. But, oddly enough, he had seemed almost pleased by her request, smiling agreeably as she knelt before him and nodding his head as she picked up her skirts and hurried away.

She gave a sigh of exasperation as a stubborn knot refused to yield to her tugging, shrugging her shoulders free of the bodice of the gown so that she could twist the skirt about to get a better hold on the strings.

"May I help you?"

Juliana gave a gasp and spun round, her colour fading as she saw John standing in the centre of the room, his feet planted firmly apart, his hands resting lightly on his hips.

"Sire! What are you doing here? I did not hear you at the door. You cannot. . . ."

John gave a low laugh as he walked over to her.

"You were not meant to hear me, girl, and as to what I am doing here, why that is simple enough. I have come to help you rid yourself of your gown. Here, let me do that."

"No!"

Hastily Juliana pulled the robe about her, blushing quickly as she felt John's fingers on her shoulder. He was so close to her that she could see the grey flecks in his beard and smell the heaviness of the wine on his breath. It was then that she

183

began to be afraid. Sober, John might be capable of being controlled; drunk he would not be. She kept her voice low so that he should not hear the panic in it.

"No, your grace, no! I need no help. I can manage, and soon my maids will come and. . . ."

"They will not; I have seen to that."

"What!"

"They will not come. But you shall not be robbed of a tire-woman, for I am used to such a role." He chuckled again and caught hold of her. "I have been watching you tonight."

"I am aware of it." She tried not to struggle but she could feel the damp heat of his hands through her gown. "I do not know why you found me of such interest."

"Do you not? Then your mirror is blind and fails in its purpose if it has not shown you the gifts with which Nature has endowed you." His free hand entwined her long hair through his fingers and he gave a deep sigh. "Such tresses too. Softer than any silk and so pure and pale."

"Please let me go." She jerked away from him, pulling her hair free of his hold. "Sire, you must see how improper this is and how. . . ."

"Improper!" He pulled a face. "Is that all that bothers you? Life is too short for such nonsense. Learn now, while you are young, to take what you want and hold fast to it."

"But I do not want. . . ."

"You do not want me? Ah, but then I want you. I was sore at heart this day until you came. When I saw you, I felt new life flow through my veins once more and I was young again. If one glance can do that, what might a taste of your body do for me? God, you shall not refuse me."

He grabbed her by the arms and pulled her towards him, forcing his mouth against hers. She recoiled as if she had been struck, growing frigid and stiff in his hold, unable to move yet not bending one fraction to his caress.

Suddenly he thrust her away and the leering desire was replaced by a black scowl.

"So! You are like all the others. You proud, impudent

184

creatures who flaunt your bodies at a man and then scream of your virginity if you are touched."

"I have not screamed."

"But you would like to have done. I felt your shudder when our lips met. You would liked to have screamed then; you wanted to cry out and remind me of your honour. You longed to spit on me and shout to me of your loathing."

Juliana was petrified. He was drunker than she had supposed, yet he was neither incapable of mischief nor deaf to his own words. Her lips were parched as she edged away from him, and a small exclamation escaped her as he seized her wrist and wrenched her round to face him.

"You have offered me insult and you shall pay the price. Marry you shall, but not Carlingford. I have a better idea than that. I'll find some Flemish mercenary of low birth and he shall have you in payment for his services to me."

"You cannot do that!" Her eyes were stricken and she could feel the words choking in her throat. "You cannot give me to a man such as that."

"Of course I can." He was satisfied now for he had made her whimper and her stark fear was satisfyingly obvious. "I have done it before, many times. Ask my barons. They are always complaining of my habit of paying my dues with rich heiresses. They've even written clauses into their precious charter on the subject. Heiresses shall not be disparaged." His eyes grew cold. "But you shall be, madam. Oh yes, you shall be. The charter is not sealed yet, nor will it be if I have my way. I am still master of this kingdom and I do what I like with my own. You are mine; you and all your property. If you refuse me, you shall have a *routier* instead." He gave a coarse laugh. "He'll stand no nonsense from you. These Flemings have no such tender feelings as I have and they're hot-blooded fellows. He'll not coax you, unless it be with a stick. If I do not take you now, he will do so later."

Juliana watched John as he stalked angrily to the door and as it slammed behind him her knees buckled under her as she collapsed by the side of the bed and began to weep in relief.

She had no time then to concern herself with the threat of the future; all her thoughts were for the present and for her overwhelming thankfulness that John had gone. Tomorrow's evil could wait. For tonight at least she was safe.

Three days later John sent Juliana back to Rockingham. It was recognized by all at court that she had returned to her home in disgrace, although none could get a hint of the reason for her sudden fall from favour. Even to Melisenda Juliana could say nothing at first, giving some unconvincing excuse in a tone which prohibited further questions.

Two days after her departure, Miles Carlingford arrived at court to ask the king a few questions of his own. He had received a message from John in which the king had told him that it was no longer possible for Juliana Ducarel to be his bride, but that soon some other and equally suitable heiress would be found for him.

Miles did not entirely understand the reason for the quick anger he felt on reading the king's letter. Since he had never set eyes on the Ducarel girl it could not be a question of her charm, and as he had placed a good deal of undeserved and irrational blame on her for putting an end to his relationship with Galiena he ought to have felt a sense of relief when John's courier arrived. But curiously enough he had felt no such thing. Instead, he felt in some strange way cheated of something which was already his and, since he disliked mysteries, he had mounted up and called his knights about him, setting off to Bury St. Edmund's with all speed.

John was not entirely surprised to see him, for he was well-versed in the reactions of his nobles, and as his stinging wrath at the Ducarel girl's rebuff had not yet died down, he had already decided to have some quiet fun at the expense of the pair of them. John's sense of humour at the best of times verged on the vindictive, and now he was feeling sore and out of countenance. He knew he had supped too well on potent wines the night he had gone to Juliana's room, but her revulsion had been so obvious that he was determined to make her smart for it. Furthermore, he was growing increasingly tired of the barons' high opinion of themselves, and even though he had a fair measure of affection for Miles Carlingford, he too must be taught not to question his sovereign's decisions.

"Miles." The wolfish smile was misleadingly gentle. "We had not thought to see you at court at this time. Did you not receive our message?"

"I did, sire, and that is why I am here."

Miles rose to his feet and gave the king a straight look.

"Oh? Did we not make ourselves clear?"

"Abundantly, yet your grace gave no reasons."

"Are we required to do so?"

Miles ignored the danger signals in John's tone.

"Not required to do so, yet is there cause why I should not know why the decision has been taken?"

The eyes of the two men met for a long moment. Then John shrugged.

"None, I suppose."

"Then I would have you tell me, my lord."

"She is not good enough for you."

"She was when you arranged the match."

"That was before I saw her, and found out what kind of woman she was."

"Oh?" Miles was wary. There was something about the king's manner which he found difficult to analyse. Something odd about the half-smile lurking at the corners of the sensual mouth and the light which flickered behind the slanting eyes. "What kind of woman is she?"

"A beauty." John was offhand. "But beauty is only skin deep."

"And beneath the skin?"

"A haughty creature, filled with self-pride which the manner of her life does not warrant."

Carlingford's brows met in a frown.

"Your grace's riddles perplex me. In what way does her life fall short? A certain pride was to be expected. She bears a distinguished name."

187

"Which she has not kept untarnished."

"Juliana Ducarel?" Miles was faintly incredulous. "You say that she is a. . . ."

"I say she is a whore if you want bluntness, as clearly you do."

"Your grace!"

John sniggered. "I shock you? Oh come, Miles, you are not so naïve as to believe every woman is like your sainted mother. Not all of them are as chaste and pure as she. Juliana Ducarel is not, for one."

"I cannot believe it."

"You doubt our word?"

"No, no, of course not, yet. . . ."

John's flash of anger died again as his lips curved once more into a satisfied smile.

"I see that it is hard for you to accept, yet it is as well that I discovered it now, for you and your father are dear to me and I would not have had you tied to one so unworthy. The girl I choose for you, Miles, shall be a virgin."

Miles's eyes widened fractionally and John felt a warm glow of triumph spread inside himself. Yes, that would give the young cockerel something to think about. He would want no more to do with the impudent strumpet now, nor would he fly to her defence when he heard the fate which awaited her.

"I'll not keep you waiting long. As soon as some suitable woman can be found, you shall have her."

"There is no need. I did not ask for a wife."

"Nor did you, but you shall have one nevertheless. My word is given. My word is given to the Ducarel wench too."

Miles grew more cautious still.

"What is that?"

"Can this be of interest to you?" John was cool. "She is no longer your concern."

"But she was, and I would know, your grace willing."

"She is to marry a *routier*. A fitting and just reward for her."

Miles Carlingford stiffened. The king was justified in his reminder that what happened to Juliana Ducarel was none of

188

his business, and the mode of her life, which shocked him as much as it surprised him, was ample reason for him to put her out of his mind once and for all, but somehow he could not do it.

He looked at John's obvious amusement and the unkindly glint in his eye and something began to worry at his mind. What if John were lying? It was well-known that the king loved nothing better than a heartless prank and there was no proof that the girl was corrupt other than John's unsupported word. What if she were innocent and John was merely finding an excuse to break the betrothal in order to reward one of his hirelings?

For the first time in his life he began to understand the rage of the barons, and his cousin Doun's words began to hammer in his brain. 'You have not suffered under John's monstrous demands' Doun had said, and he had been right. He had not been forced to pay heavy fines or dues, but he had thought it merely because he had followed the king without question. Now, despite his loyalty, the woman offered to him was to be disparaged and given to a foreigner of humble birth. Miles felt anger burn along his veins like a slow, smouldering fire. It was not that he had sought Juliana, or even wanted her, but she had been promised to him and now she was to be snatched away.

At last some inkling of understanding began to dawn on him as he faced the smug monarch, powerless to reverse the decision which John had made, feeling somehow reduced and denigrated by it.

Then he remembered Doun's odd tale of how the Lady Ducarel kept to her chamber, never venturing out nor receiving callers as she mourned her dead mother and father. His frown deepened.

"Are you quite certain that she is wanton, sire?"

"Quite certain. I heard it from her own lips." John began to embroider as he saw the doubt grow in Carlingford. "Why, she even dared to boast in my presence of her lover."

"Who is he?" The words were rapped out, and now Miles was really furious beneath his icy exterior. "Who is this man?"

"She did not say and I did not ask. It was enough that he existed. I knew then that I would have to find another for you."

Carlingford took a deep breath and relaxed. John was getting too much of his own way in this exchange and had succeeded in stirring up hot passion, a wholly unexpected jealousy, and an even more unlooked for sympathy with the barons and their complaints. But whether John was aware of the storm which he had aroused Miles had no way of knowing, neither could he be sure whether the king was speaking the truth or deliberately lying.

There was one sure way to find out, however, and that was to see Juliana Ducarel himself so that he could make his own judgment, and with a brief word he made his obeisance to the king and rode off from court, leaving John laughing uproariously at the result of his fabrication, and planning further malicious embellishments to add on some future occasion.

It was growing dark when Miles arrived at Rockingham two days later. Juliana had not touched the meal which Sibile had brought to her, but the parchment she still held in her hand she had read time and time again. It was another message from John, couched in terms both crude and resolute, informing her of his fixed intention to carry out his threat and adding that Miles Carlingford fully supported the decision made.

When she had read the last few words, penned in the hand of John's meticulous secretary, she had shed a few tears, for her last hope of escape from John's sentence seemed to have gone. She had not wanted anything to do with Earl Hamelin's son but after her terrifying experience with the king and his vicious reaction to her refusal, she had pinned her faith on the fact that Carlingford would try to force John to change his mind. She had told John she was unaware of the barons' rumblings but this was not entirely true, for it was impossible to be in total ignorance of so strong a movement, and she had been certain that Carlingford, probably as fiercely greedy and brutally determined as his fellows, would insist on his right to marry her. But he had not. He had tamely given in to John, bowing

190

to a proposal which made him a traitor to his class. Now her tears had all dried as anger took their place and she began at once to consider ways and means of escaping from the king's trap.

When Sibile came to whisper to her of Carlingford's arrival she found her heart was racing oddly, and it was with mixed feelings that she straightened her gown and made her way slowly down the stairs.

As she entered the great hall, Carlingford turned from his contemplation of a tapestry on the wall and walked towards her and for a minute neither of them spoke.

Juliana stared up at Miles, bewildered by the startling difference between the picture she had drawn for herself and the reality of the tall, lean man who moved so gracefully yet in a way which spoke silently of power and authority. His thin, slightly tanned face and bright blue eyes were a direct contrast to the heavy-jowled, choleric complexion she had anticipated, and the slim jewelled fingers which rested on his sword-hilt made her lips part in blank amazement.

For his part, Miles was reduced to silence by the beauty of Juliana's face and the clear, wonderfully coloured eyes fringed with thick, curling lashes. He had been told she was lovely, of course, but he had not imagined anything as devastating as this and for no reason at all his anger began to grow. If she were a high-born prostitute she hid the fact well, for she had a strange kind of serenity about her which was at once restful and disturbing. A man could find his heart's desire in a woman such as this, yet despite his admiration he was not such a fool as to be taken in by an exquisite face, and his tone was suitably chilly as he said shortly:

"I regret that I came without warning, madam."

Juliana pulled herself together. The fact that he was not the manner of man she had expected but was handsome in a way which made a queer shiver run through her must not lead her to forget that he had agreed to her marriage to a Flemish bowman, and her own voice was as frosty as his as she answered him.

191

"I had not expected you at all, my lord, with or without warning. Why have you come?"

"Is that not obvious?"

"Not to me."

He felt his ire rising again. Yes, she was a bewitching creature, but haughty as John had said. If the king were right about that, perhaps he was also right about her reputation.

"We were to marry."

"It was not my choice."

"Nor mine. It was the king's."

"And now the king has decided on another course."

He hesitated. He wanted to ask her outright whether John's accusations were true and to offer his protection if they were not, but the light in her eye stifled the question at birth.

"And that, sire, is a matter between his grace and me."

Carlingford ground his teeth. She was telling him to mind his own business in no uncertain terms, and he longed to take her by the shoulders and give her a good shaking. Instead he said bleakly:

"The prospect does not seem to concern you."

"No, nor need it trouble you."

She had no intention of pleading with him for his help, and since he had already acquiesced in John's scheme, there was no alternative but to keep him at arm's length and to be rid of him as soon as possible. She could not understand the sudden weakness in her which made her want to stretch out her hand and feel his close over hers, and the absurdity of her thoughts made her tarter still.

"I have no doubt that his grace will find another means of rewarding you for your services. If money and land are what you want, there are other women as well-endowed as I."

He thrust down the spurt of anger which made his hand twitch at his side. John had been right after all. A haughty, proud woman, quite capable of taking a lover and concealing the fact, for she had no softness in her at all. So different from Galiena, who was meek and pliable and submissive in her love. This girl would never be submissive nor even lovable, and meekness was a virtue of which she had clearly never heard.

"I do not need land or money, as well you know."

"Then perhaps the king would have done better to offer you a new horse."

"Perhaps he would. A horse can be broken."

"But I cannot be."

"Time will show. The spur to be applied to your flanks may well be sharper than mine."

He saw her flush and paused in the middle of his exasperation to gaze in wonder at the effect of the pink streaks of colour along the perfectly-formed cheekbones and the way it lit up the crystal clearness of her eyes. Whatever the girl had done, and however irritating she might be, she did not deserve a *routier* for a master, and somewhere deep down inside himself a determination was beginning to harden.

"That remains to be seen. And now, my lord, if that is all you have come to say...."

"Are you alone here?" he asked abruptly. "Is there no one with you?"

"Of course. I have my cousin, my women, my servants, my knights and the king's own captain, Guibert de Bray."

"No one else? No one to whom you could turn if help were needed?"

Juliana looked at him quickly and in that fraction of time saw something beneath his frost which made her tremble. It was whilst she was trying to recover herself that she remembered Guy de Montauban, and her lips parted in a small reserved smile as a flood of relief washed through her.

"Oh yes, sir, there is someone else. You need have no fears for me, for I know where to go for aid."

He saw the sudden thawing and heard the warmth in her voice and was instantly outraged again. He wanted to shout a demand for the name of the man who could make her look like that, but he had no intention of making a fool of himself and schooled himself to silence. John had been entirely right: not only about her pride and arrogance but about her lewdness too. He swallowed the gall which rose in his throat as he thought about the unknown lover who had already taken her slender, sweetly-curved body for his own, and he was curt to the point of rudeness as he bade her farewell.

"Then, as you say, there is nothing left for me to do. I bid you good-night, madam."

He strode through the hall, leaving Juliana shaken and uncertain, but when she had thrown off the inexplicable depression which his departure had brought about, she went in search of Melisenda and Sibile and bade them help her prepare for a journey on the following day.

"Guy will help me." Juliana beckoned to the hovering Sibile to follow her as she hurried back to her room. "He will know what to do."

"But what help do you need?" Melisenda's eyes were dark with worry. "If the Sire de Montauban can help you, why cannot I do so? Love, will you not tell me what is wrong, for I am fearful, not knowing what troubles you so?"

All at once it seemed easy to relate to Melisenda the ugly scene in her bedroom and not difficult at all to tell her of the king's threat and although Melisenda wept a few tears for her, these were soon dried and forgotten in the bustle and hurry of packing their belongings.

"Guy is a powerful man." Juliana looked happier than she had done for many days as she helped Sibile to fold a gown. "I cannot think why I was so foolish not to think of him before. I knew him when I was a child and although I have not seen him for several years, he will not have forgotten the bond of friendship which was once between us."

"But would it not be better to seek the aid of Carlingford?"

Juliana's eyes flashed dangerously.

"Had you seen him, you would not ask such a question, and the king has told me that the earl's son is content enough to see me married to a serf. Would you ask such a man as that for succour?"

"No." Melisenda was dubious. "But what manner of man was he?"

"Cold and insensitive and unbearably rude. I hope I shall never see him again."

Melisenda looked at her cousin carefully. There was something in the way Juliana had said that which was puzzling, but there was no time then for further enquiries for Juliana and Sibile were opening yet another chest, rummaging amongst the perfumed silks for a missing cote, and she forgot her doubts as she went on with the folding of linen shifts and gossamer-fine veils.

As they approached Montauban's castle at Oakham on the following day, Melisenda ventured another thought.

"What if the lord Montauban refuses to help? He may be shocked by such a tale as we have to tell."

Juliana, wrapped in a fur pelisson and mounted securely on her palfrey, Grisel, gave a smothered laugh which had true amusement in its depths, and Melisenda brightened. It was the first time she had heard Juliana laugh like that since she had joined her and it was vastly encouraging.

"He will not be shocked?"

"It takes a great deal to shock John's magnates and most of all Guy." Juliana sobered. "In fact, it is he who may shock us, and perhaps I am wrong and selfish to bring you with me, for it is no secret that Guy has a bad reputation."

"Which baron has not?" Melisenda had all the world-weary understanding of a seventeen-year old in her voice. "And I would not have let you come without me. Has he many bastards?"

"Probably. He does not talk of them."

"But others do it would seem."

"Frequently, I believe, yet he is a good soldier too. His family comes from southern Poitou, but they have deserted John. Only Guy remains loyal to the king. Whatever else men may say of him, they cannot accuse him of cowardice or treachery."

"Is he handsome?"

"I suppose so. I have never thought about it."

Melisenda said no more, but when they reached Oakham and were helped from their horses by Juliana's knights, she found she was strangely excited at the prospect of meeting the lord of the great castle which reared up in front of her like a towering sentinel clad in stone. Her curiosity was not to be satisfied at once, however, for the eager servants who ushered them into the great hall and drew them to the blazing log fire chattered of their regret that their master was out hunting, but they soon procured hot food which they served on heavy silver dishes which made Melisenda stare in awe.

"He must be wealthy, Juliana. See how heavy these platters are. Why, even one of them could ransom an earl."

"Well, a knight or two at least." Juliana was dry. "Yes, Guy is rich, but how he came by his fortune no one knows."

"Perhaps he stole it. Is he wicked enough for that?"

"Quite wicked enough. He has no moral sense at all. That is why I have come to him for help."

"I do not understand."

"It is as well that you do not. Eat your fowl, Melisenda, I want to think."

Obediently Melisenda spooned the richly spiced morsels into her mouth but she hardly tasted them for her eyes were too busy wandering round the hall admiring the quality of the brightly coloured tapestries and the expert workmanship of the carved sideboards which bore goblets and flagons of silver and gold and beautifully wrought aquamaniles shaped like birds with wings of lapis-lazuli and eyes of emerald and ruby.

When Guy de Montauban returned in a riot of shouts, clatter of hooves on cobbles and the deep satisfied bays of the hounds, he made his way casually into the hall and strolled over to the fire to make his bow to his guests.

He was a large man of five and twenty years, broad of shoulder and chest and, even in his habit stained and torn by the fierce rigours of the chase, he contrived to look impressive. He had hair the colour of a fallen chestnut, light hazel eyes topped by straight brows, with an aquiline nose and thin, well-shaped lips.

"Bring me wine, Ralph." He glanced over his shoulder to his steward. "And make the brew a strong one. I have had a fair tussle with the boar today and my throat is parched. Now, my dear Juliana, what are you doing here? I had thought to catch no more than the red or fallow deer this morning, yet now I find I have netted no less than two enchanting women. I am not complaining, as I am sure you will understand, but merely curious to know why I am so honoured."

His eyes moved to Melisenda and she blushed delightfully.

"But tell me first, who is this you bring with you?"

"My cousin, Melisenda de Gressi. Melisenda, this is the lord de Montauban."

"Of whom no doubt you have heard much." Guy was still considering Melisenda thoughtfully. "Has Juliana told you that I am a hopeless degenerate and that I seduce women as frequently as I hunt?"

Melisenda knew she should have been shocked, or at least reduced to silence by his words, but from the moment he had looked in her direction she had felt completely at home with him, as if she had known and understood him for a long time.

"Yes, she has told me, my lord, and I have been impatient to meet you."

"Have you indeed?" His brows rose a fraction. "Then I can see that you have not been properly reared. No woman who has been well brought up would permit herself to visit me. Are you a shameless hussy, Melisenda?"

"I think I must be, for I am very happy to be here."

"Melisenda!"

Juliana was impatient, and Guy turned back to her with a slight smile.

"Ah yes, my dear, you were about to tell me why you have come. And how is it that Captain de Bray is not with you? I am surprised that he should let you leave Rockingham."

"He does not know that I am here," said Juliana shortly. "He has gone away for a few days, but I should have come in any event."

"How determined you are." He was faintly mocking. "But then you were always self-willed, even as a child. Well, what is it all about?"

197

Juliana waited until the steward had served Montauban, hesitating until he was out of earshot. Then she said quietly:

"You have heard of the death of my father?"

Guy took an unhurried mouthful of wine.

"Yes, I had heard."

"And . . . and of my mother?"

"Yes."

"She could not live without him."

"She did not even try." Montauban put his goblet down on the table. "Don't be sentimental, Juliana. If you have come to me for sympathy you have wasted your time. Your father died bravely and with honour; these things must be accepted. Your mother was merely selfish."

Melisenda looked quickly at Juliana but to her relief her cousin was not wilting beneath Montauban's harsh truths.

"I do not think so, but that is not why I have come. I do not want commiseration; I need help. I could think of no one but you to whom I could turn."

"I am flattered, but what of your betrothed? Did I not hear that you were to marry Carlingford?"

"No longer."

"Why not? Have you quarrelled with him?"

"Yes I have," she snapped, "but the betrothal was already broken when I did so."

"By whom?"

"The king."

Montauban's eyes narrowed.

"I see. Why?"

Juliana hesitated again. "It is not easy to speak of it."

"Then we shall not make much progress, for my help will be somewhat limited if I do not know what we are talking about."

"You are very hard."

"I always was, and you knew it when you came. Don't be a fool. Tell me what is the matter with you."

For a moment longer she said nothing; then she gave a reluctant laugh.

"Yes, you are a heartless creature, Guy, but as you say I knew it when I came. Very well, I will tell you."

He listened in silence until she had finished, no flicker of expression on his face as she stammered through her tale of John's visit to her room and went on to relate her unfortunate interview with Miles Carlingford.

When she had completed her story he gave her a caustic smile and reached for his wine.

"What a capacity you have developed for falling foul of important men, my dear. Can you not confine your quarrels to those of less consequence?"

"This is no matter for laughter."

"Nor am I laughing, as you will observe. Of course I have only heard your side of the story and every tale has at least two facets, but I will grant you that Carlingford sounds a stiff-necked boor."

"And the king?"

"I cannot find it in my heart to blame him."

"What!"

"You are enough to make the most continent of men turn to thoughts of rape, and John is notoriously fond of beautiful women. It was a compliment in a way."

"I did not see it as such."

"No you would not, of course. Well, now let us see the situation at which we have arrived. You have insulted the king and he proposes to wed you to one of his hirelings. You have crossed swords with Carlingford, who obviously has no further interest in you, and you have come here without the permission of your royal guardian's captain, and brought with you your innocent young cousin who ought to be protected from a man such as I."

He glanced back at Melisenda who was listening to him with unwavering attention.

"It is not encouraging, is it?"

Melisenda shook her head. Guy was being very off-hand and casual, but somehow she was no longer worried by Juliana's predicament. Montauban would find a solution to it and she gave him a wide smile which held his attention for a long moment before he returned to Juliana.

"What would you have me do about this tangle? Take up arms against the king? Storm Carlingford's castle and teach him his manners?"

"Neither. I want you to offer for my hand."

He said nothing for a while, not noticing Melisenda's sudden look of consternation nor the anxiety in Juliana's eyes, staring into the fire reflectively and rubbing his chin slowly with one long forefinger.

"I am not of a mind to marry. Not even you, my dear."

"There will be no question of marriage. I merely want you to offer for my hand. John will heed your request, for it is well-known that he favours you and is grateful for your support. If you offer him enough marks he will agree."

"Oh? I am to pay for the privilege into the bargain, eh?"

"No, I will pay, but the king will not know that."

"But if he is determined to punish you, he will insist on a Fleming for your spouse."

"Not if you explain to him that I was greatly distressed by the death of my father. You could make him change his mind."

"I am not sure that I wish to do so."

"Guy! You would stand by and see me given to a peasant?"

"Rather than get caught in the toils of wedlock myself, yes."

"I have told you, there would be no marriage."

"Betrothal is as binding as marriage itself."

"But we could find reasons later why the bond should be broken. There must be a hundred ways. Meanwhile something must be done, for John is still angry."

"I don't doubt it. You pricked his pride and made him look a fool. Why could you not have bent a little?"

She stiffened. "You can ask me that?"

"Yes I can, although I do not expect a rational answer. You will have to give me time to think, Juliana."

"There is no time."

"There will be enough. Has the king sent word yet of whom he has chosen for you from amongst his men?"

"No."

"Then there is time. He has many other things on his mind at the moment. He has had one meeting with the barons at Bury St. Edmund's and they are to meet him again in London at the Epiphany. Do not imagine that John is entirely wrapped up in thoughts of a fitting revenge against you. He has much more urgent things to hold his attention. He is being hard-pressed by FitzWalter, de Vesci and their followers."

"How much time do you need to consider what I have asked of you?"

"A week or two."

"But if the king should. . . ."

"Do not fuss. He will not move that swiftly. You have too fine a conceit of yourself. You are not really important. It is his kingdom which matters to him. You are not his enemy: you are merely a tiresome girl who is his ward. He can deal with you at any time by the stroke of a pen, but if he wants to master the barons he will eventually have to take up arms against them."

"You are every bit as rude as Carlingford," declared Juliana hotly as she rose to her feet. "You have not offered so much as a word of comfort since I arrived."

"You do not need comfort; you need aid. You said so yourself. In any event, I have not refused my help. I simply need time to think about your follies."

"And I must wait upon your deliberations?"

"You have no choice, have you? And now perhaps you should rest. Doubtless my servants have prepared rooms for you; they are remarkably efficient although I seldom rouse myself to give them orders."

"We shall not stay here."

He got up and stared down at her in mild surprise.

"Then where, pray, will you stay? The day is wearing on and it will soon be dark. Do you imagine that I will let you travel the roads by night with a handful of men?"

"We shall stay at the Convent of the Sacred Heart. It is only two miles away and we shall reach it easily before night falls."

"It will not offer such comforts as my castle."

"Nor yet such risks."

"Ah, I see. Are you thinking of your reputation again which you are determined shall remain unsullied, or are you considering the Lady Melisenda's?"

He raised Melisenda's hand to his lips.

"We have had no opportunity to talk this day," he said softly, "but this will be remedied on another occasion. Perhaps when next we meet your cousin's problems will have been resolved and we can give our minds to other things."

Melisenda felt a quiver of delight run through her at his touch, and she was neither nervous nor coy as she answered him.

"I hope it will be so, my lord," she said in a low voice. "I would be sad if I could not see you again."

"No need to fear. You will see me again; many times."

He led her towards the door where Juliana was already waiting restively.

"Ride with care." He snapped his fingers at the grooms. "Juliana, do not let your fears make you reckless. Be patient and wait." He took her hand in his and his face softened. "I will consider what can be done, so you have no further need to worry."

She nodded, holding tightly to his fingers.

"I know. That is why I came to you. At first I was desperate for I could think of no one who could help. Then I remembered you, and I knew that you would think of something."

"You would trust me with your life, if not with your virtue, is that it?"

She had the grace to laugh.

"Perhaps. Send word to me soon, I beg you."

"I will."

The small procession moved off into the darkening afternoon and Melisenda was sorely tempted to turn her head to wave to Montauban. She was hardly conscious of the bite of the wind for she seemed to glow inside as if a warm fire had been lit within her breast. She had only talked to him for so short a while, and the touch of his hand on hers had been of the briefest, yet already she felt as if there was a deep intimacy between them and his promise of a renewal of their acquaintanceship had not been a polite, conventional parting. He had meant it. She had wondered, as they had journeyed towards Oakham, what kind of man he was and now she knew. Handsome, as she had hoped, but with no time for platitudes or weak emotions. On the surface idle in his manner, yet with great strength not far beneath the skin which made him almost frightening. A vastly attractive creature for whom she had felt an instant and overwhelming longing, although she had known at once that he would have no like feeling for her.

She stole a glance at Juliana, busy with her own thoughts as the horses trotted briskly along the rough road leading down to the valley where the convent lay.

"He does not mean to be unkind, Juliana." Somehow she felt impelled to excuse Guy's blunt turn of speech. "It is clear that he is fond of you."

Juliana chuckled. "No need to explain him to me, sweet, I have known him too long. I admit at times he rouses me to anger with his tongue, but that is because I am a simpleton. I should ignore his taunts because they mean nothing. Yes, I am sure he will help."

Clearly Juliana had found the meeting with Montauban worthwhile and was not unduly put out by his bracing words. Melisenda sighed with relief. Now she could return to her own secret and exciting meditations, hugging the remembrance of the last hour close to her heart, dwelling lovingly on each word and gesture as the convent came in sight and Juliana's squires began to canter quickly ahead to give due warning of their coming.

CHAPTER NINE

AFTER the Christmas festivities of 1214 were over, John left
Worcester, hurrying to London to take up residence at New
Temple. There, on the feast of the Epiphany, the barons came
to him, armed as if for war, and put their terms to him once
again in a manner which brooked neither delay nor argument.

There were no more than forty-five or so of the magnates
opposed to John and of these Robert FitzWalter, lord of
Dunmow, was the leader. He brought with him a number of
barons, some of first rank, others of lesser importance, allied
to him by blood or marriage, including Geoffrey de Mandeville,
Earl of Essex; Henry Bohun, Earl of Hereford; Robert de Vere,
Earl of Oxford, and Geoffrey de Say who was accompanied by
his friends and close neighbours from the houses of Clare and
Bigod.

On that occasion de Vesci was not present, but Richard Percy,
a northern magnate, was amongst the number which crowded
into the chamber to face the king, and so were Robert de Ros,
who had married a bastard of William the Lion of Scotland;
Saer de Quincy, Earl of Winchester and lately one of John's
justiciars; Richard, Earl of Clare and his son Gilbert; William
Mowbray, Clare's nephew; William Mallett, proudly claiming
descent from the Conqueror; William de Beauchamp, lord of
Bedford, and William Marshal the younger, Pembroke's son.

When they boldly required John to restore the charter of the
first Henry as he had sworn to do at Winchester two years
before, John spoke to them calmly and in soothing tones. He
had no intention of bending to their will but it was an angry
and formidable gathering shuffling restively before him, and he
knew that an open quarrel must be avoided.

When he told them that what they asked posed so grave a problem that he would have to have time to consider it, proposing a truce until Low Sunday, they shouted so loudly that the very rafters rang with their discontent for they were used to John's prevarications and were in no mood to tolerate such an idea.

Finally he managed to persuade them that there was a real need to consult those who advised him, and when the archbishop, the Earl of Pembroke and the Bishop of Ely stood surety for his good intentions, the barons took themselves off, grumbling and far from satisfied, but at least prepared to hold their hand for the time being.

John watched them go. He would have liked to have taken each and every one of them by the throat and choked the life out of them but although their numbers were small, they were growing in power and their followers were increasing daily. What had once been merely an irritating buzzing in the ear was now a very real threat and he sank his chin into his hand as he dwelt upon the situation with darkened brow.

Men said it was the northern barons who had begun the trouble but if this were true it had soon spread to Lincoln and to Essex. There had been a rising in Devonshire and others in Shropshire, Herefordshire, Gloucestershire and Somersetshire.

John knew the midlands and the counties in the central and southern parts of the realm were safe enough, for in those areas his own power was strong and he still held men there in a grip of iron but, where his influence was weaker, the barons had found receptive ears for their seditious talk and had coaxed many to join their own knights and men in their stand against the crown.

"If I were to take FitzWalter, half my troubles would be over," said John finally to Stephen Langton when the hall had been cleared. "It is he and that rogue de Vesci who have stirred my people against me."

"You cannot do that, sire." Langton was sharp. "You have given your word that they will not be molested until Low Sunday. The earl and I stand as guarantors of that promise."

"And you will see that I keep it, eh? Sometimes I wonder if you and Pembroke are not as guilty as FitzWalter and de Vesci, for you encourage them with your weakness."

"It is not weakness to seek justice, your grace," returned Langton coldly. "Have Marshal and I not warned you time and time again that trouble would come if you did not put right the wrongs of which your people complain?"

"My people do not complain. It is the barons who do that, including your own son, my lord Pembroke."

William Marshal looked faintly uncomfortable.

"I have begged him to reconsider, but he is young and hot for the reforms which FitzWalter seeks."

"Reforms! FitzWalter! Never tell me that you are taken in by what Sir Robert says."

"No, I understand the temper of FitzWalter, but though his motives may be at fault, much of what he asks for is right for the kingdom. Your people grow restive beneath the crushing burden they have to bear. We have tried to make this clear to you, but you will not heed us. Is it to be wondered that many look to FitzWalter as a saviour?"

"It is a wonder to me." John glared at Pembroke. "Why should they follow a scoundrel like him when they have a king to lead them?"

"We have told you why, your grace, time and time again." The archbishop's voice was weary. "They will turn anywhere, to any man, for relief. You will have to consider what the barons ask. You cannot ignore their requests for ever for they will not let you do so. We must talk seriously of this charter."

"You have already talked of it, my lord archbishop." John bared his teeth. "But for you, no one would have remembered its existence. You are much to blame for this present outcry."

"I believe the terms of the charter to be right and just. They define most precisely the way in which a king should rule within the law of the land. There are still some matters to be added, for all men should benefit from it, but I think the magnates will see the wisdom of this in time."

"I make the law, for I am king, and if you are trying to tell me that Henry ruled in accordance with such a charter I will call you a liar to your face."

"I am not unused to such abuse," retorted Langton with spirit, "but if King Henry did not abide by the clauses, you will have to do so. I beg you to heed us. We are not rebels, men such as Pembroke and myself. We are not greedy for worldly goods for ourselves nor do we seek to harm the crown; you know it well. If you will but see reason and accept the charter, men will revere you and serve you loyally."

"A piece of parchment will alter the pattern of a lifetime? Is that what you are saying?" John gave a short laugh. "Archbishop, men have never served me loyally, at least very few of them have done so. I have been deserted in my greatest hour of need and spurned by those who should have fought by my side. Normandy was lost, not through my inertia as some said, but because the barons there left me and turned to Philip. Look at the threat offered me when I would have put down the Welsh rebellion. What of the expedition to Poitou? A charter will not change this. But mark my words. When I die, I will leave to my son a kingdom intact. I will have no man dictate terms to me, nor will I allow ruffians to sap my power and leave me defenceless."

"You may have no choice."

"There is always a choice and I am not afraid to fight for what is mine. Preach peace and goodwill all you wish, but do not look for it at my expense."

With that John rose abruptly from his chair and stamped noisily out of the room, leaving the archbishop and earl gazing hopelessly after him.

At the beginning of February Juliana and Melisenda went to visit Guy de Montauban again. Fortune was with them once more, for Guibert de Bray had been called to London to see the king, and they found no difficulty in persuading his deputies that they were going to visit the Convent of the Sacred Heart to offer special prayers for the souls of Gervase Ducarel and his wife.

This time the journey was more arduous, for the snow had fallen thickly during the previous week, and they were cold and tired when they reached Oakham, thankful to see the warmth of Montauban's fire and the bright forest of candles which lit the hall.

There had been no hunting that day and Montauban and his men were playing dice by the hearth, but as Juliana and her cousin were brought to him he waved his companions away and got to his feet.

"What an impatient creature you are, Juliana," he said, as if it had been a mere two days since they had last met. "Did I not tell you to contain your restlessness and wait until you had word from me?"

"You did, but time passes and each hour is as long as a week. Do you not understand my anxiety?"

"Clearly, but you have no need to fear. I told you I would do something and I have. I was about to send couriers to Rockingham with a message for you."

"Oh Guy!" Juliana caught his hand. "I am sorry if I have seemed to lose faith, but in truth I have been afraid."

"There was never need for that."

"Perhaps not, but I have not got your strength. What have you been able to do?"

He took Melisenda's hand in his for a moment, squeezing it slightly as he seated her on a stool.

"I have gained the king's consent to you becoming my ward."

"Your ward?" Juliana frowned. "But how will that help?"

"It will help in many ways. First, you are freed from Guibert de Bray's custody, and secondly it is likely that in the end the king will permit me to choose your husband, provided he receives a sufficiently generous fine at the time of your marriage."

"You mean he has forgiven me? He will not insist on my union with a *routier*?"

Guy looked at Juliana's tense face and pursed his lips.

"I would not say that he has forgiven you, nor is the threat of a Fleming entirely over, but the king has need of men from Poitou and I am in a position to get them for him, despite my family's hostile influence. I think he may be persuaded that the idea is not a good one, particularly as the magnates grow so fevered at the present time about such things."

"Guy!" Juliana rose and planted a kiss on Montauban's cheek. "I do not know what to say."

"Then hold your tongue, my love, for it has done enough harm already. And do not think that you will find in me a weak guardian. I can be a good deal more severe than de Bray as you will soon discover."

"I do not care." Juliana returned to her seat and clasped her hands together in thankfulness. "I do not mind what you do, as long as you can induce the king to change his mind."

"I will do what I can, but not if you persist in riding all over the countryside in such weather as this. Tomorrow you will return to Rockingham and stay there. In a week or two I will come to see you and we will talk again."

"I will do anything you wish."

"So you say now."

"I truly mean to obey you."

"I shall see that you do. Now I suppose you wish to go to the convent for the night, since your passionate gratitude does not extend to trusting me with your person."

Juliana gave a small smile and suddenly it occurred to Melisenda how much her cousin had changed in the last two months. The frozen grief which had held her in its grip for so long seemed completely to have melted. Although Juliana had been worried and concerned, she had pushed away her phantoms and her eyes were no longer dead and blank. She almost envied Juliana her easy relationship with Guy, for whilst they used no soft words to one another, it was clear that the affection was there. Yet it was not mere affection that she, Melisenda, wanted from Montauban and she resolutely thrust aside the stab of jealousy as Guy went to give orders to his grooms.

In a few minutes, however, he was back again to tell them of the heavy snow which had started to fall, waving aside Juliana's protests as he sent his servants scurrying to prepare rooms for them.

209

"Be done with your arguments. It is clear that you cannot travel in weather such as this. Do you want to die in a drift of snow?"

"It is not proper that we should stay here alone." Juliana was stubborn. "It is not far to the convent."

"It is too far in a blizzard and I shall not permit you to go."

"How can you stop us?"

"Very easily. You are my ward; have you forgotten so soon?"

"That is absurd. You cannot. . . ."

"Indeed I can. Be quiet, or I will take other measures to convince you of our respective positions."

"But there are no other women here."

"Of course there are." Guy gave her an exasperated look. "The kitchens are full of them. You may have any number of females to share your chamber if you will, and I will swear on the gospels not to break down your door. Really, Juliana, you are quite ridiculous. I have told you before you have too much conceit of yourself. I have not the slightest desire to sleep with you tonight or on any other occasion."

Juliana said no more, reduced to silence by his snub, and after the evening meal was over she and Melisenda were led to a richly-appointed room with thick straw spread over the floor and a splendidly furnished bed dominating one wall. Two rosy-cheeked maids with a well-scrubbed look had prepared the hot water for the tubs in the adjoining garderobes and it was no surprise to Juliana to find that Montauban's household was able to supply their every need, even down to ivory combs and tiny silver phials of heady perfume which filled the room with musky odours.

A fire had been lit in the centre of the room and it was blazing cheerfully as Juliana and Melisenda returned warm and sweet from their ablutions. They pulled up two stools close to the logs and sipped the spiced wine which Guy had sent to lull them to sleep.

Soon Juliana was yawning, almost unable to find the energy to stumble to the bed and nestle down amongst the linen sheets, drifting off into deep slumber almost as soon as her head touched the spotless pillow.

But Melisenda was in no mood for sleep. Somewhere along the corridor beyond the closed door, Guy would be making preparations for the night. He would be stripping off the elaborate tunic and mantle and his servants would be loosening the ties of the expensive shirt, placing a warm night robe near to hand. She dared to wonder what his body would be like, and blushed at her own temerity, but then a new and unpleasantly disturbing thought occurred to her which made her mouth droop disconsolately. What if Guy were not alone? What if he had a woman with him? One of his pretty serving wenches perhaps, or a girl from the village who had found favour with him.

She tried to push the notion out of her mind but it clung persistently. Juliana had said he was wholly immoral; that his reputation with women was a scandal even in an age when such things were held to be of slight importance. Was it really likely that he would be content to sleep alone?

She covered her eyes with her hands in an effort to blot out pictures she did not want to see and was unconscious that the door had opened until she heard the faint rustle of straw at her side and turned with a quick exclamation on her lips.

Montauban raised one cautionary hand.

"Do not cry out. Juliana rests soundly but it would be a pity to wake her."

She got up quickly, not in the least afraid now that he was there, and looked towards the shadows where her cousin lay.

"She may stir, my lord."

"I doubt it. The wine was very potent."

"But I drank of it and I am not sleeping."

"No, but then your cup was not doctored and hers was."

Melisenda's eyes widened. "She will not come to harm?"

"None at all. Perhaps a small headache in the morning, but it is in a good cause. She would never let you come with me were she wide-awake and in possession of her senses."

"Come with you?"

211

"Yes, of course. You want to, do you not? You wanted to come to me on that first day we met but it was not possible then. Now it is possible; I have made it so. Come, we waste time."

He led her unresisting from the room and along the darkened passage to his own chamber, drawing her to the bed.

"You know what sort of man I am." He pulled her down beside him. "Juliana has made that plain enough. She says I am a lecher."

She giggled. "And are you?"

"Sometimes. No, in truth, many times. And I have no interest in marriage."

She sobered. "No, sir, so you said."

"This does not trouble you?"

"No."

"Perhaps it should. There is still time for you to change your mind. You can go back to your cousin if you will. There is ample room in the bed for both of you, and she will not harm you as I shall do."

"I do not think you would harm me." She was conscious of his closeness and it made her helplessly weak. "I am growing accustomed to your rough tongue, as Juliana has done. I do not think your words are a true indication of the quality of your heart."

"Perhaps not, but you should read my intents for what they are. I have not brought you here to chatter the night away. I will take from you that which you should hold most dear."

"I do not care what you take from me. I would offer you anything I had, most willingly."

He put an arm round her and held her closer.

"You are very young for such generosity. I wonder if you know the value of what you would give."

She leaned against his chest, a smile of pure contentment touching her mouth as her hand found its way into his.

"It is not much. I do not overvalue it."

"Your humility is touching. Juliana will be very angry."

"With me as well as with you."

212

He raised her face with his free hand and said almost under his breath:

"Be sure, sweet; be very sure."

"I am, my lord. I was sure from the first moment I saw you."

When their lips met she felt the room spin round and was hardly conscious of the cold as he pulled the wrap from her shoulders.

"You have the body of a child," he said after a moment, "yet it arouses something in me which I have not felt before. How odd that is. Why should it be so?"

She smiled again but did not waste time with words as he propped himself up on one elbow to blow out the candles and then turned back to pull her fiercely into his arms.

When Juliana discovered the truth on the following morning her wrath was high and the scorn which she poured on the unrepentant Montauban was scalding in its heat.

"How dared you?" Her eyes were furious as she turned on him with fresh vigour. "How dared you seduce my cousin under your own roof? Have you no sense of shame at all?"

"None." He lay back in his chair and watched her pace the room. "I did not rape her you know."

"Are you saying she was willing? Do you expect me to believe such a tale?"

"No, but then you were never very perceptive, my dear Juliana. You are too wrapped up in your own affairs to notice what others are doing or thinking or feeling. But there is no need to take my word for it. Here is Melisenda. Ask her yourself."

Juliana's lips were tight with displeasure as she waited for Melisenda to come to Guy's side, but even as she opened her mouth to continue her tirade, Melisenda smiled at Montauban in a way which was quite unmistakable and put a small loving hand on his shoulder.

"Do you scold Lord Montauban, Juliana?" She seemed slightly amused. "You should not do so, for it was not his fault."

"Then whose fault was it?"

"Mine, of course."

"Melisenda!"

"You are angry, as I knew you would be, but I beg you not to be for I have never been happier in my life."

"You are too young to know what you were doing. Montauban is not. Guy, what you have done is beyond forgiveness. I shall leave at once and you, Melisenda, will come with me."

"I cannot, dearest." Melisenda was gentle but very definite. "I would not have hurt you if there had been any other way, but there was none for me. Try to understand."

"I find it well-nigh impossible to do so."

"Make an effort," advised Montauban as he kissed Melisenda's hand and rose to his feet. "You will not find it too difficult if you use a measure of imagination. I will see that your horses are made ready."

"And Melisenda?"

"She stays with me. I will bring her to see you when I come to Rockingham to talk of your own future. Rest assured. She is under my protection and will come to no harm."

When he had gone, Melisenda said quietly:

"Do not grieve, Juliana. I am so happy that I would not have you fret for me."

Juliana made a helpless gesture.

"I feel that I am responsible. But for me, you would not have met him."

"You are responsible, dear one, and my debt of gratitude to you can never be repaid. Oh, Juliana, I never thought to feel as I do now. I had never dreamed that love could mean so much. He is all I will ever want or need as long as my life shall last."

Juliana, staring at her cousin's wrapt expression, grew cold inside. Such a passion had been her mother's for Gervase Ducarel and, when he was no longer there, she had put an end to an existence in which he had no part. Her lips were stiff and her words sounded stilted in her own ears, but she had to give the final warning.

"What if he should tire of you? You are not the first."

"No." Melisenda was comforting. "I know that, but you

must not worry. Even should it last for only a short time, it will be enough. I shall not ask for anything which he is not willing to give."

"He does not intend marriage."

"No, he said so plainly, but it does not matter."

"Oh, Melisenda, it should! It should matter."

"But it does not. Nothing will ever matter again. Go now, love, and do not let me be a burden on your thoughts. There is no need for that. Remember that I am happy and that I desire him with all that is in me."

Juliana went slowly downstairs to join Montauban and together they stood for a while looking out on to the crisp blanket of snow. A weak sun was shining that morning and it made the delicate frost flowers on the bare branches of the trees glitter like objects from a fairy world.

"She will not come with me."

"No. Her heart is here and you cannot ask her to leave it, taking only an empty body and mind back to Rockingham with you."

"I do not understand her." Juliana was almost in tears. "I thought I knew her, but this morning she is like a stranger to me."

Guy put an arm round her shoulders and hugged her gently.

"One day you will understand, at least I pray that you will, for you are too beautiful to go through life not knowing what love can do."

"I have seen what it can do. It killed my mother."

"It is not always so destructive."

She looked up from the shelter of his arm.

"I pray it will not be this time. It is clear enough what Melisenda feels for you, but I am no more able to read your thoughts now than I have ever been. Do you care for her, Guy? She is not just another woman of the night for you?"

He laughed softly. "No, not just that."

"Do not hurt her."

"I shall not do so."

215

"She is very young."

"She is older than you in many ways. She could teach you much, if you would listen."

He bent and kissed her brow.

"Go now, Juliana, you have a long ride."

"You will come and see me." She looked at him doubtfully. "You will not forget your promise?"

"No, I will not forget."

The squires helped her into the high-backed saddle and she raised her hand to wave to Montauban, but soon the horses had quickened speed and the castle was lost to sight as they descended the hill. Juliana felt utterly alone as the miles fell behind her. Melisenda had not lived with her for long but she had grown very fond of her cousin during the time she had been at Rockingham, and now she would have to return to the empty hollowness of her castle without the gaiety and companionship on which she had come to rely so much.

She knew that Melisenda had much fondness for her and so had Guy, yet it was obvious that they had both been anxious to see her go, for she played no part in the binding union which had been forged for them on the previous night. She was merely an intruder who had had to be hastened on her way so that their magical, intimate world should not be disturbed by her presence.

She was shut out again, just as she had been when her father and mother were alive: cut off, because she had no place in their existence. She wondered if this inexplicable thing called love was always so cruel and selfish and, if she were ever to discover it herself, whether it would exclude other human beings so completely from her heart and mind.

Suddenly she no longer cared whether Montauban could solve the problem of her own future, and she could even contemplate with indifference marriage with a bowman from Flanders, for all her emotions seemed to have withered again. They were as hard and lifeless as the snow churning up beneath the horses' hooves, and when she finally reached Rockingham she almost welcomed the eerie stillness which greeted her. At least here she would not see the glow of joy in Melisenda's eyes, nor the faint smile on Guy's lips as his gaze had lingered possessively on the slender body he had taken for his own the night before.

No, it was better to be here at Rockingham than to watch the alchemy of love at work, and her face was blankly impassive as she mounted the stairs to the chilly bower and gave herself over to the deadly silence of solitude.

At the end of February Miles returned home again. There was an odd restlessness in him which was wholly foreign to his nature and which he found extremely disturbing. He could not put his finger on the cause, although he entertained for some time the thought that it was the general unrest in the air and the fact that the rebel barons were clearly bent on further action. He tried to push all other reasons out of his mind because they were quite absurd and warranted no attention, but every now and again he caught himself thinking of the gaunt castle at Rockingham and the defiant girl who had such sadness in the depths of her eyes.

He found his father hobbling about with the aid of a gnarled stick which he was wont to brandish threateningly at any who came within striking distance of his injured leg but, since his servants were nimble creatures, none had come to any great harm from their irascible master.

"Well, Miles?" Clemence, busy with her embroidery, looked ravishing in a gown of pale violet silk with a richly decorated bliaut of matching brocade and a gold cretone studded with amethysts over her white wimple. "Tell us your news."

"It does not make good telling." Miles looked at her with troubled eyes. "There is much disquiet and the pressure upon the king grows daily."

Clemence threaded her needle and considered her son carefully.

"There is disquiet in you too. Something has happened to you since you were last here."

For once Miles wished his mother were a little less perceptive

but before he could dismiss her observation with a few meaningless words, Hamelin had limped over to him.

"What is it, boy? Do you fear for the king?"

Carlingford shrugged. "He is not without his followers."

"That is no answer. What of FitzWalter and de Vesci? I hear
they are gaining more support."

"So I believe, and now I understand why."

"What!"

Hamelin's face grew flushed and Clemence put up a restrain-
ing hand.

"Hush, dear, hush. Let Miles tell it his way."

"Tell what?" snapped the earl. "I will have no such talk in
my presence. Whatever John has done, we are his men."

"Are we?" Miles sounded almost weary. "I thought so, sir,
until recently. Now I am not so sure. Doun said that I did not
know what it was like to feel the royal lash and he was right.
Now I do, and I wonder about this charter for which men ask."

Hamelin's cheeks grew congested with anger.

"God's teeth! Do you dare to stand there and say. . . ."

"Quietly, my sweet, quietly." Clemence put aside her work
and went to her husband's side, laying her hand on his arm as
she gave him a quick smile. "Hear what Miles has to say. You
know him well enough to realize that there must be a reason for
his words. Listen, I beg you, before you make harsh judgments."

The earl grunted but the dangerous colour faded from his
face.

"Very well. I will listen but your reasons had better be good
ones, boy, or I shall. . . ."

"They are good enough." Miles was curt as he related the
tale of Juliana Ducarel and John's threat to marry her off to a
routier. "And whatever she has done," he concluded, "the king
has no right to do this. She is of noble birth and deserves
better."

Hamelin went back to his chair and sat down, tugging at his
beard in perplexity.

"I know not what to say. If she is a woman of the kind which

218

the king says, then he is right to stop the marriage between you."

"If she is." Miles looked at his father sombrely. "But what if she is not? And whether she be wanton or not, a Fleming is no fit mate for her."

"The king may not mean it. Perhaps he was angered and said it in the heat of the moment."

"Perhaps. Again perhaps not." Miles began to pace the chamber, his hand on his sword hilt. "I do not know, my lord, I do not know. Yet if he does mean it, then FitzWalter and the others are right. There should be some way to stop such things and I am of a mind to help them do it."

"That you must not do." The earl was definite. He was no longer irate but anxious as he leaned forward quickly. "Miles, you cannot ally yourself to such men. I would not pretend that John is a saint, and I can see as readily as the next man that reforms are needed, but not FitzWalter's way."

"Then how? How shall it be stopped, father, for although I want no union with a whore, if that is what she is, I see now the justice of some of the complaints which are made against John's unfettered will."

"Heed the archbishop and Pembroke." Hamelin lay back in his chair and sighed. "If you are hot for reforms, listen to them."

"What have they to say that FitzWalter and de Vesci have not already said?"

"They speak with the voice of truth and honesty. What they seek is good for all men; what FitzWalter wants is for himself." Suddenly the earl looked old. "Do not let them make a fool of you. I do not know the truth of what has happened between this girl and the king and it would seem that you are not much better versed than I. It is natural that you should be angered but do not let that anger make a traitor of you. Your allegiance belongs to the king, no matter what he has done, and in the last resort you must fight for him."

"Even against Pembroke and Langton?" Miles's lips twisted slightly. "What if it comes to that, sir? What if John cannot

219

satisfy even the moderates amongst his critics and what if those moderate voices are right? What then?"

"You must still fight for John," returned Hamelin steadily. "You have no other choice. This family has been loyal to the crown since it first received its lands from royal hands. No son of mine will break this tradition. I would kill you myself before I would let you take up arms against the king."

"Even if John is in the wrong?"

"I do not accept that he is wholly wrong. I do not pretend that the Angevins have been easy masters. They have demanded much, too much perhaps, yet they have given things in return which not all men recognize for their true value. John has said he will hold this realm intact for his son, and he is right to do so. Would you serve a foreign lord? Do you want Louis of France on our throne to give us orders? Are we to become an appendage of Philip Augustus's? A people of no importance, ruled by a Frenchman? Think well what you are doing. Fitz-Walter and his men already correspond with France. Even here at Renfell I know that and you cannot be unaware of it either. Do you want to bow the knee to Philip?"

Miles said nothing for a moment. Then he gave a deep sigh.

"No, my lord, I do not."

"Then be done with your doubts. Drive them out of your heart and your mind, for they are dangerous. If you can follow such men as Pembroke and Langton and still remain John's man, then you have my blessing, but, if not, then follow John. I will have your word on it."

Slowly Miles inclined his head.

"You have it."

"Then I am satisfied." Hamelin rose awkwardly to his feet. "Now I have things to do. Talk to your mother for a while, for if I know her she has a hundred questions to ask you." He gave Miles a warm grin. "Take care; she'll turn your soul inside out and you'll never notice it until it's too late."

Clemence chuckled as the earl closed the door behind him, and held out her hand to Miles.

"I shall do no such thing, but tell me of this girl of yours."

220

"Not mine."

Her smile was gentle. "No?"

"You heard my story."

"I heard your words which said one thing but I watched your eyes and they said another. What is she like?"

"Haughty and cold. I was not welcomed."

"Did you deserve to be?"

"Madam?"

"I know you, Miles. Did you go as a supplicant or a conqueror?"

"Neither." He gave her an irritated look. "Our meeting was a short one and far from friendly."

"But that of course was not your fault." She looked wickedly innocent. "What she beautiful?"

It was useless to lie to Clemence and he did not try.

"Very." He hesitated. "She was also lonely and sad underneath the anger. She lives in her father's castle with a cousin and her servants, but she is still lonely."

"Perhaps that is why you found her cold."

"No, she was also hostile." He was frowning as the memory of his interview with Juliana Ducarel came back to him. "No, there was something else which I did not understand then, and no more do I now. Also I believe she has a lover."

"Miles!"

"John said she had and she did not deny it."

Clemence was silent for a moment. "John might have been lying."

"He might, but why did she not refute the charge?"

"Did you ask her outright if she had a lover?"

"No. No, I did not, but she spoke as if there were someone."

"And this angered you?"

"Naturally."

"Then you must have some feeling for her, otherwise you would not have cared."

"I have no feeling for her. Good God, I had only then met her."

Clemence's lips parted and her eyes were kind.

"Dearest, I only saw your father for a few minutes at our first meeting but I knew at once that I loved him and I made up my mind there and then to marry him. A second or two was all that I needed. Perhaps it was the same for you."

"I doubt it," began Miles, when the door opened and Doun came in raising his hand in greeting.

"Doun? You are here again?"

"Why not?" FitzAnthony bent to kiss his aunt's cheek. "I am a dutiful nephew visiting my much-beloved Clemence."

"Are you? You have not shown such solicitude for many years. Are you sure it is not because your friends are here?"

"My friends?" Doun's voice was light but he gave his cousin a cautious look. "What friends?"

"These eastern counties have joined with the northern barons, and your sympathies lie with them."

"You are too suspicious by far." Doun straightened up. "And by now I should have thought you too would be considering a change of heart. What is this I hear about the Ducarel girl? John has taken her from you, so it is said."

"That is none of your affair. If the king has had a change of mind it is not for me to question it. I would have wished he had not chosen a Fleming for her husband but. . . ."

"But he has not. You are behind the times, my dear Miles. Juliana Ducarel is now Guy de Montauban's ward, and rumour has it that he will marry her in time."

"Montauban?" Carlingford was sharp. "I had not heard this."

"No? Then you do lag behind in current gossip, cousin. Yes, she is Montauban's charge, and need I remind you what manner of reputation he has?"

"You need not." Carlingford was shorter still. "Did she agree to this?"

"I have no idea. I doubt that her opinion was sought. Why, does it trouble you?"

Miles controlled the sudden anger within himself and gave his cousin a cool look.

"Not in the least. It is not my business. And now shall we talk of other things, for this subject begins to weary me."

He listened with half an ear to Clemence and Doun as they chattered away, their words flowing over him almost unheeded. He could not understand why his heart felt so leaden nor why there was a sour, grinding anger lying on his mind like a dead weight.

Why should he care that Juliana Ducarel was Montauban's ward, his prospective bride, or even his mistress? It was no affair of his any longer, and he cursed himself for his weakness, but the cursing did no good and the anger remained.

Certainly she had spoken softly of an unknown man but was it Montauban? If so John was right, for Montauban's reputation was a by-word and if Juliana looked to him for help then she was probably as depraved as the king had claimed.

He was on the point of dismissing the whole matter from his mind, determined not to make a fool of himself over a woman who clearly had detested him on sight and who was probably a high-born whore into the bargain, when he had a sudden vision of Juliana's face and the wide grey eyes which had betrayed something more than indignation and dislike.

No, it could not rest like this; he had to be sure before he consigned Juliana to the devil. He came back to reality with a rush to find Doun and his mother looking at him quizzically.

"Forgive me. Did you ask me something?"

Clemence's mouth curved slightly.

"I asked when you were going to see the Lord Montauban."

Miles showed his teeth. It was quite impossible to conceal the slightest thing from Clemence, even a half-formed resolution which had only just occurred to him.

"Soon."

"That is good." Clemence looked remarkably pleased with herself. "Now I would have you leave me for a while, for I have a letter of some importance to write and if you stay you will distract me from my task."

She shooed them off with a loving smile, returning to the fireside where a small table stood furnished with quill and parchment. For a moment she sat with the quill in her hand, her eyes half-closed in thought. Then with a slight nod she began to write in her impeccable Latin a brief but decidedly pointed letter to Guy de Montauban.

John's initial rage had died down following his meeting with the barons at Epiphany and he began to manoeuvre cautiously and with great skill towards his target. Now was not the time for hot words and bluster; now was the season for inspired statesmanship and quiet diplomacy, and John was truly his father's son as he laid his carefully calculated plans.

His first move was to renew the charter to the Church in an effort to get the clergy behind him, quick to send a copy of the document to the pope by emissaries who were charged to tell Innocent of the problems which beset his royal vassal, and though the magnates were soon packing off their own envoys, John merely laughed at their efforts for he had no doubt at all as to whose side Innocent would take.

Then there were the neutral barons to consider; those men who had watched thoughtfully the struggle which was taking place between John and the rebels, but who had not so far come to a decision as to the part they would play in the final conflict, nor committed themselves to either party. They were important, for they far outweighed the numbers which FitzWalter and de Vesci could command, and they had to be coaxed with gentle words and convincing deeds. To assure them of his good intentions, John sent to Ireland under the leadership of Savaric de Mauléon the Poitevin mercenaries whom he had summoned to his aid. It was essential that the magnates still undecided should not be alarmed by the sight of hordes of soldiers in arms. They must not be allowed to believe that the king was building up a foreign army to use against them. England had to remain peaceful, yet the lances he might still require had to be reasonably close at hand, for in the end diplomacy might well fail and cold steel become the only solution.

But John's master stroke came on the 4th March when, unexpectedly and somewhat smugly, he took the Cross, making his vows as a crusader and putting his person and all that he owned firmly under the protection of the Holy Church, thus gaining for himself the customary three years' breathing space in which to meet his secular debts and liabilities.

Langton was furious, resenting the brilliance of John's latest trick, and speaking out harshly against it, but John responded with even softer words and conciliatory actions, going so far as to send home some of the mercenaries already in England to prove to the archbishop the honesty of his intentions.

Langton was not fooled by John's activities but it was hard to find anything on which he could justifiably take issue with the king. John was being too clever, more than a match for the archbishop and his supporters, and the primate fumed silently until mid-April when the pope's response to John's messages arrived in England in the form of two letters.

Innocent, now completely won over to John's cause, expressed surprise and disappointment that neither Langton nor his fellow-bishops had succeeded in their task of making peace between the king and those in rebellion against him. It had been their task, he wrote severely, to show the disaffected nobles the error of their ways and to ensure that the remorseful king was reconciled with those who had held him blameworthy for the earlier rift with Rome.

Stephen Langton read the pope's missive with grim despair. Innocent, who had once spoken so hotly of John's failings, could now see no wrong in his submissive vassal, and he had ended his letter with a sharp personal rebuke to Langton himself, charging him to make an end of factions and conspiracies and to bring about peace without delay. There was also a further reprimand for Langton for his continued support of the men who were seeking an unlawful charter from their sovereign, and Langton gave a deep, heartfelt sigh as he rubbed his tired eyes and lay back in his chair.

It was clear that Innocent was blithely unconscious of the truth. He could have no conception of the real state of affairs in England, his newly-acquired fief of which he was so proud. To him, England was merely the place where a contrite king had expressed his sorrow in spectacular style, and where madmen were rising up against their monarch who had received full and complete absolution for his sins. How could he know the manner of John's rule? How could the pope even begin to understand what lay behind the discontent? How could he possibly comprehend what manner of man John was?

The archbishop moved uneasily in his seat. The conflagration was growing nearer. The meeting between the king and some of the barons which had been held at Oxford earlier that spring had been entirely fruitless. The magnates had shouted loudly for a fulfilment of the promise made by John at the Epiphany, but though John had answered them quietly enough he had given none of the undertakings which they had sought and they had gone away snarling and as dissatisfied as ever.

It could not go on. They would not wait much longer, these bitter, thwarted men who had marched so far along the road of rebellion. They would not go tamely back to their homes now and forget what he, Langton, had shown them might be theirs.

And Langton's fears were justified, for when Eustace de Vesci returned from Rome bearing a third letter from the pontiff, this time addressed to the barons of England, reproving them for their contumacy, there was not one amongst FitzWalter's followers who did not realize that John had won the day in gaining Innocent's support and that their cause was hopelessly lost in Rome.

They had come too far to turn back, as Langton had seen, and they knew they could expect no mercy from John should they weaken now. There would be no forgiveness for them even were they to humble themselves before the king; he would exact the most terrible penalties for their previous defiance and in any event none of them were ready to give up the struggle for what they stoutly believed to be their rights.

And so, between the 19th and 26th April, the rebels assembled in arms at Stamford; some forty barons, five earls and two thousand knights, served by serjeants, squires and pages and accompanied by numerous foot soldiers and well-trained horsemen.

The pope's letters which had been designed to bring an end to conflict and to resolve the differences between the king and his barons had proved, in fact, a weapon with a frightening double-edge, for they had driven the hopes of peace further away and had brought England trembling to the threshold of civil war.

CHAPTER TEN

WHILE the barons were gathering at Stamford, Miles Carlingford rode off to see Guy de Montauban. It had taken him some time to make up his mind to confront Montauban for his feelings were still somewhat mixed, and he was well aware that the future of Juliana Ducarel was none of his business. But in the end he had realized that there was no choice for him, and he braced himself as Montauban's servants led him through the great doors into the hall where their master was waiting.

"My lord, you are welcome." Montauban ran his eye slowly and speculatively over his visitor. "I have been expecting you."

Miles raised an eyebrow. He had not anticipated such a greeting, and Montauban himself was something of a surprise, but he let nothing of his fleeting emotions show as he bowed slightly.

"Indeed? I gave no warning of my coming."

"Yet it was inevitable that you should do so, once you heard that Juliana was my ward. Come, sit here and take some wine. There is no reason for us to discuss the matter in discomfort." He waved Miles to a stool by the table and nodded to the attendant pages to fill the goblets. "You must meet Juliana's cousin, Melisenda. My dear, come here and greet Earl Hamelin's son."

Carlingford rose again, blankly astonished as Melisenda came forward to curtsy gracefully to him. She was positively radiant in a gown of green silk and the look she gave Montauban as he took her hand left no doubt as to the nature of their relationship.

"Madam." Miles was very distant. "I had thought you were with the Lady Juliana at Rockingham."

"So she was." Montauban was patently amused. "Drink your wine, for I think you will need its comfort."

Miles obeyed but he was still wary. The light in Montauban's eye was gently satirical and Carlingford had the feeling that it would not take much to make Guy burst into outright laughter. Since it appeared that he, Carlingford, was the cause of the humour, his face grew studiedly blank as he put up an invisible shield between himself and his host.

"Your wine is excellent, and so is your taste in women." Miles hit out directly and without hesitation. "I had been told this was so."

"Had you now? Do you approve of my choice?"

"My approval is not necessary nor sought, I suspect."

"Perhaps not, but it is encouraging to have one's judgment confirmed. For myself I find her quite enchanting."

Miles turned to look at Melisenda, expecting to find her covered with confusion, but she was smiling happily as she held tightly to Guy's hand.

"You have left your cousin?" Miles was abrupt. "I would have thought, in the circumstances, that your place was with her."

"She had no choice." Montauban released her hold and sat down. "Do not censure her, my lord, the fault was mine. I would not let her go. But did you come here to discuss my affairs or those of Juliana?"

"Which you are about to tell me are no more my business than the choice of your mistress."

Guy shook his head. "No, you are wrong, I was not going to say that. I can see your right to ask about Juliana. After all, she was to be your wife."

"And now she is your ward."

"She is, but I am a lax guardian. You may visit her if you wish."

"I am grateful." Miles would not let himself grow enraged at the casual, almost indifferent permission. "I shall take

229

advantage of your kindness at the earliest opportunity, but there is something else I have to ask."

"You are free to ask what you will."

The eyes of the two men met.

"Do you intend to marry Juliana."

Montauban pulled a face. "An awkward question."

"I should not have thought so." Carlingford's voice was even. "After all, you must know whether you wish to make her your wife."

"Ah, now that is the problem you see. I do not know." Montauban ran his forefinger round the top of his goblet. "She is lovely enough I grant you and rich too, of course, but I have other problems to solve first."

"What to do with her cousin, perhaps?" Miles was cruel as he shot Melisenda another glance. "Can you not discard her as easily as you have discarded others in the past?"

Melisenda giggled and Carlingford said sharply:

"You take these circumstances very oddly, madam. Does it mean nothing to you that you have thrown away your reputation?"

"You must not be angry, my lord." Melisenda came to sit beside him and looked earnestly into his face. "I know what you are feeling but there is a solution for you and one day you will realize it. As for me; I am more than content."

"Then you are a most unusual woman." Miles turned back to Montauban. "If you are not prepared to give me an answer, I must tell you this. I will not stand by and see Juliana treated thus. If you do not want her, let her go. Make clear to her that you will not marry her, and release her from her doubts."

Guy's mouth moved fractionally.

"What makes you think she has doubts? Juliana is devoted to me."

"Devoted enough to come and live with you and her cousin?" Miles was scathing. "Never tell me her affections have such depths for I will not believe it."

"You are not required to. Sufficient to say that I am satisfied with the way things are."

Miles stood up and slammed the goblet down on the table.

"Well I am not. I will give you one week to tell the king you no longer wish to have her as your ward; seven days to tell Juliana you will make no claim on her."

"And if I do not?" Montauban was looking up at Miles with interest. "What then?"

"Then I will kill you."

"Harsh words, my lord."

"And harshly meant."

"A week is not long enough. I have other things to attend to. Tomorrow I return to Poitou to deal with personal business. I shall have no time to settle Juliana's future before I go."

"How long will you be gone?"

"Three weeks, perhaps longer."

"Then I will give you a month, but no more."

"That should suffice." Guy rose idly, nodding amiably. "Yes, I think I can settle affairs in France by then. Are you always so determined to have your own way?"

"When the issue is important enough, yes."

"And Juliana is important to you?"

"I did not say that she mattered to me; merely that she was important."

"I see." Montauban rubbed his jaw thoughtfully. "How fortunate Juliana is to have such a fierce champion, and one who demands nothing for himself. I had not expected to find such altruism in you, my lord."

Once again Miles had the distinct feeling that Guy was laughing at him, although the reason for the concealed mirth was not apparent to him, and, since he disliked being the butt of another man's merriment, he made his *adieux* brief and cold, striding out of the hall in some irritation.

Montauban had not been what he had expected at all. If he were a degenerate as men claimed he hid the fact remarkably well, for he bore none of the signs of dissipation which Miles had thought to see in him. True, he had obviously seduced Juliana's young cousin in a most reprehensible way but, angry though he was, Miles had not been blind to the obvious devotion

231

in Melisenda's eyes, nor the affection with which Montauban had squeezed her hand. But, if Montauban was fully satisfied with his latest conquest, why did he refuse to release Juliana? Why should he still be considering marriage with her whilst he shared his bed with another?

Miles shrugged resignedly as he accepted the truth with reluctance. After all, why should Guy not? Few marriages sprang from love. Most were designed to unite powerful houses or to provide impoverished peers with wealthy brides. But Guy was not in the least impoverished nor did his house need the support of Juliana's, such as was left of it.

He mounted up, still vexed and puzzled, and was about to ride off when he saw a horseman cantering into the courtyard. In an instant he was out of the saddle and running for cover behind the stables as he watched his cousin Doun leap to the ground and hand his roan over to the grooms.

Doun here at Montauban's castle? Doun, who had spent so much time at Renfell of late; who had urged his cousin to reconsider his loyalties; who had spoken openly and critically of John's shortcomings.

He waited until Doun was out of sight before remounting. Now Guy de Montauban was planning to return to Poitou. For what purpose? To raise troops against the king from amongst his many enemies in southern Poitou? Guy's own family was known to be hostile, although Guy himself had always claimed to be loyal. Was that loyalty a false one, or wearing thin, and had Doun come from Robert FitzWalter to urge Montauban on his way?

If Juliana was really considering marriage with her guardian it was high time that she learned the truth about him, and with a brief command to his mount Miles drove in his prick spurs and raced quickly off to Rockingham, there to seek another confrontation with the Lady Juliana Ducarel.

When he reached Juliana's castle Miles found that John's men had gone and Guy de Montauban's had taken their place. He was greeted in a friendly fashion and instantly offered the freedom of the castle. Although a trifle surprised by such a welcome, Miles was not slow to take advantage of it as he made his way upstairs to tap on the door of Juliana's bower. The castle seemed strangely quiet and deserted to him, for apart from a few servants and knights in the lower hall he met no one as he wandered along the corridors. There were no stewards, no maids-in-waiting, not a sight of a secretary or chaplain. It was a queer feeling, almost as if he were alone, and when he got no response to his knock, he turned the handle of the door and went inside. The chamber felt cool and smelt of a delicate perfume but Juliana was not there and so he turned on his heel and began to investigate the other rooms. After a while his eye caught a half-open door at the end of a passage and he walked quietly towards it, pushing it open slightly as he entered the room.

His heart quickened as he saw Juliana but for a moment he did not speak. She had her back to him and seemed wholly absorbed in her thoughts as she stroked the sleeve of a velvet gown hanging on a perch at one end of the room. He glanced about him. The room had a stale and musty smell, quite unlike Juliana's own bower, and although he was not given to imagining things, he felt a *frisson* of unease along his spine which he did not understand.

Clearly it was a woman's chamber, for there was a small table by the window covered with jewels and cosmetics, all slightly dusty, and the neglected garments hanging about the walls were of silk and satin, trimmed with gems and costly fur. As he moved slowly across the floor he could see the dirt which marred the heavily embroidered bedspread, noting the jug and ewer by the side of the couch which were tarnished with age and disuse.

"Madam."

He said it softly, hoping not to startle her, but she turned with a quick exclamation of alarm, her face white and drawn as she stared at him. He frowned as he took the final steps towards her, filled with sudden angry concern that she should look so wan.

"Forgive me. I frightened you."

"No . . . no." She controlled herself with an effort. "No, it is all right. I had not expected you."

She could not take her eyes off his face. That day had been a long one and she had been oddly depressed since early morning. She had woken at dawn when the sun was just coming up over the horizon and sleep had eluded her as she had tossed and turned in her bed, wondering how to endure another day of solitude and painful thoughts. When she had first returned home she had been completely withdrawn in her misery, shocked and bewildered by Melisenda's desertion and by the calm, untroubled way in which Guy had sent her back to Rockingham by herself, as if he had not cared at all what became of her. For days she could not bear to think of Guy and Melisenda in their happiness, but then the paralysis had left her and with it her protective shell.

She was not quite sure when she had begun to remember Miles Carlingford again. She had only seen him once, and that meeting had been far from friendly, yet she found herself thinking more and more of the thin, handsome face, his tall, spare form, and the inexplicable sense of security which she had felt when he was with her.

She had not expected to see him any more and had chided herself for her foolishness in dwelling on their meeting, but now he was here and he was looking at her in a way which made her want to throw aside her reserve and weep on his shoulder.

"No, I had no time to warn you."

"It does not matter."

She was aware that he had taken her hand, but completely unconscious of the fact that her own fingers had tightened over his. It seemed to her that he was the only real thing in the world at that moment, and she could feel the phantoms retreating in the face of his vigorous and vital presence.

"What is this room?"

He was looking about him in distaste, and she shivered.

"It was my mother's."

"Why are you here?"

"I come here often."

"You should not do so. These things ought to be cleared away." He made a quick gesture with his hand. "How can you hope to forget when you have such reminders?"

"I do not want to forget. She and my father are all I have left."

"They are dead."

"Not to me."

He took a deep breath. "Then they should be, Juliana, they should be. You cannot live with memories all your life."

"I have nothing else."

She sounded remarkably forlorn and he looked grim again.

"You speak of Melisenda?"

"You know she is not here?"

"Indeed I do. I saw her when I went to Montauban's castle."

"You have been to see Guy?" Her eyes were startled. "But why, my lord?"

"We had things to discuss. Did you know Melisenda was his mistress?"

"Of course." She gave a tremulous sigh. "Is it possible to be with them and not know it? I should not have taken her with me."

"You took her to Montauban?" He was terse. "Why? Why did you go yourself?"

She flushed. "I . . . I . . . cannot speak of it."

"You will have to. I have not come here to avoid unpleasant words."

"I did not ask you to come at all." She was defensive. "I have nothing to say."

"But I have." He caught her shoulders and pulled her closer to him. "Montauban is trying to make up his mind whether to marry you. Does that mean nothing to you?"

She could not speak at first, for his hold on her made her tremble. She could feel the strength run through the long fingers gripping her arms, charging her with energy, and was thoroughly alive for the first time in many months.

"I cannot speak of it."

235

"He has a mistress; your cousin."

"So you have said. What of it, my lord? Marriage and mistresses have nothing in common."

"They do if you love him." Miles let her go. "If you have some other reason for wanting to be Montauban's wife, so be it, but if you love him God help you. He has nothing left for you."

"He would be better than a mercenary from Flanders."

He stared at her blankly. "A mercenary? Is that why you would marry him? Simply to escape John's sentence? If that is so, you would do better to marry me."

She felt herself shivering again but she would not let him see what his suggestion was doing to her.

"Marry you? But that the king has forbidden."

"He could be persuaded to change his mind."

"You could make him do that?"

"I think so."

"Because you pity me?" Her voice was suddenly harsh as she thrust down the longing inside herself. How close she had been to missing the obvious. For a few wonderful moments she had been dull-witted enough to imagine that Carlingford wanted her, but then, just in time, reason came to her aid. "You feel some compassion is that it, and would rescue me from John's hireling and from Guy at one and the same time?"

"If you choose to think that, yes." He wanted to shout his denials at her and silence her words with a kiss but he dared not do so for she might well be as infatuated with Montauban as her cousin was. "For pity then, if for nothing else."

She drew back, her eyes blank and cold.

"I need no pity. No woman who is Lord Montauban's mistress requires that."

He felt the world tilt uncomfortably and was beset by a devastating urge to grab at her and shake her hard until she stopped what she was saying, but all he could do was to let his hands fall to his sides as he said quietly:

"I see. I had not realized."

"Now that you do, is there more to say?"

236

"No." He was pulling on his jewelled gauntlets. "It seems it has all been said." He turned to look about him and then for a second their eyes met. "Yet you should not stay here. You are too much alone."

"Perhaps I shall not be alone for much longer."

"Perhaps not." The moment of softness was gone and he was as frigid as she. "My pardon for intruding upon you. It will not happen again."

He did not bother to stay to tell her of his suspicions of Montauban's loyalty to the king, for this was of no importance to him at that moment. All that mattered to him then was that Juliana was lost to him for good and that he loved her.

As Juliana watched him go the tears were pouring down her cheeks, the ring of his boots on the stone passage outside violent in her ears. She had no idea why she had lied to him. Why she had allowed him to think that Guy was her lover. It was a kind of momentary madness which had overcome her when she realized that he felt nothing for her but sympathy. A defence against something which was so savage in its quality that she had crumpled instantly beneath its first blow.

She wanted to run after him and tell him the truth but that would do no more than lift the anger from his face. It would not dispel the unpalatable fact that he had nothing to give her but his name and protection, and they were not enough. Better to live at Rockingham in a tomb than dwell with a man whom one loved but who had no response to make but kindliness and a measure of concern.

The thought came into her mind before she could stop it, but once it was there she could not rid herself of it nor blind herself to its veracity. Yes, she did love him. It was wildly absurd but it was true. She had seen him so few times; knew so little about him; had quarrelled with him when they met. But it made no difference. She loved him and the very thought took her breath away and left her dazed and bewildered.

She sat on the stool in front of her mother's table and stared blankly at herself in the dusty hand-mirror. Could one really love at first sight? Was it truly possible, or was it just a fevered

237

longing of the lonely? She could just see the outline of her face, white and misty, and the glint of the ruby brooch she wore at her throat. Yes, it was possible, for had not Melisenda felt just such an instant passion for Guy? These things could happen, although she had never thought to find herself a victim. She could see at last why she had been able to remember every line of Miles's face with such clarity, and why she had trembled when he touched her. It was painfully obvious now, and she almost laughed at her own blindness.

The top of one of the scent bottles had become dislodged and the heady perfume, long dried up, was still strong in her nostrils. All at once she could feel the shadows thick about her as if they were moving towards her and she rose quickly to her feet, almost running out of the room before they could lay their spectral hands on her shoulder.

As she hurried back to her own room she felt new tears on her cheeks. The ghosts were still there, waiting behind the door she had slammed behind her, but the creature of warm flesh and blood who might have saved her from their destruction she had sent out of her life with an absurd lie. Now she would have to spend the rest of her days with the consequence of her own folly, and with a sob of despair she threw herself down on the bed and began to weep.

On the 27th April 1215 the rebel barons broke camp at Stamford and rode off to Brackley in Northamptonshire. As soon as he heard of the move, John sent Stephen Langton and William Marshal to parley with them and to discover in precise terms what demands the recalcitrant nobles made of him and since Miles Carlingford was with the king when the emissaries set forth, he too was sent with his knights to stiffen the guard about the royal messengers.

By now John had no hesitation in asking for the barons' requirements in a definite form for he was already confident that he could dismiss each and every one of them as being unlawful, nor did it take the barons very long for their part to present the schedule to the primate, for Langton himself had drafted the document during his meetings with the insurgents in the previous week.

The first rough draft of the Articles of the Barons was something of a triumph for Langton, for he had been faced with hot-tempered men who regarded John as a personal enemy and who spent a good deal of their time reciting the evils done to them by the king and his predecessors. But the archbishop's wisdom could not be ignored, and even the most fiery of the magnates were shrewd enough to see that Langton's enlarged version of their Articles had an almost constitutional flavour about them and would thus be likely to appeal, not only to the moderates of their own class, but to the prosperous townsfolk, lesser knights, and to every man in the realm entitled to call himself free.

The most selfish amongst John's enemies began to talk smugly of the rights of man and felt themselves politically secure as they went through the ritual of handing to Langton the document which he himself had helped to prepare.

When Langton and Marshal returned to the king in Wiltshire he listened with a sardonic smile to the list of ancient laws and customs of the realm which he and his successors were required to confirm and uphold under seal. When Langton's voice died away into silence, John said tightly:

"And that is all?"

"All, save that if your grace's agreement cannot be secured by voluntary means, the barons will find another way."

"They threaten us?"

"They can see no other way to gain justice." It was Pembroke who spoke, taking a step nearer to the king whose face was growing mottled with wrath. "They would secure their rights by peaceful means if they could, but if not. . . ."

"Damn you, do you defend them?" John leapt out of his chair, his hands clenched by his sides. "Do you presume to stand there and tell us that we should pay heed to such insolence?"

"Some heed must be paid." Langton was firm. "This has gone too far for hot words to melt away reason. Your people only ask for justice from you, sire, no more."

"Justice! Reason! You are mad, archbishop, mad! Do you imagine that we will agree to place ourselves in the hands of men like FitzWalter and de Vesci? Are we to hand over the sovereignty of our crown to monsters like them? Why don't these impudent rascals seek our kingdom here and now, for that is what they really want?"

The veins in John's temples were standing out like ugly knots as he began to shout.

"Never, I tell you; never! We will not grant so much as one of their demands, never mind these baronial Articles which you, archbishop, have connived to produce. We will not give them liberties and rights which would make us their slave. They shall not dictate their will to us nor twist us about their finger to do with us what they will. Never, d'you hear me; never!"

"I beg you to reconsider before it is too late." Stephen Langton's face was tense but it was a vital moment and he recognized its significance only too well. "At least take time to think of the consequences of refusal, your grace. Do not reject what is asked of you without weighing carefully what may come. I have warned you many times that such reforms must be effected; the voice of your people must be heard."

"The voice of FitzWalter you mean, and your bleating whisper behind him!" John thrust his face into the archbishop's, his eyes bloodshot and glazed with passion. "Take your Articles, lord archbishop, and begone. Take them back to our enemies and tell them in words which they will not mistake that we will never accept them. Take them away! Do you hear me? Take them away!"

The king's voice rose to a scream as he began to stamp like a mad bull, and Pembroke and Langton exchanged a hopeless glance. It was useless. John would never listen. He would not even take time to reflect calmly on what was asked of him. Slowly they backed out of his presence and on the following day set out with their escort once more to inform the barons of their failure.

Miles Carlingford listened silently as Langton began to speak to the assembled magnates. Standing in front of the others was

Robert FitzWalter, a thick-set, burly man, over sixty-five years of age with a weather-beaten face and iron grey hair under his steel helm. His eyes had grown colourless with time but they were sharply alert and his jaw was ramrod hard as he waited for the primate to finish. By his side was Saer de Quincy, of a similiar age to FitzWalter, and on his left was de Vesci, a comely man of forty-four. Not all the men gathered about Pembroke and Langton that day were so mature: many of the men were young, such as Pembroke's own son, Maurice de Ghent, and William de Fortibus, yet there were enough there of middle years to hold the balance between reckless youth and stubborn intractable old age. Robert de Vere, Geoffrey de Say, Henry de Bohun, Robert de Ros, Geoffrey and William de Mandeville were but a few of the men who stood firmly behind their leaders and listened to the king's fierce rebuttal of their terms.

Miles watched FitzWalter through narrowed eyes. Whatever the archbishop might say about the justice of the magnates' cause, and whatever benefit might accrue to lesser men, it was quite obvious that FitzWalter was concerned with nothing but his own interests. He was a coarse brute of a man, loud of voice, ugly of temper and selfish to the core, and when Langton had delivered John's message, FitzWalter said roughly:

"And that is his last word?"

Langton's face was sad. "I fear so. Pembroke and I did what we could, but we could not make his grace heed us."

"When did he ever heed anything but his own voice? I warned you it would be useless. Did I not say that our time and effort would be wasted?"

"It is never a waste of time to work for peace." The archbishop looked more worried still. "I think there might yet be hope if we. . . ."

"Well I do not!" FitzWalter's eyes flashed. Peace was not really to his liking and he felt remarkably confident and strong with his companions at his back. "I say the time has come to force the issue."

There was a roar of approval from the crowd."

"So say I." De Vesci's hand was twitching at his sword.

"Enough of words, my lords, or else we shall drown in them and with us our hopes. Let steel and fire be our weapons now, for they will not bend and flicker like soft phrases." He turned to the others, his eyes alight. "I say the time has come to defy the king. He has had our loyalty too long and misused it grossly. He has bled us white with his taxes and fines and taken our castles from us, even as his father and brother did before him. He has made oaths and broken them, laughing and jeering at us for our gullibility. He has tricked us and made fools of us; he has made our reputation shabby in Rome with his lies. Are we to endure more? Shall it be never ending?"

"No! No! Defy the king! An end to it!"

The cry went up all round and Miles grimaced. There would be no holding them now; it was too late. If John had been bluffing he had misjudged his men. If he had not been, then he would have his war.

When the shouting died down, de Mandeville waved his hands to gain attention.

"Sirs, since we are now of one mind we must act with due propriety. If we would renounce our allegiance and make an end of our homage it must be done in proper form. The good canon of Durham who is with us today shall release us from our vows, and then we must choose one of our number to lead us in our just fight."

Again the magnates cheered, and when the canon of Durham had duly mumbled the necessary words, Robert FitzWalter was unanimously elected as the leader of the barons and given the resounding but meaningless title of 'Marshal of the Army of God and of Holy Church'.

"Take back our decision to the king," said FitzWalter finally, his face flushed with pride and triumph. "Tell his grace that we no longer acknowledge him as our suzerain and have made formal renunciation of our fealty. Tell him also that we march to Northampton Castle to lay siege to it. If he would make war on us, he will find us there."

With that he strode over to his horse and called to his knights to follow, and with a faint sigh Carlingford watched the camp break up as one by one the insurgents rode jauntily away to begin their struggle against the king.

When John heard the news he did not fly into another fit of rage, but sat down calmly to consider the situation. He could have moved at once to quash the rebellion with force, but he was not yet ready to abandon politics in favour of conflict. Yet he was not so careless as to allow military preparations to be neglected and directed his supporters at Gloucester to proceed to Cirencester, there to await his further commands, whilst at the same time he issued orders for the strengthening of cities such as London, Oxford, Norwich, Bristol and Salisbury. The Earls of Salisbury, Warenne and Pembroke were despatched to scour the countryside to ensure that all royal castles were well-fortified, and on the 8th May news came that troops were on their way from Flanders under the banner of Gerard of Gravelines, in addition to foot and horse from Poitou.

Secure in the knowledge that help was on its way if needed, John then proceeded to issue letters to those of the barons who still waited passively in their own castles, for there was yet time to win them over to the crown.

"Write this," said John to his scribbling clerk. "Despite the rebellion in our kingdom, we are nevertheless willing to put all grievances before our rightful suzerain, Pope Innocent III, and, so that men shall have trust in our good faith, we undertake and give our solemn word that we will take no action against those who defy us without prior judgment. We will not take our barons by force, nor their men, nor will we disseise them nor take up arms against them except by the law of our realm or by the judgment of their peers in our court."

To secure the support of the capital, John returned to the city long enough to confirm its liberties and to add the sop of a properly constituted municipality and the right of the citizens to elect a mayor each year from amongst their own numbers.

Whilst John was proving to all men how reasonable were his intents, the defiant magnates had failed to make the slightest dent in the walls of Northampton Castle and, somewhat discouraged, had moved on to Bedford where the castle held by

243

William de Beauchamp was readily handed over to them. Despite their poor showing at Northampton, the numbers of the barons were swelling daily. They had not succeeded in moving the stolid neutrals, but they quickly gained the sympathy and support of the young sons and nephews of the great houses of England, whose high spirits and ideals sent them in droves to join FitzWalter's forces.

By the 16th May John was seeking Stephen Langton's aid in the arranging of a brief truce, for he was beginning to be suspicious of the loyalty of the capital and wanted his half-brother, Salisbury, to act as his emissary and to have further discussions with the mayor, aldermen and barons of London.

But John had left it too late. He had had every opportunity to crush the insurgents in the field whilst they battled hopelessly against the keep of Northampton, but he had not done so. He had made a few decisive moves, giving orders for the lands and castles of the rebels to be seized, and had arrested some known sympathizers. He had put down a rising in Devon and sent men to other doubtful areas, but for the most part he had been concerned to convince the pope and the moderates that the rebels were wholly to blame for the outbreak of hostilities and that he himself was showing commendable restraint and reasonableness.

Whilst he was engaged in writing further letters to his overlord, the rebels had brewed a plot which was to change the whole tenor of the struggle and bring the magnates on to an equal footing with the king. For some time secret messages had been passing between FitzWalter's men and the capital, and even as Salisbury was riding towards London the barons arrived in full force and were admitted through Aldgate early on the morning of the 17th May when honest citizens were still on their knees hearing mass. Shouting and screaming with exultation the barons quickly secured all the gates of the city and began to plunder the houses of John's supporters. They demolished the dwellings of the Jews and repaired the city walls with the rubble, taking silver and valuables from the money-lenders and even their precious stores of food.

Only the garrison in the Tower withstood them. The remainder of the citizens were either too poor to defy the invaders or were rich enough to be won over by FitzWalter's creed.

Once inside the safety of the city walls the barons began to send letters to the moderates. They did not bother to coax and placate as the king had done, but told their brethren frankly that unless they joined the movement their houses, castles and barns would be destroyed and all their possessions wrested from them. Few heeded the threats, but the situation was an ugly one, and the normal business of the realm faltered as sheriffs' courts ceased to function and judicial and administrative business ground slowly to a halt.

John himself was at his hunting lodge of Fremantle in Wiltshire, waiting cautiously for the next move to be made. He had diverted Salisbury to Exeter in an attempt to save the castle, and on the 19th he welcomed a contingent of knights from Flanders led by Robert de Béthune.

He was angered by the way things had gone. His plan for cornering the nobles not yet committed to rebellion had been carefully thought out, and his letters to Innocent could have done nothing but convince the pope of the righteousness of his intents, yet what had at first been a mere handful of rebels fruitlessly battering at the walls of one castle had become a sizeable army which had won a race against Salisbury to London and was now on comfortable and equal terms with him from behind the safety of the walls of the capital.

Miles Carlingford, staying at Fremantle for a day or two, felt some sympathy with John's frustration. He had no illusions about John's motives, yet his recent meeting with FitzWalter had quelled once and for all his desire to join the barons. That Langton, Pembroke and the Earls of Salisbury, Chester and Albemarle and men like them fought for principles and ideals and for the good of all men, he did not doubt. That FitzWalter and de Vesci were outright brigands, utterly selfish and motivated only by a desire for personal gain and prestige, was equally clear. Even had he made no oath to his father, Miles had no further time for FitzWalter and his pretensions, and his hopes were now pinned on the slim chance that Langton and those who supported him might salvage some good from the turbulence and chaos now tearing the country apart.

It was difficult to fault John's diplomacy; hard to censure him for trying peaceful means, for whatever reasons, but, equally, it was almost impossible to avoid the temptation of measuring the king's handling of the situation with the methods which his father and brother would most undoubtedly have adopted. Neither Henry nor Richard would have wasted time writing letters or convincing men of their good intentions: either one of them would have led their army of hard, experienced mercenaries up to the walls of Northampton Castle and battered FitzWalter's mob into oblivion.

Towards the end of May John had called one section of his army to muster at Marlborough and thence to ride to Odiham and Farnham, whilst others were held back from the approaches to Reading to await his orders. He had begged Stephen Langton to hand over to him Rochester Castle and to forego his rights as custodian in order that royal troops might be garrisoned there and, upon receiving the archbishop's agreement, John had accepted the terms of a new truce negotiated by the primate and had given Langton letters of safe-conduct for himself and those who would go with him to Staines to discuss further peace moves between the king and the barons.

But, even as he discussed peace with Langton, John was issuing urgent messages to the continent calling urgently upon his friends and allies to join him with all speed, and was penning yet another letter to Innocent, plaintively pointing out the impossibility of fulfilling his crusader's vows whilst one section of the baronage was in wilful rebellion against him. Even as late as Whitsun eve, the 6th June, the king was ordering Fawkes de Bréauté to send four hundred Welsh troops to join Salisbury by the following Tuesday when the truce was to expire, flexing his sinews and preparing for battle as the eleventh hour drew nearer.

And whilst the barons in London entrenched themselves more

firmly and John held his mercenaries in check, Langton and his helpers seized with both hands the opportunity provided by the lull. Patiently but determinedly they rode the distance between London and Windsor, offering first one suggestion then another to the two opposing parties, never discouraged by a blank refusal and always ready to try again with an alternative. Slowly but surely they made some progress: a measure of agreement here, a grudging acceptance there. Clauses were strengthened and others re-drafted; new safeguards were inserted and inflammatory passages removed and replaced with less contentious words.

The barons felt themselves to be winning and by now John had come to a conclusion as to the policy he must pursue in the light of prevailing events. An open fight at the present time was too hazardous. He was not certain enough of his own strength nor yet sure of the numbers who would join the insurgents should war break out. He had to have a more commanding position before the gauntlet was finally flung down and for that he needed time.

Time could be purchased at a price. He would heed the clamour of the rebels and the insistent persuasion of Langton, if he must. He would accede to their demands for the time being and grant the concessions they sought, but not for long. Grimly John smiled to himself as he made his way on the 10th June to the water meadows which flanked the Thames at Staines. Sourly he nodded acceptance of the draft thrust before him and permitted his clerks to affix the Great Seal to the Articles of the Barons as a binding promise of his intentions, agreeing to meet the whole body of the magnates again on the 15th June when there would be a grand and formal ceremony to mark the sealing of the charter.

FitzWalter and de Vesci were blatantly triumphant, making no bones about their delight. Langton was tired but content. War had been averted and the Articles of the Barons now bore some semblance to the contract he had fought for for so long. It was no longer a list of selfish baronial demands but a charter which would benefit all free men, and he was praying softly under his breath as he watched the royal clerks affix the Seal.

But John was not praying. His agile mind was already planning ahead, and when he saw the satisfaction on Fitz-Walter's red face his lips moved in a small, cold smile. Let the Marshal of the Army of God puff himself up with self-pride while he could. The promise now forced from him could be invalidated by Innocent in the same time as it had taken his own men to seal the Articles. Let them smirk and look at him with scorn. He would soon have gathered an army about him which would make them laugh on the other side of their faces. They had the whip-hand for the moment but their victory was illusory and would be short-lived. Innocent was solidly behind his royal vassal, and England was a papal fief which the pontiff would protect to the utmost limits, whilst the continent abounded with tough mercenaries who would welcome John's silver as much as a rousing fight.

Let them gloat; his time would come. Without a backward glance at his enemies, John mounted up and rode off to wait for the 15th June and its aftermath.

CHAPTER ELEVEN

ON the day that John met the leaders of the baronial party at Staines, Miles Carlingford returned to Guy de Montauban's castle. The month which he had given Montauban to free Juliana Ducarel had long elapsed as Miles had been kept busy with errands for the king, and it was not until preliminary agreement had been reached between the opposing parties that Miles was free to ride off to attend to personal business. Perhaps there was no longer any hope for him with Juliana, yet he did not intend to let Montauban misuse her, and there was still the matter of Guy's visit to Poitou to be investigated.

When he arrived, Montauban himself was out hunting but Melisenda came to greet him with a sunny smile and a warm welcome.

"It is good to see you again, my lord." She led Carlingford to the window embrasure. "Come, sit here with me and we can watch for Lord Montauban's return. We had expected you before."

"I have been in attendance on the king." Miles sat beside her reluctantly. Since he had come to make a reckoning with her lover, he felt mildly uncomfortable at the situation in which he now found himself, but Melisenda seemed wholly unconscious of his embarrassment.

"Rumour has come to us that the king has reached conclusions with the barons. I am glad that it is not to be war."

"Not yet, at least."

Miles was guarded. He had no faith in the king's present acceptance of the terms, for he knew John too well. Not even the Great Seal on the Articles of the Barons would save them when John was ready to make his move.

"You are too pessimistic by far." Melisenda was bracing. "All will be well; you will see. Why have you come back, sir? To make an end of Guy?"

Miles gave her a sharp look.

"You find that prospect amusing? I thought you loved him."

"So I do, with all my heart, but then I doubt that he is in any danger."

"Your optimism is without limit it would seem." He was acid. "But whether you be right about peace or not, you are most certainly in error in judging my intents."

"I am not such a simpleton as you think." She turned to look out of the narrow slit of a window on to the green grass below. "Is it not a beautiful day? I wish I could have gone hunting too, but Guy says it is no fit sport for a woman."

"He is right." Miles gazed at her severely. "And I am glad to hear that Montauban has some concern for your welfare."

"He is most solicitous, I can assure you." She dimpled. "I had not thought to find him so, yet I am most shamefully pampered. Why do you want to kill him?"

"You know full well the reason."

"Because he is Juliana's guardian? That seems a small enough crime and not one to warrant death."

"That is not why."

"Then because you believe he wishes to marry her? Have no fear, my lord, he has no intention of doing so."

"Nor that either. He has no need to wed her. He has already violated her, and that is why I have come." His eyes were savage. "You may find it insufficient reason, madam, but I do not."

Melisenda went off into a sudden peal of laughter and Miles stiffened angrily.

"There is nothing in the least humorous. . . ."

"My lord, my lord!" She held up one hand to stem his protests. "Patience, I pray you." She sobered. "I did not mean to offend, nor yet to seem without heart, but the notion that Guy would treat Juliana in such a way is so absurd that I could not help myself."

250

"Absurd or not, she is his mistress."

"Has he said so?"

"No, but Juliana has."

Melisenda was silent for a moment; then she nodded.

"Ah yes, I see. Was she angry with you when she said it?"

"Angry? Well . . . yes, I suppose so, but what difference does it make what humour she was in? It does not alter the fact that. . . ."

"But anger can make fact of fiction." She leaned forward to pat his hand. "Juliana is not Guy's mistress. My lord, use your wits! When could they have become so closely intimate? Guy has not been to Rockingham for years and Juliana came here only twice. The first occasion we spent not more than an hour in the castle." She gave a rosy blush. "The second time it was I who was in Guy's bed whilst poor Juliana slept heavily, for Guy had drugged her wine."

Carlingford stared at her.

"Drugged her wine?"

"Why yes. It was the only way, you see. Juliana would never have allowed me to go to Guy if she had been conscious. She was very strict with me." The demure sauciness was gone. "You have no need to worry. Juliana is no one's mistress, not even the king's, although he tried to make her so, and that is why she needed Lord Montauban's aid. It is why John was angered with her, and threatened to marry her to a mercenary. He tried to seduce her, did she not tell you? Did she not also mention that John had told her you had agreed to such a course?"

"God! No." Miles slumped back against the embrasure and raised his hands helplessly. "No, she did not. I assumed. . . ."

"But of course. Who would not in such circumstances? Do you love her?"

"That is none of your affair," he said tartly, "and in any event it is beside the point, for she most certainly has no affection for me."

"I expect you have been as dense about her feelings as you have been about the rest of this tangle." She was comforting as she laid her hand over his again. "Juliana has been very sad

251

these last few months. She still grieves for her father, and her mother's death seems almost to haunt her. Is it any wonder that you found her cold and even quarrelsome? And since you had already made up your mind as to the kind of woman she was, I have no doubt that you were equally rough of tongue. Do not fret; a lovers' quarrel is soon mended."

"How would you know? I do not permit you to quarrel with me."

Carlingford and Melisenda turned quickly and found Montauban eyeing them with amusement. The heat of the sun had tanned his face a golden brown, making his hazel eyes brighter than ever, and his customary elegance was only slightly marred by the coating of dust which covered his riding boots and stained the hem of his tunic.

"My lord." Melisenda rose at once and Guy put an arm round her, bending to touch her forehead with his lips. "We have a guest; a most welcome one."

"Indeed. Have you come to kill me?" Montauban was smiling. "I seem to remember that such a promise was made."

Carlingford rose slowly to his feet.

"Yes, such a promise was made."

"Do you favour sword or mace?"

Miles laughed reluctantly. "My threats appear to have been of an idle nature, and my information less than accurate."

"Ah, then Melisenda has told you the truth. It is a pity in a way for I should have enjoyed combat with you, but then perhaps I should incur more disfavour with Juliana were I to wound you."

"Or I the everlasting hatred of her cousin were I to be the victor." Miles gave Melisenda a faint smile. "I have harboured unjust thoughts about you, my lord. I owe you an apology."

"Hardly that. You were deliberately misled, partly by John out of sheer malice, partly by Juliana who is in no state at present to recognize truth from falsehood, and partly by me."

"But your state of mind is sound enough, and I do not believe you malicious."

252

"No, but I was not sure about you. I had to be certain whether you really cared about her before I let her go. She is very dear to me." He grinned. "Not, may I hasten to assure you, in the way that Melisenda is, but I have known Juliana since she was a child and she sought my help. I was under an obligation to give it to her. I would not have allowed the king to give her to a *routier*, but neither was I prepared to hand her over to you until I was satisfied as to your feeling towards her."

"And now you are satisfied?"

"Oh yes. Men do not offer mortal combat unless there is good reason. I doubt that you would bother to fight for her fortune; you are not that kind of man."

"I asked Sir Miles if he loved Juliana," said Melisenda guilelessly, "but he would not tell me. He said it was not my business."

"Nor is it." Guy gave her a lazy look. "But such a question was quite unnecessary, for the answer is obvious."

"I still cannot conceive why Juliana should lie to me." Miles shook his head. "She implied that you were her lover."

"And you believed her, of course?"

"I thought I was justified in doing so."

"I cannot think why love makes such fools of some men," observed Montauban to no one in particular. "I have never found passion affects my mental faculties. Even if my reputation is a trifle sullied, surely it was clear to you that Juliana's was not. A more innocent looking girl I have yet to see."

Miles gave Melisenda a brief glance.

"The Lady Melisenda looks innocent too."

"Oh come, my lord, I swear you must be either totally blind or bereft of your senses. Melisenda is a baggage and looks it. Juliana is quite different."

Melisenda crowed with delight.

"Do I really look a baggage?"

"Every inch of you. Now be quiet, for I think Sir Miles has something else to say."

"On the subject of Lady Melisenda's virtue, nothing. On the question of Juliana, well, I still confess myself to be puzzled.

Why could she not tell me the truth? Am I so formidable that she had to lie?"

"I do not find you formidable," Guy gave a slight laugh, "but then my situation is somewhat different from Juliana's." The smile died. "She is very much afraid of being hurt, did you know that? She is trying to shut herself away in that castle of hers so that no one can harm her. Hers is a bruised spirit; she is very vulnerable."

"She seemed so at times." Miles was musing half to himself. "Yet at others she was completely her own mistress, very forbidding and keeping me at arm's length."

"And why should she bother to do that?"

"I have no idea."

"Miles!" Montauban shook his head. "Truly, you cannot be so obtuse. Why should she hold anyone off unless she knew they could hurt her? She knew you could."

"In so short a time?"

"In the space of a single minute. Are you now convinced?"

Carlingford nodded, still somewhat taken aback by the sudden lifting of the weight from his mind and the breathtaking possibilities of Montauban's words. Then his expression changed.

"About Juliana, perhaps, but there is another matter to settle between us. You have been to Poitou?"

"Yes. I told you I was going."

"To collect together men and arms?"

"That was my purpose."

"Then tell me, my lord," said Miles very quietly, "for whom were those men intended?"

Montauban raised his eyebrows. "For whom do you imagine they were intended?"

"I am not sure. That is why I ask. We may yet have our combat if I am not satisfied with your reply."

"I trust we shall not, for I have decided that the afternoon is too hot after all, and I have had enough of fighting for one day. The boar was most disobliging." Guy took a seat in the window and stretched his arms above his head. "But if you must have an answer, and I can see that this is so, then I will

254

give you one. They were for John." His light-hearted manner dropped quite suddenly and his eyes were as cold as ice. "You may trample my reputation with women in the dust if you will, although the tales told of me are much exaggerated, but if you call into question my honour and my fealty to the king, Juliana will be a widow before she is a bride."

"My cousin Doun was here." Miles's voice was still low and dangerous. "I saw him with my own eyes. His sympathies are not with the king. He rides with FitzWalter."

"But I do not, and never shall." Montauban relaxed and began to smile again. "That is why you doubted me? Because you saw FitzAnthony here?"

"It is."

"He was a messenger, nothing more."

"From FitzWalter?"

"Indeed no. From someone far more formidable than Sir Robert. Someone whose command I would not dare to disobey."

"Doun would not carry messages for the king."

"I did not say he did. The letter was from your mother."

"My mother!" Carlingford was thunderstruck. "But . . . but . . . why should she write to you? You do not know her."

"Oh but I do." Guy gave Miles a slow, knowing smile. "I know all the really beautiful women in England, and your mother is amongst the loveliest. We are old friends."

"But. . . ."

"Why did she write? Simple enough. She wrote to tell me that you loved Juliana and that I was not to torment you. Did you imagine she did not know what you felt? Clemence knows everything. I have always held that she was a witch, and I have told her so on many occasions. She laughs at me, but she does not deny it."

Miles gave up in despair.

"It seems I must yet again offer my regrets. I had not thought you a traitor, but I had to be sure."

"And rightly. You will ride with John when war comes?"

"You too think war will come?"

"Certainly. Don't you?"

"I believe it is inevitable. John will not really accept the terms of this charter. It is my belief that he is already making other plans."

"I do not doubt for a moment that you are right. Yes, we shall have war, and you will ride with the king?"

"I shall. I have given my word."

"To John?"

"To my father also."

"And if you had not done so?"

"It would have made no difference. John has many faults, I know that, and much of what Langton and Pembroke seek is good and sound, but John is right to fight for his crown. Were I he, I would not let men like FitzWalter rob my son of his inheritance, nor would I permit them to tie my hands with their selfish greed."

"No more would I. We may well fight together when the time comes."

"I would deem it an honour."

Guy walked with Miles into the courtyard and waited for him to get into the saddle.

"You will go to Juliana?"

"Soon. There is to be another meeting on the 15th." Miles looked wry. "All men are to witness the agreement made between the king and the barons and I am commanded by his grace to attend upon him."

"It is as well that I am not, for I should break the peace ere it had begun were I to clap eyes on FitzWalter. But thereafter you will go to Rockingham?"

"I will."

"Give my ward my love, and tell her she did not really need my help at all. Nature has a remarkable way of settling these things without man's aid."

Montauban raised his hand in salute as Miles rode off and then returned to Melisenda.

"That is that," he said as he pulled her close to him. "And now that Juliana's problem is solved, we must decide what to do about you."

Melisenda's face paled, her normal high spirits suddenly subdued as she searched his face.

"About me, my lord? But why? Do you tire of me so soon?"

He bent his head and kissed her gently on the lips.

"Not in the least, my love, I find you most diverting, but since you are carrying my child, some thought must be given to its future."

Her eyes grew round and startled.

"But . . . but . . . how did you know? I have said nothing to anyone, not even the women who serve me."

He laid one hand lightly on her cheek.

"I needed no one to tell me such a thing. I was aware of it almost as soon as you were yourself. Not all men are so comfortably blinkered as the good Miles."

Her eyes filled with tears.

"Now you will send me away. You will not want me here any longer, for I shall grow fat and ungainly."

"Yes you will, unless of course you are a freak and can bear a child without outward and visible sign."

"You make mock of me."

A small sob escaped her and he hugged her to him again.

"If I do, sweet, it is only because you are being foolish. I have no intention of sending you away, but I have enough bastards to my name already."

"You would not harm the child?" She was terrified as her fingers gripped his arm. "You would not. . . ."

"God Almighty, Melisenda, what manner of man do you think I am?" He gave her a slight shake. "Of course I shall not not harm the child. He will be a part of you, and of me too, and I need an heir. I may need one sooner than I had anticipated, for the conflict which we face will be a bloody one. I will have none of my family laying claim to what is mine. That shall belong to my son."

"But . . . but. . . ." Melisenda was still holding on to him tightly. "But if he is to be your heir, we should have to marry."

"It is quite a common custom. Even the Church approves of it."

"But you do not."

"How fortunate for you that it has not found favour with me before."

"My lord, you cannot mean it."

"My lady, I do. You shall no longer play the exciting role of courtesan, much as you may have enjoyed it. You shall become a most respectable and dutiful wife, seemly in your conduct as will befit the mother of my heir. Will you find that dull?"

"Oh no! I could never find life dull with you."

"We shall see." He tilted her chin with his forefinger. "Meanwhile, we have a certain amount of time left in which to enjoy our illicit pleasures. Let us make the most of it."

And with that he lifted her in his arms and made for the stairs, laughing quietly to himself as Melisenda buried her head in his shoulder and began to cry.

It was a perfect June day. Dawn had come rosily and wreathed in a mist which promised fierce heat by noon-tide, but at the hour of seven the air was cool and fresh and alive with the stirrings of a summer morning. The sky was a painted canopy overhead and on either side of the river the long stretches of flat grassland were as emerald carpets sprinkled with diamond dew.

Already columns of men were appearing in the distance; the king's party riding proudly from Windsor with all the pomp and circumstance of majesty as John's banners flew boldly overhead and heralds sounded their brazen trumpets to give warning of his coming. The barons, no less impressive, cantered up from Staines, steel-clad, with flat-topped helms and surcoats of war over their armour so that none should mistake the manner of their coming.

They had accepted Runnymede willingly as the place of rendezvous with John for, despite the extended truce which had been arranged a few days before, the magnates still doubted his good faith and were glad to have the marshy valley of the Colne on their flank for protection, welcoming the natural defences of Runnymede itself with its low-lying ground to the east and south and the barrier of a minor stream which flowed swiftly down to the Thames from the hills to the west.

From Cooper's Hill, the highest point of the gently-rising range, to the flat land below there was a chain of shimmering ponds, all that remained of an old river course, and when the barons approached the water meadows from the east they were able confidently to assure themselves that the king could not come upon them suddenly and with treacherous intent, for his sole route was along the southern bank from the west, with only Staines Bridge to link the two sides of the Thames.

Within an hour of the arrival of the two parties, tents had been pitched, John's at one end of the grassy bank, the barons' at the other. The king's tent was made of bright silk with a ball of gold to top it, and grouped protectively round the royal retreat were the standards of his supporters, fluttering defiantly in the bright sunshine. By the time John himself rode in, all was ready. His great chair had been mounted on a hastily constructed platform, a footstool placed nearby, the Great Seal ready and waiting and in the safe custody of the king's spigurnel.

John grunted as he swung himself out of the saddle and made his way into the tent to take refreshment. He showed no outward sign of the terrible fury which gripped him inwardly and made him scream and thresh about the floor in the privacy of his own quarters. There he did not have to pretend. Alone with Petit or with a few of his chosen intimates he could be starkly honest in his emotions. He had no need to adopt the fixed smile and control the redness of his eye. He could swear and shout and raised clenched fists to heaven as he poured vituperation over the uncaring heads of the barons who had forced him to this pass.

He was resentful that he had to meet them again; sour that they had insisted on a full and public gathering at which he would have to repeat his oath and watch once more as fresh seals were affixed to the charter which had been hastily prepared from the Articles of the Barons. They wanted to humiliate him. They wanted to watch gloatingly as each clause was read, waiting for him to nod assent, basking in the certain knowledge that every word was like a knife-thrust through his belly.

When he had drunk a second goblet of wine he rose to his feet. The moment could not be put off for ever and the longer he hesitated the more difficult it would be to walk out to face his foes. There would be no peace that day, of course, for the barons were still in a state of rebellion. Reconciliation would come later, when the clerks, advisers and officials had hammered out the details of the charter, and scribes had made fair transcripts to send to all quarters of the realm. Today was merely the reiteration of their demands and the re-affirmation of his promises, and his mouth was ugly as he thrust aside the flap of the tent and strode up to the platform.

He was conscious of their eyes as he walked firmly up the steps towards his chair. He could feel their triumph wrapped round him like a suffocating blanket as he turned to face the silent ranks of magnates resting hands mittened with steel on the hilts of their swords, their faces as hard and unyielding as the chain-mail which clung about their heads.

He felt completely alone, although of course he was not. Standing close by were the Archbishops of Canterbury and Dublin with seven bishops in attendance. Pandulf, the papal legate, was there, worried and restless, and by the side of his mercenary captains were the Earls of Pembroke, Salisbury, Warenne and Arundel, relieved to have reached a settlement which, in their view, offered so much to so many.

The ceremony was not a long one. The hard work would come later when the negotiations of details began behind the scenes. All that was required now was the formality of royal acceptance before the face of all men; a commitment in public and under seal which would bind the king in perpetuity.

John almost laughed aloud. Little did they know, these treacherous, greedy, insulting men who stood in front of him and stared him out, how short a time it would be before he tore their precious charter into shreds and flung the pieces in their faces. He would need some weeks; time to get his foreign mercenaries across the Channel and to call his loyal Englishmen to him; a while to get Innocent's support confirmed. Then he would show them what he thought about their Articles and their insolence. Innocent would readily absolve him from an oath made under duress, and he had not forgotten how to fight for what was his.

Stephen Langton watched John uneasily. He could read the king very well by now and was not fooled by the blank bright eyes and faint curve of the lips. John was very angry, and when John was angry he was also dangerous.

Langton sighed. It had been a difficult time for him. No one was more aware than he of the motives which had led men like FitzWalter to press for the charter. They were not interested in men's liberty or the raising of crushing burdens from the poor. They were satisfied with the Articles because the sixty-one clauses of the resulting charter went a long way to rectify the flaws which they felt existed in the relationship between the king and his vassals. Henry II and Richard had been too strong and clever for them and had found many chinks in the armour of the feudal bargain through which they had shot their arrows and brought even the most powerful of magnates to the ground. The charter would end such opportunities as it repaired the rents and tears in the feudal contract, making it impossible in the future for a tyrant to impose his will unhampered upon his people or to seize too much from reluctant vassals.

John listened to the clauses in silence. As he had told Petit previously they dealt with every aspect and each was to John's disadvantage. Reliefs, rights of custody, forest laws, scutage, administration, removal of foreign mercenary captains. Nothing was forgotten, not even the election of twenty-five barons to ensure John kept his promise, and the sting in the tail which could deprive him of his possessions if he broke his oath. Langton might be satisfied that lesser men would benefit, for here and there the purely feudal nature of the document was broken down by sheer expediency, but to John it was nothing less than an iron chain fettered to his ankle.

He caught Langton's eye. He would have something to say to the pope about this troublesome prelate who had aided and abetted the rebels in their mounstrous act. He felt the blood pounding in his temples, knocking like iron hammers inside his skull as he watched the nods of satisfaction amongst the waiting crowd.

He, John, King of England and Lord of Ireland, hemmed about by a handful of insurgents with power in their grasping hands to rob him of goods and chattels should he fail to obey their orders. He, sovereign by divine right, dictated to by loutish upstarts and rogues who had no more concern for the people they pretended to represent than they had for law and justice.

He stood up quickly, fearful lest the curdling wrath inside himself should burst out too soon and give warning to his adversaries of what was to come. It would not do to let them see what lay behind the glance he gave them as he stepped forward to the edge of the dais.

"Thus it is agreed," he said after a brief pause, and his voice was commendably calm. "This charter is given freely by our hand in the field which is called Runnymede on this, the 15th day of June, in the year of Our Lord 1215 and in the seventeenth year of our reign. Our seal shall be affixed to it and our officials and advisers shall confer with those appointed by our magnates, so that all points of dispute may be resolved. Then will we meet again in this place to conclude our peace."

On the 19th June, when all arguments and altercations were finished, and fair copies of the charter had been made, the barons came before John once more to renew their homage and fealty, to be received back into his favour as his loyal men. When he had clasped the last pair of hands between his own, John looked up and smiled. It was not a pleasant sight, for it was the smile of a hungry tiger, but the barons were too pleased and self-satisfied to notice it as the king gave orders for letters patent to be despatched to all sheriffs in the kingdom, requiring them to display copies of the charter where all men might see them and know what had come to pass.

At last the barons' rebellion was over and peace had been declared once more; the charter had been hotly sought and granted under royal seal. But there was a price to be paid.

262

England had at last taken the final step towards disaster and now stood precariously on the brink of a bloody civil war from which there could be no possible escape.

When Miles Carlingford left Runnymede he rode straight to Rockingham, for he judged it would not be long before the king would have need of his services. He had found the ceremonies at Runnymede both distasteful and disquieting. It was one thing to take steps to clip the wings of a despot, if in fact John was the oppressor his barons claimed him to be. It was quite another matter to put unlimited power into the reckless keeping of the magnates and to reduce the crown of England to a trifling bauble to be tossed irresponsibly from one pair of bloodstained hands to another. Either Langton and his peace-makers were a pack of fools or they had seriously misjudged the situation and, in particular, John's reaction to the pressure put upon him. Miles had also watched the king at Runnymede and was amazed that the magnates could bask complacently in the glow of their own success with death staring out at them so blatantly from a pair of frigid blue eyes.

When he arrived at Rockingham Juliana was nowhere to be seen but after he had paced impatiently about the hall for a while, the steward returned, rather pale of face, to announce that the Lady Juliana was refusing to receive visitors and had requested that Sir Miles should leave her castle without delay.

Miles swore under his breath and brushed past the man.

"I will give her an answer to that myself," he said as he made for the stairs, ignoring the steward's shocked protests. "Stay here and do not interfere unless you want to feel the point of my sword at your throat."

He hurried quickly along the upper passage and knocked peremptorily at Juliana's door, waiting a mere moment or two before turning the handle and marching in.

Juliana turned from the window and watched him walk towards her. She had been sure she would never see him again, and the sight of his face, even set in menacing lines, made her heart begin to beat like a drum. She wished she had had warning

263

of his coming, for she would have liked to have changed into her newest red gown, touching her face with a suspicion of rouge and dabbing her ears and wrists with perfume to give herself confidence. As it was, she felt almost drab in her dark kirtle, conscious of the shadows beneath her eyes and the unnatural pallor of her face as she made herself speak calmly.

"Did you not receive my message? I told my steward that I would see no one."

"I received it, but I have no time to waste. There are things to be settled before war begins."

"War?" She was shocked out of the preoccupation with her own personal problems. "But we were told that the king and the barons were reconciled. Is this not so? Hasn't John accepted the charter?"

"No. He has sealed it, but he has not accepted it. Harbour no delusions on this score; there will be war."

"I cannot believe it."

"You had better try to do so. Now we have other things to talk about."

"I doubt it, my lord." The alarm in Juliana's eyes was gone and she looked at him coldly. "It was all said at our last meeting."

"So it was." He gave her a brief, calculating smile. "You said then, if I recall, that you were Guy de Montauban's mistress."

She flushed, for the lie still made her wince.

"I did not say that, but. . . ."

"You said precisely that. And now I have come to a conclusion about you."

"Oh?" She looked at him suspiciously. "What is that?"

"Well, since I am now convinced that you are entirely without moral scruples and the plaything of any man who cares to seek your favours, I shall myself take advantage of this happy state of affairs."

Her eyes dilated. "Take advantage? What do you mean?"

"Exactly what I say." He was beginning to enjoy himself as he took another step nearer to her. "I shall take you; by force if I have to. You are very lovely and I shall derive much satisfaction from your body for it is most marvellously formed. For your part, madam, since you are addicted to profligates, or so John tells me, you will have no quarrel with such a course, I am sure."

She gasped as he caught her by the arms and pulled her close to him.

"You cannot!" Now she was quietly frantic. "I do not know what you are talking about."

"Then I will make it plainer." He had one arm round her waist, holding her tightly so that she could not draw back. "John said you were a strumpet and that you were not good enough for me." He paused for a moment and contemplated her face thoughtfully. "Perhaps he was right, yet you are damnably good to look at and, since we are not discussing marriage, the point is not of much importance."

She struggled to free herself, aghast by the look in his eyes.

"Please . . . please. . . . Let me go."

"Certainly not. I wish to kiss you as a prelude to more gratifying pleasures, and how can I do so if I let you go?"

"You . . . you cannot mean what you say." She found her arms pinned to her side and his mouth was very close to her own. "You cannot. . . ."

When at last he raised his head he gave a faint laugh.

"You are quite wrong, you see."

Juliana's lips parted. She was still afraid of what he might do, but his kiss had roused her to something she had never felt before, and one hand caught at his surcoat and held it fast.

"You . . . you said the king told you that I was unchaste?" She managed to get the words out at last, fighting down the almost irresistible temptation to raise her mouth to his again. "Is that really true?"

"It is."

"When you first saw me, you were angry. Is that why? Because you believed the king?"

He shrugged. "I wasn't sure then. I thought he might be indulging in a measure of spite. Then, of course, you confirmed his tale yourself when you told me of Montauban. But enough of words, madam. You are here and there is a bed for our use. What more do we need?"

"No!"

She gave a cry of dismay as he caught her wrist and dragged her unceremoniously across the room.

"No, my lord, no!"

"Yes, madam, yes. Why should I be deprived of a taste of that which you have offered so freely to Montauban?" He threw her across the bed and leaned over her. "Well? Will you disrobe yourself, or must I do it for you?"

Juliana thought she was going to faint and closed her eyes tightly. The world had suddenly become a nightmare place where flesh and blood had proved to be more dreadful than ghosts after all. That she had wanted Miles Carlingford she could not deny, but that he should seek to take her in such a way brought her to the brink of helpless despair.

She kept her eyes shut, waiting for the touch of his hand on her again, ready to scream or to attempt an escape if opportunity afforded itself. After a long minute, when he had neither moved nor spoken, she dared to raise her lids and glance up at him, the fear receding as she found him gazing at her in quiet amusement.

"My lord?"

"Yes?"

"Are you not going to. . . ."

"To rape you? That rather depends upon you. There is an alternative if you will take it."

She sat up and straightened the starched fillet which had become dislodged in their undignified struggle.

"I will hear it." She tried to ignore his smile. It was difficult to do so, but somehow she was no longer afraid of him. "What is it you offer? It could scarcely be worse than that which you first threatened."

"Oh but it is, I assure you." He bent down and kissed her lightly on the cheek. "The alternative is marriage. It lasts much longer than seduction and is binding both in the sight of God and man."

"Marriage?" She said it vaguely, not really taking in what he was saying until he came to sit beside her and she could see the laughter in his eyes. "Do you seriously ask this?"

"Most seriously."

"But the king has forbidden it, and he said you had accepted the suggestion of my disparagement."

"He will agree. He has more important things to worry about than you and me, my love, and by now he will have forgotten that you refused him so roughly. Furthermore, I gave no such agreement about your marriage to a *routier*. My opinion was never asked."

She turned to stare at him.

"How did you know about my refusal of the king's attentions?"

"Your cousin told me. It was also obvious that you were not Montauban's mistress for, if I am not mistaken, your guardian's affections are genuine this time."

Her eyes filled with sudden comprehension.

"Then . . . then when you came here today, you were aware of the truth. You knew I was not a . . . not . . . a. . . ."

"Whore?"

"If you will; a whore."

"I knew it."

"And yet you would have taken me by force?"

"Do you really think so?"

She gazed at his quizzical face, torn between indignation and relief. Then she gave a small laugh.

"No. No, I do not think you would, but for a while you frightened me greatly."

"A fitting punishment for lying to me." His smile faded. "Do you know how I felt when you told me Montauban was your lover?"

She shook her head, feeling an odd quickening of her pulse.

"No, my lord. How did you feel?"

"As though my world had fallen apart."

"But you did not know me. We had only met once before."

"My mother says once is enough."

Immediately her face grew stricken and he frowned as he saw her shiver.

"What is it, Juliana?"

"My . . . my mother found it enough too."

"Ghosts again?" He drew her nearer. "You must forget them, sweet. They lived their lives and now you must live yours, free of the shadows they have cast about you. They are gone and you have mourned them long enough."

"I know that and I will try to do as you say. It is simply that I could find it in myself to love you as my mother loved my father and that is dangerous."

"Could? I had hoped for something more than that."

She blushed again and buried her head against his chest.

"I confess that I do so already, but I am afraid."

"There is no need to be." Gently he raised her up to face him. "Not all love ends in tragedy. There will be much happiness for us, as you will see. I shall take you to my home. Spectres cannot live there, for my father deafens them with his bellowing and my mother has a witchcraft of her own which they cannot withstand. Well, my love, which is it to be? Shall I make a harlot of you, or will you marry me?"

Juliana sat up straight and looked at him. Suddenly she felt ridiculously happy and the sadness and sense of foreboding which had dogged her footsteps since her parents' death seemed to fall away as if it had never existed. She turned to look about her. Even the room was different. The dark corners had mysteriously vanished and she knew beyond doubt that were she to walk into her mother's chamber she would find nothing more sinister than a few insignificant trinkets and some dusty garments hanging harmlessly on their pegs.

Her lips parted in wonderment and there was a new brightness in her eyes which Miles had not seen before.

"Well?" he repeated after a moment. "Which is it to be?"

She gave a demure smile.

"Well, my lord, as marriage lasts the longer that would be my choice."

"You sound uncertain."

268

"Do I?" She was absurdly light-hearted as she held his hand against her cheek. "Well, it is not every day one has two such interesting offers put to one, and I confess the choice was hard to make."

"Juliana!"

"Yes?"

"Are you a trollop after all?"

"I really do not know." She rested her lips against his fingers for a second. "I am not certain, of course, but I rather think perhaps I may be. Are you prepared to take the risk?"

"I never turn my back on hazards," he assured her gravely as his arms tightened about her, "but now be quiet, my love, for this is no time for talking."

And Juliana, silenced by the violence of his kiss and the comforting strength of his hold, was more than inclined to agree.

At the beginning of July John was preparing to leave Winchester whence he had gone from Windsor. Petit watched him as he paced his chamber, his eyes dark with anger, his mouth distorted in fury.

"It is beginning," he said, and shot his body-servant a baleful glance. "D'you see it, Petit? We are almost at the end of this hollow peace which has lasted for so short a time, and I for one am glad of it. Christ, what I have had to endure! First the charter which is designed to hem me in and make a slave of me. Then a body of petty under-kings to watch my every word and action. Even my mercenaries mock us for our folly, for where else would one find a monarch in such chains as I wear?"

"There was the appointment of a further body of men," ventured Petit doubtfully. "Thirty-eight of them, set to watch the committee of twenty-five, lest they break their own vows."

"God's legs! Should this give me comfort. To begin with twenty-five and then thirty-eight. All making oaths and promises to one another, swearing obedience and fidelity like a pack of old women. But I am the king." He rounded suddenly and Petit coughed nervously. "I, John, am sovereign of this realm. I want no charter or a flock of watchdogs to aid me in my task of

269

holding fast this kingdom. It is mine, and mine is the duty to preserve it intact.

"What manner of men are these who puff themselves up with pride; these demi-kings who strut before me? Have you forgotten so soon how they treated me when I was laid low with gout? I had done their bidding, unwilling though I was to do so. I had ordered my Flemish and Poitevin captains home; sent hence the mercenaries, and removed from office those sheriffs FitzWalter claimed were corrupted by my will. But was it enough that I showed my good faith? No, it was not! As I lay there, racked with pain, they sent word to me to attend the *curia regis* that a judgment might be confirmed. Did I not send back word that I could not move and sought their presence in my chamber?"

Petit nodded. "You did, sire."

"Did they agree?" John's face was growing mottled. "No, they did not. They sent their messengers to bid me come on a litter for, they claimed, it was against their rights to come to me. Their rights! God Almighty!"

The sweat was standing out on his brow and now his eyes were beginning to roll fiercely.

"So I went, ill though I was, and had myself borne on a litter to the council chamber. And then! What then?"

John's voice rose to a near scream.

"Did they rise to greet their king? Did they give one sign that their sovereign was amongst them? No, they did not. They heaped upon me injury and insult which I shall never forget. They sat on their benches, lolling and idle, as if I were some serf brought before them for trial. When I spoke to them sharply they were curt of tongue and told me yet again of their privileges which permitted them to sit in my presence."

He sank to his knees, his clenched fists pounding on the straw, the tears rolling down his cheeks as his words grew hoarse.

"As God is my witness, I will destroy them all for this. And do you know they are already sending messages to Louis, the French king's son, asking him to join them? So much must I do and promise for the good of all men and for the kingdom, but

270

they may play with treason, flirting openly with our enemies, and who is there to stay their hand?"

"I do not know, your grace."

Petit stared at the king sadly. He had not understood all that had gone on during the difficult days at Windsor and Runnymede but it was clear enough that John had been badly mauled by the barons. Clear enough also that John would not sit down calmly beneath such treatment nor abide by a charter which reduced him to a puppet of vicious, unscrupulous men.

"But I do." John got to his feet and the flurry of passion was gone. The heat had left his voice and his face was its normal sallow hue as he took his seat again. "There is only one man who can make an end of them, Petit, and that is me."

"It will not be easy."

"Perhaps not."

"It will mean violence, lord king."

"Violence is all they understand. They are deaf to reason and persuasion but their ears shall be opened to the clash of steel and they shall hear my trumpets loudly enough as I ride out against them. If I have to, I will set all England afire. They have called me Softsword, doubting my ability to fight, but they shall now learn how wrong they were to judge me so. I will storm their castles, burn their barns and fields, destroy their cattle and slaughter their sons. I will bring them cringing to their knees; they shall cry out for pardon and their anguish will be as music to my ears. Yet mercy shall not come easily."

"You will need help."

"I shall have it. There are still men in England loyal to me. Men who believe that kings are born to their task, not created by futile, worthless charters; men who will not bow down to a French princeling. I will bring back the troops from Flanders and Poitou, and Innocent shall condemn my enemies for what they do. England is a papal fief, and the pope will fight for it, never fear. Oh yes; I shall have help.

"Now send my secretaries to me for there is much to do and a dozen or more letters must be despatched."

271

He looked up again and he was smiling in a way which made Petit shiver in fear.

"Do as I bid you," said John very quietly. "There is no time to lose. Not a moment must be wasted for the hour is upon us. The waiting is done; the talk is over; the false peace finished; the pretence shattered. Go quickly, Petit; now does my war begin."